SWEETWATER

KNUT FALDBAKKEN

Sweetwater

Translated from the Norwegian by
JOAN TATE

PETER OWEN • London
UNESCO Publishing • Paris

PETER OWEN PUBLISHERS
73 Kenway Road London SW5 0RE
Peter Owen books are distributed in the USA by
Dufour Editions Inc. Chester Springs PA 19425–0449

Translated from the Norwegian *Uår: Sweetwater*
© Knut Faldbakken 1976
Originally published as *Uår: Sweetwater*
© Gyldendal Norsk Forlag A/S 1976
English translation © Joan Tate 1994
First published in Great Britain 1994

UNESCO Collection of Representative Works
European Series

Peter Owen Limited gratefully acknowledge the assistance of NORLA and
Gyldendal Norsk Forlag in the publication of this book.

ISBN 0–7206–0911–9
UNESCO ISBN 92–3–102936–3

A catalogue record for this book is available from
the British Library

Printed and made in Great Britain by
Biddles of Guildford and King's Lynn

PART ONE

1

Jonathan Bean, sergeant in the Peacekeeping Force, was displeased with the morning's action.

Ever since he had at last managed to get the stigma of deserter removed from his brother's good name and have him listed under officers missing in suspicious circumstances, then at long last convince his superiors the reason why an investigation should be made so long after his disappearance, he had been looking forward to this day with passionate eagerness.

He had no knowledge of the Dump and had never been out there before today. But all the evidence he had managed to collect on his brother Joseph's activities immediately before his disappearance pointed in that direction. The last words scribbled in the notebook found in the glove department of his patrol car had been: *Followed them to the gate. So they live on the Dump. Nothing to do but wait. . . .*

In the three years since his brother had gone, Jonathan Bean had worked tirelessly for an investigation into the circumstances round this mysterious disappearance, and at long last his efforts had borne fruit. The results of his private investigations had shown that his brother had in all likelihood been the victim of a crime, not, as the routine verdict had stated, 'Absent without leave. Present address unknown. Presumed deserted.' After only a little pressure, he had finally been given the green light to begin inquiries.

But the Dump had shattered his hopes. He kicked angrily out at the trash as he made his way as last man out along the rough roadway like a cart-track to the rusty iron gate where the patrol car was parked. Garbage and junk lay strewn everywhere, the wheel ruts deep in the stinking grey sludge clinging to his boots, making

5

walking heavy going. Bean was in a wretched mood. They had not found a single scrap-collector or vagrant, no one they could question. They had found no trace of human beings, or rather, far too *many* traces. . . . Naturally he had been perfectly aware the area was large. They had seen that on the map and he knew that in present circumstances he could take only a limited number of men with him on such an assignment. But he could never have imagined that with four men he would feel *so* helpless when faced with the huge extent of the Dump, this apparently endless landscape of junk, flotsam and mass of garbage. He knew people roamed round the garbage tips, people from the city making their way out to look for things they could use or sell. He had even found out there was supposed to be a colony of permanent residents living on the Dump, and that they got by on trading in used goods. They were the people he was particularly interested in tracking down and bringing in for questioning, to find out whether their consciences were clear (which he doubted very much), and getting out of them everything they knew about the people roaming the Dump over the last few years, especially foreigners: Jonathan Bean knew his brother had been tracking down illegal immigrants when he suddenly disappeared. But they had not found any, or seen a living soul. All morning they had combed the mounds and between the heaps, a nerve-racking, useless effort, as this barren, monotonous but shifting landscape of garbage made it almost impossible to orientate properly. Two of the men had almost gone mad when they had lost sight of each other for a moment. Their attempt to divide the area into zones and systematically search one zone after another had also ended in disarray. The landscape itself, the whole peculiar topography created by man, seemed to resist every purposeful encroachment.

He would simply have to admit their attempt to investigate the Dump had gone wrong first time round. The area was impossible to search in the ordinary way – unless he had a whole army of men at his disposal. Anger rose in him as his eyes ranged over the parts of the vast area they had not even set foot in. But at the same time he had a gnawing sense of fear when he thought about that panic-stricken moment when he had felt the ground giving way under his feet and had slipped and fallen into what had seemed like an abyss of loose refuse, cardboard boxes, shredded paper, cans, sacks and plastic containers, with and without their stinking contents, a mass of immeasurable size and depth heaving like a sea all round him, threatening to drown him.

Last man out, he was trudging back towards the rusty iron gate, his men already impatiently waiting by the car for orders to go back to the station. They had made no attempt to conceal their dislike of this assignment and were probably hoping the day's fiasco would mean this part of the investigation would be abandoned. But he was still convinced the answer to the mystery of his missing brother was to be found on the Dump, and this made him persist, because he was a proud and purposeful man, not easily persuaded that he was wrong.

'You can go,' he said tersely to the blank, questioning faces, 'the cream of the nation's young men', as it said in the recruiting campaign. He had often criticized recruits for their unnecessary use of force, their lack of both imagination and capacity for independent thought, and he occasionally found it difficult to conceal that he considered himself above their smug indifference. Morale in the Force was not what it ought to be, and when he looked into those regular, smooth-shaven faces, the taut young skin, the bulging jaw muscles, flushed with vitamins, the underlying egoism and brutal indifference behind their taciturn obedience, the reluctance behind their well-disciplined behaviour, he again felt a gnawing inside himself, as if from fear. How could one stick to the letter of the law in a just and responsible way and bring social ills to light with a force based on human material of that kind?

'We'll continue with the search tomorrow in the south area of the tip, working our way as far out as possible. You can go.'

He watched the patrol car driving away, for a moment incapable of deciding whether to get into his own car and drive home. The huge brackish area behind him, its vastness, its impregnability, both angered and depressed him, but it also exercised a strange fascination. He had considered the possibilities of discovering traces of his brother – or his murderer, for he had long since given up hope of finding Joseph alive – there so often, he found the fact that he was now actually *there* on the Dump and after a whole day's fruitless searching behind him, unreal, almost absurd. Again he had to turn round and gaze over the endless expanse of death and destruction. God, how the sight repelled him! It made him feel sick, the uselessness, the decay, the rottenness, the smells . . . the stench had almost finished them, although it was still only early spring, still not too hot even in the middle of the day. He thought with horror of what it must be like in midsummer, scorching in the heat, the flies. . . .

Jonathan Bean detested the thought of decay. If there were any philosophy behind his tireless efforts in the Peacekeeping Force, it was the desire to counteract the tendency to decay in society, to help restore the dignity of human beings, what he called their 'moral instincts', which he considered were in ruins wherever he turned, even within the ranks of the Force.

The sun was behind an impenetrable layer of cloud and sulphur-yellow smog, not a breeze rippling the dull, glassy surface of Paradise Bay. He could see a thin column of smoke rising above the garbage heaps somewhere in the south-east. He had seen similar columns earlier that day and thought excitedly *now* . . . but it was self-combustion playing tricks with his eagerness to find what he was seeking. His senses were always constantly on the alert, as if he had some idea that what he was looking for (What *was* it really? Did he himself know?) was just beyond his range of vision and would make itself known only if he made just a little more effort, a *little* . . .

Involuntarily, he had gone a short way back along the rough track. Hadn't he also heard a pattering noise, as if someone were rummaging and poking around in waste paper? Sure to be rats; they had come across some truly magnificent specimens in the course of the day. The men had amused themselves kicking a couple to death. His disgust at the primitive instincts of the recruits and the repulsive animals had been so strong, he had been forced to turn away.

Nevertheless, his vigilant senses drew him in the direction of the rustling sound, telling him he was a fool for not giving up the impossible, at the same time he quickly calculated that, alone and unarmed as he was, it would perhaps be unfortunate should he come across something *now*, 'something' in reality meaning these people whose existence he knew of only by rumour and speculation, but on whom he had still unconsciously based his hopes. But he went on ahead despite the difficulties in covering the rugged terrain, putting one foot cautiously in front of the other, noting with sorrow even more soil and muck sticking to his already filthy boots . . . then he slipped and nearly fell, and as he flung out a hand to save himself, he set off a veritable avalanche by striking a tottering heap of corrugated iron and twisted rusty pipes. The noise was deafening in the silence and he cursed inwardly.

Then he saw the boy, a small figure in colourless rags, his skin and hair so filthy he completely merged with the grey mountain of garbage of the Dump. But his eyes were bright and lively. For a moment they looked at each other, then the boy swung round and ran off between the mounds with incredible speed and agility. Jonathan Bean regained his balance and ran after him, his hand fumbling at his belt for his baton. At that moment, he wished he had a gun, although on principle he was against the use of arms and had voted against a proposal to make guns part of the Force's regular equipment. Jonathan Bean was in good physical shape. He swam and went running twice a week, but he had no chance against the speed of this creature. He could still just see his back – the impression was of a boy – and made a supreme effort, but the distance between them increased. Desperately, Bean tried shouting when he realized he was losing sight of his victim, but his *'Stop'* was scarcely audible, like a gasp in his heavy breathing. In no more than a few seconds, this untamed child, who had shown him that his theory none the less held water, would be out of reach, presumably for ever. The failures of the day gnawed at his sense of pride. Raging, he scooped up a stone as he ran, keeping his eyes fixed on the slim back ahead, the head with long tangled hair stiff with dirt, then with a wild curse he flung the stone with all his strength. The stone soared up into the yellow sky with no chance of succeeding, for the fugitive would soon be behind a shack beyond a couple of mounds and the battle would be lost. But the stone reached the peak of its curve and came down with merciless and incomprehensible logic in the right direction – he could feel it with his whole body, and jubilation rose in him. It struck the fugitive on the shoulder and he heard the dull thump, then saw the thin body fall and roll around on the ground.

He reached the boy as he was trying to struggle to his feet, his expression distorted with the pain in his shoulder, which was clearly inhibiting his movements, but he managed to get to his feet when he saw the policeman coming towards him. Bean leapt forward and kicked out just as the boy was about to flee. Then he stood over the tiny, curled-up figure, his baton raised, but did not hit him, in the end incapable of setting about a child. But how was he to pacify his prisoner? The boy was on the ground, his hand clutching his injured shoulder, his lips drawn back as he twisted and kicked out, hissing like a wild animal. He stopped for a brief moment as if listening, then let out a sharp, shrill scream. Bean glanced hastily round, but could see no one, nothing moving in the deadly monotony of the macabre landscape, not a sound breaking the stillness, apart from the boy's gasps of fear and pain. But the posture of the boy had changed and he seemed to be waiting, his eyes bright and shifting, fixed watchfully on the face of his pursuer. Irresolutely, Bean raised and lowered his baton. Should he arrest the boy and take him to the station, or should he try to question him on the spot to see if he could get out of him what he knew (if he had any speech – none of the sounds coming from him indicated that he had), and try to find out where the others were, the others, those semi-mysterious 'others' whom Jonathan Bean had spent years of his life trying to track down, of whom he *had* now found traces. . . .

He got no further with his thoughts. The blow came from behind and fell heavily and accurately. Coarse, greyish-yellow soil filled his open mouth. The sun went out.

2

He woke, freezing on the cold ground. Opening his eyes brought on explosions of pain in the back of his head. The darkness round him was broken here and there by strange patterns of lighter patches, and their utter lack of symmetry frightened him. He closed his eyes tight again, the pain in his head threatening to finish him as he tried to sit up. He noticed the collar of his uniform jacket sticking to his cheek. His chin was wet with saliva and slime and, surrounded as he was by a suffocating stink, he realized he was lying in his own vomit. The thought was so repulsive, he almost vomited again. He fumbled round, his eyes still closed, but all he could feel was an uneven floor. As he tried unsteadily to get to his feet, he hit his head on something so hard he fell again and lay there in a miserable, helpless heap.

His eyes fixed on those patterns of light, those strange, faint shining points which were apparently imperceptibly moving but so indefinite in origin, form and extent, that he could not connect them with anything real. He sat there for a while trying to gather his wits. He had been struck down as he was about to arrest a suspect, a boy he had hoped would clarify the question whether there really were people living on the Dump who might have had something to do with his brother's disappearance. Someone had hit him and brought him there. So there are several of them, he thought, almost mechanically. But there was no satisfaction in having his theory confirmed. All he could feel was that his strength had failed him and a numbness more disquieting than the nauseating pain in his head had set in his body and put a stop to every inclination to act. He sat without moving, his eyes wide open and fixed on that incomprehensible system of light points which occasionally moved rather faintly, their strength increasing and decreasing in a rhythm beyond all reason. This illogical lack of anything recognizable filled him with a weakness he had never felt before, rendering him helpless.

He concentrated, trying to clear his mind, trying to survey his situation. He was a prisoner. That was obvious. He had crawled round on all fours in his stockinged feet (his boots had gone, but he ignored that). How long ago? He had fumbled round with one hand while crawling over the uneven floor and felt nothing but massive walls of cold, uneven stone. And the ceiling, that was also of rough bricks and stones, in some places so low he had hardly been able to sit upright. He had tried orientating himself according to the lighter patches (painstakingly avoiding them), trying to decide the shape and extent of his prison, but with no success. The darkness seemed to be enclosing him in a space with no fixed dimensions. The terrible thought struck him that he might be buried alive, that he was sitting here in a chance hollow under tons of scrap and garbage with no chance of getting out, left to die of suffocation under the city's mountains of refuse, or to die slowly, painfully, of hunger and thirst.

He was cold. He was shaking, shuddering. He wrapped his arms round his legs, his knees under his chin, but that was no help. The cold seeped up into him from the raw earth floor he was sitting on, from the darkness pressing in on him all round in this terrible prison, unendurable because it had no known definition, apparently contracting and expanding all round him in time with his breath whistling through his throat, a spasmodic, almost soundless wail.

Time passed – several hours? He could not determine how long. The light patches changed character before his eyes, constantly outlined more clearly, becoming sharper – were they also growing? The hoarse, hacking sounds, the only break in the silence, were his own breathing. For the first time in his adult life he experienced anguish, and the naked terror he felt when faced with something totally incomprehensible reduced him to a whimpering, motionless bundle. He did not even notice that the bottomless darkness was beginning to lighten all around him.

He must have dozed off, for he woke to narrow rays of sunlight falling on his face, and he took in his surroundings at a glance. He was lying on the floor of something resembling a cellar with partly collapsed walls and a sharply sloping, partly fallen ceiling. Daylight was trickling in through a few cracks in the wall, the wall behind him the only one more or less intact and the ceiling there high enough for a short man to stand upright. He saw a door. All this, caught in single glance, totally changed the picture he had formed of his situation. The nightmare of the night vanished. Although he was shaking with cold, his head ached, he was feeling sick and was stiff after lying all night on an earth floor, some of his self-confidence and courage returned, and a few minutes later he had collected himself sufficiently to start systematically examining the place in which he was imprisoned.

The door was wooden, but heavy and massive, locked or bolted on the outside. The walls were thick and apparently impenetrable even where there were cracks and holes. The ceiling sloped danger-ously down to a corner of the little room, and had collapsed com-pletely, resembling most of all a heap of stones. That was where he could glimpse the sky through a crack as wide as his hand. As he crawled over and put his face to it, he also saw something else – vegetation, clusters of green leaves on thick branches, swinging and swaying out in the bright air! A few stalks came right in through the crack, creeping along the damp wall and sending out pale shoots in the semi-darkness, the leaves, branches and stems forming a net-work between him and the misty sky.

Where was he? That must be undergrowth out there, plants he had never seen before, though he had to admit he knew little about plants. Was this the Dump? But nothing grew on the Dump, so he must be somewhere else. But where had they taken him, and why was he being held prisoner?

In the middle of these thoughts, he suddenly made a discovery so obvious he had to laugh. The daylight trickling through the foliage outside the long crack was throwing a lively pattern of light and shade on the back wall. The points of light that had frightened him so much in the darkness! He must have glimpsed the first light of dawn and its reflection on the wall.

But that solved none of the riddles about where he was, who had taken him and kept him prisoner there, or why. He was hungry. It was almost twenty-four hours since he had eaten anything. He guessed it was about midday. He wanted to look at the time but discovered his watch had gone. Someone had stolen his wrist-watch. And his boots. Of course, that was why they had gone. He swore. Theft angered him more than anything else. Infringement of someone else's private property! For a moment, his indignation at having been exposed to anything like it briefly overshadowed his anxieties about his situation. Damned pack of thieves! He thumped the floor with his fist and ground his teeth. Then exhaustion over-came him again and his thoughts started racing. Stella. What would she think? He remembered their agreement, and two bottles of chemical wine for which he had been lucky enough to barter, now lying chilling in his apartment. Slim, short-haired, trim Stella – what would she think when no one turned up at the agreed time? What would she say if she could see him now?

For the umpteenth time he tried to reason, but again came up against the mass of questions to which there were no possible answers. But one thing remained – it was likely that the kidnappers, whoever they were, wanted to keep him alive, otherwise they would have finished him off at once and let him disappear under tons of garbage where no one would ever have found his corpse. Whoever had brought him there must have had some reason to do so. But what? And who were 'they'?

He got up from his crouching position. His examination of the dungeon had largely had to be undertaken on all fours. His uniform was creased and dirty, the collar still stiff with vomit, his cap missing. He brushed earth and straw off his trousers, wet his fingers with spit and rubbed the worst patches off his jacket. That made him feel better, although his head still ached from the blow. The swelling on the back of his head was tender and the hair below stiff with dried blood. But as far as he could make out, he was not seriously injured, at least no longer bleeding. He was weak with hunger, but told himself that was probably mostly imagination. Human beings can go incredibly long without food. Thirst was worse. If things became really bad, he could perhaps suck a little moisture off the wall, where drops kept trickling down a slimy track. But it would be long before he reached that stage. He would hold out as long as he could. He would be careful not to show any signs of weakness to these bandits. He would set his resolution and cunning against theirs and find a way out of this dilemma – they would not go unpunished for abducting an officer of the Peacekeep-ing Force. There was also the patrol he had organized the day before. His last order had been to continue the search today. They would miss him and, putting two and two together, would bring in reinforcements, fine-comb the area and not give up until they had found him.

But as the hours went by, he grew less confident, tormented by the uncertainty as to where he was. He remembered the men's reluctance to take part in this assignment out on the Dump. He remembered their inefficiency during the search, their sullen looks when he had given those last orders. He began to doubt whether they were to be trusted. They were not like him. They had no sense of responsibility, and their morale was low. They would take the easy way out and report him missing, which was much the same as burying him alive out there. Again he raged, vainly, helplessly, digging his nails into the earth floor. He had often spoken up on the inadequacy of the training his men were given, and deep down he also nourished a distrust of the recruits, the very material they were made of. He suspected several of them had joined the Force because they had neither the qualifications nor the courage to try the Army, the military units that also energetically recruited men and were able to tempt them with a more varied life, travel abroad, exciting assignments abroad. The Allied powers were constantly involved in policing activities all over the world. Rivalry between the Army and the Force was great, and Bean was one of those who feared that the Army took on most of the more promising recruits. With disquiet, he also noticed the tendency to liberalization of traditional military attitudes, which he had heard (Force propaganda) was finding an increasingly firm foothold within the ranks of the Army.

Bean sat there feeling the stillness and inactivity like an ache in his body. The hours passed and his courage faded. The patches of sunlight on the wall had moved over towards his corner and they also faded. Hunger was a constant hollow in the region of his stomach, a pain that could be so intense he doubled up and groaned. It frightened and amazed him that his hunger could already be so considerable. He had thought its full strength would not make itself felt for two or three days. That was what he had been told on the anti-terrorist instruction course. Was it because he had been unconscious for so long, perhaps longer than one night? He caught a few drops off the wet wall on his fingers and sucked them in. That helped.

He had had to use one of the corners of his cramped prison as a latrine, and that worried him more than it would have done out in the open, here with no hope of even a modicum of hygiene.

Jonathan Bean was a man of order even when it came to his own person, a man who considered a degree of collective cleanliness an adequate aim for society's level of civilization. To have to sit like this with his own excrement, so to speak, in front of his nose and endure both the stench and the repulsive sight (the loose earth he had scratched together and tried to throw over it did not help in the slightest), shook him, assaulting something deep down in him, something fundamental, causing him actual suffering.

Thinking about his unknown kidnappers became an obsession as he sat there watching the light disappearing, fighting his anxiety, the helplessness, the vision that yet another long, dark night in this cave aroused in him. If only they had made themselves known! If only he could have seen them, talked to them, if only he had been able to fathom out why he was being held prisoner and starved. They can't have meant to bring him all this way in a state of unconsciousness just to let him starve to death?

Once again he crawled round his prison searching for some clue, some small detail that might be a pointer to what kind of creatures were deciding on his fate, to give him something to hold on to before the light vanished completely, before he was again left to the fears and uncertainties of the night. He tried the door once more, but again it refused to budge. He put his ear to it one more time to see if he could hear some human sound, if only an indistinct voice, footsteps . . . but the stillness was absolute. In his disappointment and despair, he did something he had decided never to do. He called out, hoarsely at first, then shouted loudly, beating on the door with his clenched fists. The sound of his own voice was terrible, the cries ringing inhumanly in the silence of the small space. He stopped, frightened by the noise he was making. He fell to his knees by the door, his hands pressed to his stomach to subdue the pains. The only clear thought in his head was that he would not, *must* not give in. He was an officer in the Peacekeeping Force and that also gave him some moral responsibility. He had to withstand the strongest of pressures.

Then he saw something. In the damp earth below the slanting threshold of the doorway was a footprint, a perfectly clear imprint of a foot, the first sure sign people had brought him here . . . what nonsense! What else could have? Bean did not know. All he knew was that his thoughts were grinding round and round in his head until he could hardly be sure of anything. Not one single thing.

But the imprint of a bare foot was something positive.

Bean stared, transfixed, at the footprint, the broad heel, the short, thick toes so clearly outlined in the soft earthen floor. A human being! But barefoot, he thought, as his excitement simmered down. What kind of people went around barefoot at this time of year?

They had stolen his boots, but they themselves ran around barefoot.

Anxiety and his ever-present hunger again made themselves felt and forced him down to the floor, doubled up, whimpering, as if he had already lost his determined struggle against resignation and despair.

3

The third time he woke, he could smell frying. His vivid dream about food must have woken him. He had dreamt about chicken, a dream of crisply roasted, tasty chicken dripping with fat. He had not eaten chicken of that kind for years. They had been hard to get hold of, and even long ago, before the shortages and rationing, when things could still be bought in the shops, prices had been such that his sound financial sense forbade him even to consider buying one . . . but roast chicken had once been his favourite dish and the dream had been so vivid, a smell of that inaccessible delicacy seemed to be still hanging around even after he had woken, teasing his senses.

It had turned light again, but the sun was no longer shining through cracks as on the day before. A dull, woolly half-light came through the leaves he could just see outside.

It's raining, he thought. He could feel the moisture all round him, in his clothes, on the walls, from the earth floor, more than he could see the glistening moisture in the foliage. At the same time he noticed how thirsty he was. He crawled over to the nearest wall and began eagerly slurping up the drips trickling down the cold wall. Groaning, he licked the wall, ignoring the dirt and sand coming into his mouth.

While he was still busy doing this, he sensed that something was not as before. He crawled around feeling every inch of his dungeon, his senses registering the slightest change. Then he sniffed something. The smell from his dream was still there as if real in the cramped room, the smell of frying . . . it distracted him as he stood there on all fours like an animal, sniffing and licking at wet patches on the wall.

Then he turned round and saw the dish. It had been placed just inside the door, full of something that looked like meat, large pieces of pale meat, stringy and fibrous, carelessly hacked up, burnt brown, almost black in places. He looked at it as he crawled closer, trembling with excitement, almost not daring to breathe in his agitation, in his fear that something would happen to make this unbelievable sight disappear, in his anxiety that someone would suddenly come and take it away from him . . . but he reached the dish without anything happening, the smell overwhelming him, his stomach contracting and his hand shaking as he reached out and seized the nearest piece.

He examined it closely. Although he felt sick and wretched with hunger, he forced himself to be cautious. It could be a trap. The food could be poisoned. There was stuff which even in small doses drove people mad. A man could be reduced to a feeble wreck and do whatever he was told. He had often heard about the use of poison by the guerrilla movement on their victims. Poison had long been regarded as the most effective method of making prisoners confess. Poison eliminated the necessity for rigorous interrogation. Although he didn't like thinking about it, he knew the use of some chemicals had gradually become part of the tactics of the Peacekeeping Force with particularly dangerous criminals and enemies of the State, although no official approval of such methods existed. In self-defence he had thought that these methods had to be used at a time of explosive increase in crime, when rising unrest might well have turned into civil disturbances, certainly in the cities, and the consequent social collapse appeared to be a definite danger, a possibility that had to be reckoned with.

He was kneeling in front of the suspect plate of food, his guts protesting. How could he tell if the meat were poisoned? With the last shreds of his self-discipline, he tried to make himself reason. Was it likely that these creatures out on the Dump, who had struck him down, who went around barefoot, would be in possession of advanced medical preparations at a time when even ordinary medicines were in such short apply? He simply could not believe it. But. . . .

He could not take his eyes off the piece of meat he had in his hand. It was still warm. The brown crust hypnotized him, the appetizing smell. Poisoned or not? The impossible choice made him dizzy and tears welled up in his eyes, the pain in his stomach a constant gnawing agony. He *had* to eat. The crisply roasted crust dripped warm fat on to his filthy fingers, and yet he still hesitated, still felt some of the scepticism drilled into him, the stern ethics of the Force. Never give up. Never make concessions to the Enemy. But as he sat there staring at the meat like a dog begging, he felt his will, his resolution, all his ingrained discipline giving way to the overwhelming fact that he was *starving*, as hungry as he had never been before, as hungry as he had never imagined anyone could be.

Then he noticed something about the crust of the meat, the browned skin hanging on the meat like the skin of grilled chicken. But it was not chicken. It had a strange symmetrical pattern on it, like fish scales in close rows. Yet this was not fish. It couldn't be. He felt the food, poking among the pieces of meat with his fingers and finding some more pieces of 'skin' with fine scales, soft and elastic. What kind of meat was it they wanted him to eat? Then he found a foot, a small curled foot with four toes, covered with tiny scales, and the tail, long, supple and scaly as well, but with a small crest of horny plates along the back. It was a lizard he had wanted to eat! A huge lizard.

He felt more wretched than ever, sick with disappointment and disgust. He pushed the dish of pale pieces of reptile flesh away, the sight alone nauseating him. Agitation and exhaustion made him feel faint. He wept, he called out, clenched fists pressed to his aching stomach, his face on the earth floor, shamelessly, with no pride, no resistance. What kind of perverse, devilish trick was it to try to make him eat lizards? He cursed, groaned, writhing as if with cramp, grit grinding between his teeth, panting as if the heavy, raw air in the cellar were about to run out, as if the stench from his own excrement had become gas slowly poisoning him. He finally fell asleep from utter exhaustion.

How long he had lain unconscious, he was unable to judge, but he noticed something had happened to him when he finally came round. He was feeling amazingly calm, as if a cool light were pouring through him, a clear distance from himself and his sur-roundings and the situation he was in. His calmness bordered on indifference, a sullen acceptance of everything happening to him, an indifference, a calm that was much more terrifying than his actual imprisonment and the degradations into which it had forced him.

He lay on his back, shivering with cold, the moisture making his clothes heavy and uncomfortable, dirt itching on his face, all over his body, but not even that affected him as it had before. His remaining spiritual strength was concentrated on the process developing inside him, the sneaking paralysis of despair. He regarded it from a distance, looking on himself with melancholy, lying there almost with indulgence, enfeebled and degraded, stinking, tortured by hunger. But his mind told him how dangerous this hallucination was. His knowledge of psychology and training to resist certain forms of mental torture told him, but this . . .

A sentence ground round and round in his head. He had read it or heard it . . . perhaps it was a truth, perhaps a pack of lies his tortured brain had put together, beyond his control, a pretaste of his coming collapse. He formed the words with his lips? 'Many preferred to starve to death rather than eat human flesh. . . .' 'Many preferred to starve to death . . .', '. . . starve to death. . . .' As far as he could remember, it had been in connection with an accident, a whole lot of people isolated on a mountain plateau, weeks passing before help arrived. Or perhaps it had been a failed expedition, or during some war . . . 'Many preferred to starve to death. . . .' One does not eat one's own species ('in the animal kingdom, probably only rats . . .') '. . . preferred to starve to death . . .', '. . . human flesh . . .', 'Rather die. . . .'

He was so enfeebled, he could scarcely find the strength to turn his head to look at the half-burnt pieces of lizard meat lying scattered round the cracked dish, an almost comical sight at a distance, a man dying of starvation and food only an arm's length away.

No, he would have to make his body and mind connect again. This was about himself, this was happening *now* to *him*. His reason told him that soon, very soon, he would go under, die, if he did not eat. Eating was no longer a question of habit, appetite or tactics. Eating, eating anything, was the only essential, vital function of life, in line with breathing. He *understood* that, but his insight penetrated only slowly through the paralysis of indifference that allowed him to look on his misery with irony, even amusement. A deep, deep weariness lay behind his eyelids, making him hope for oblivion, eternal rest.

Nevertheless his reason stirred something in his tortured mind, if it were not his animal instinct for survival that had come back as he again turned his attention to the meat he had flung away in digust. (When? This morning? The day before? Two, three or several days ago?) Now it was his senses and nothing else turning to the food. He was nothing but a passenger in his body, guided by the need to survive.

At last he managed to roll over, gather up elbows and knees and drag himself the short way over to the nearest pieces. He tried to sit up but passed out and keeled over. Lying, he raked a piece of pale cold meat towards him and sniffed, then licked it. Disgust and indifference overwhelmed him again, but something made him go on. He had to have some nourishment, never mind from what. He *had* to eat, no matter what, or it would be the end of him. The end of him. . . .

He bit into the meat, chewed and swallowed, bit again and chewed. In so far as he was capable of tasting anything, it was sweetish, sickly, tasting almost of nothing. He ate reluctantly, mechanically, gnawing at the meat, tender and sweetish as it was, thinking all the time '. . . some preferred to starve to death rather than. . . .' But not him. He ate lizards. He wanted to survive. It almost surprised him.

He knew he must eat slowly, that his stomach would not stand too much strain after such a long period of fasting. Keeping down what he managed to get inside him was as important as eating. But it was as if a threshold had been crossed inside him – he could feel hunger coming as he devoured even more of the meat, hunger such as he had never known before. He went on chewing the food well, but nevertheless swallowed several large chunks. He was eating lizard and it tasted good . . . he went on as if in rage, hoisting himself up on his elbows, dragging himself over to where other bits lay, raking them to him, baring his teeth and tearing the meat off the strange reptile bones. He wanted to live. He went on and on eating although he could feel his body reacting to all this sudden gorging, nausea rising . . . but he went on eating like a madman. Even when he doubled up with fearful cramp and was made to see the precious contents of his stomach on the floor in front of him, stringy, undigested pieces of meat floating in stinking yellow bile, he went on, scooping with greedy fingers what he could gather up, stuffing it into his mouth, chewing, swallowing, sour and stinging, clenching his teeth, groaning with cramp. He must keep down some, *some* of it, he simply had to. He *refused* to die of starvation. He was not one of those who preferred to die of starvation rather than eat just anything. Even lizards. Lizard flesh. . . .

4

Food was put out for him every alternate or third day, and as the days grew warmer and the damp in his dungeon gradually disappeared, at irregular intervals he was also given a mug of water which he made himself ration in small gulps, so uncertain was he of when the next supply would come.

He was given mostly a mixture of boiled vegetables, a kind of soup or stew, occasionally something like meat in it, or soaked pieces of some extraordinary kind of bread. It was unappetizing and tasteless, sometimes mouldy, but he ate it, and it kept him alive. He could feel his strength returning, to the extent that he could move around in his prison without passing out. He somehow got his mind under control again and spent long, aimless periods thinking about his situation, trying to work out what it was his kidnappers wanted of him and why they were treating him in this way. One thing seemed certain: they were being very careful to keep him alive. But for what reason? Why did they let him sit there rotting away? When would they make their presence known?

Despite his isolation, he felt that little by little he was making closer contact with them. He occasionally heard footsteps or voices on the other side of the thick door, faint, indistinct, impossible to make out from which direction, but definitely signs of human life, and as time went by, the uncertainty, which had driven him almost mad at first was almost overtaken by curiosity. Who were they? What were they up to? What did they want of him? They must be keeping an eye on him all the time, because the food and water were always put in when he was asleep. But to what purpose?

For a while he had tried to keep track of the time, but he had soon given it up. For one reason or another, his body rhythm seemed no longer to follow the rhythm of day and night. He had previously been proud of living a very regular life and had noticed his well-being depended on a sound, planned, daily routine, and now he found his sleeping and waking periods in the course of a day were quite haphazard. But this did not worry him as it would normally have done. And why should such unimportant details matter when he kept finding himself in a situation as hopeless as it was painful and degrading? Although he was being fed, he was weak and depressed and for all he knew his life was still in danger. If his guards did not have murder in mind, he might easily fall ill and die in this stinking, filthy dungeon. He was still plagued with severe diarrhoea.

But all thoughts he had had of escaping, of slipping away, let alone overpowering and seizing his guards, now seemed distant, even unreal. His long isolation and the state he was in had gradually shaped his attitude, reducing his self-confident arrogance to something close to resignation. His rage, even hatred of these unknown people, the humiliation of being maltreated and humbled in this way, which had previously filled him as he thought how they had kept him prisoner like an animal in a cage, were now nothing but a dim shadow, a shadow that did indeed occasionally settle over him and reduce him to a deep depression bordering on despair. But most of time that was pushed into the background by a strange longing for contact with his tormentors, a feeling of solidarity, almost identification with them. He would sit for long spells close to the door, his ear pressed to the dry wood, listening, listening for the slightest sound that would tell him something about them. How many of them were there? Did they include any women? Were they older or younger people? The boy he had seen could not have been more than seven or eight, but it was no boy who had knocked him out — the tender spot on the back of his head told him that.

He examined the food, the dish, the mug of water. Half-cooked vegetables with rancid fat or hard bread, on rare occasions pieces of that white, sweetish lizard meat. Who ate such things? The dish was a deep, plate-like, earthenware bowl, with no characteristics at all, a type found everywhere. The battered mug was of rust-spotted enamel and seemed old-fashioned, almost antique, with a large curved handle and broad lip, things no one used any longer. When he studied these objects and tried to put his impressions together into some kind of pattern, it gave him a feeling of unreality, increasing his confusion. Nothing in his situation appeared to have any connection whatsoever with forms of human existence with which he was familiar and were beyond anything he was able to conceive. On the contrary, his habitual ideas kept being undermined, the whole situation so irrational it was difficult to imagine that it had really happened. The fact that it *had* happened, and had happened to *him*, brought his logically trained mind close to disintegration. He kept being overcome by a feeling of utter absurdity, so strong that he seemed to have begun to doubt his own existence, a nameless anxiety resembling what he had felt that first night when he had stared crazily at the pattern of stars projected on the wall. The perceptions in his mind seemed to bind him even more strongly to his despised, hateful, tormenting spirits in a desperate, feeble dependency.

He noticed it was becoming steadily more difficult for him to think coherently about the past, life as he had lived it – he had missed it sorely, uninhibitedly at first. But now and again when he had been given food and lay dozing in a kind of semi-apathetic contentment, Stella would suddenly appear to him, Stella's trim, firm white body, Stella's breasts, pointed, undeveloped like a young girl's, and burning desire would pour through him, stronger than he thought he had ever experienced, maybe because of his situation, his degradation, the despair he felt at his helplessness, the ever-present anguish, his only outlet sexual activity. When he seemed to see Stella before him, he remembered her as she had been with him, coolly considerate and clever, uncomplicated and slightly demanding, and so blessedly trim and neat he seemed to experience being aroused, sexually excited again for the first time. He had to masturbate, despising that primitive, degrading ritual, and at the same time recalling the smell of soap from her clean body.

Then, in the course of a short time, two things happened that briefly changed the picture again.

First he found the opening in the wall.

Tormented by hunger, he crawled across and forced his fingers out through the crack in the thick wall in the collapsed corner to get some of the fresh green leaves and stalks, then devoured them. One day as he was making an extra effort to get hold of a whole branch that had grown half-way inside, he noticed the formation of the crack made it possible to knock out a piece of the wall right down to the floor. This discovery again turned his ideas upside-down: the hole looked as if it could be made big enough for a grown man to slip through. Suddenly, there was a chance of escaping.

A sense of triumph mixed with fear shook him: was it really possible? Would he make it? What was there to stop him? But if he got out, what would he do then? How would he find his way back to civilization? And what if they had guards out . . . and what if they were already peering in on him through secret peep-holes and had already realized what he was thinking of doing? If they could see him kneeling there rocking the loose piece of wrecked wall, if they already . . . the very thought that he was probably being watched gradually began to seem like some kind of perverse consolation in his loneliness, but now the possibility filled him with an almost sickly anxiety. What if this one chance was now taken away from him?

Trembling, he tried to smooth out all traces of his 'investigation', sweeping earth over the place where he had found the loose piece of wall. He made an effort to make his movements slow and 'natural', and yet could feel every muscle tensing, saw his hands trembling, while the imagined gaze he always felt was following him held him firmly by the back of the neck. It was a bright day. From the reflections of daylight on the walls, he could make out that the sun was high in the sky. The room was warm and he was sweating with agitation and from the heat, pretending not to notice anything, just waiting, waiting until dark. And then. . . .

He dragged himself around for the rest of the day in a fever of restlessness, almost incapable of keeping his body under control. Two days had also passed since he had been fed, and that did not calm him either. He kept making little trips over to the crack to reach out for a leaf or two, their faintly sweetish taste providing him at least with an illusion of taking in nourishment. He was trembling with the desire to tear the piece of wall away and start digging, shovelling, boring his way out into freedom, but he curbed himself. Everything depended on his not arousing suspicion, if they were keeping an eye on him. In any case, he would have to plan his steps carefully, so as not to risk being surprised in his attempt to escape, and a doubt was still gnawing at the back of his mind: would he make it?

Towards evening he fell into an uneasy doze. Through his sleep he could hear voices and footsteps and a sound he had not heard before, like a clink of metal against metal, a creaking of boards . . . half-way between dream and waking, he realized a key was being turned in the lock. The thought woke him like lightning, every muscle in his body freezing, paralysing him with terror and ex- pectation. As long as he controlled himself and lay still, pretending to be asleep, they would come in. . . .

He ceased thinking, noticing from almost inaudible sounds, no- thing but changes in the air around him, that the door had opened. The stillness changed the echo of the blood thudding in his ear- drums; his hearing had gradually been so starved of impressions, he thought he could hear *everything*, spiders running below the ceiling, plants growing through the cracks . . . now he could hear someone stepping into the room. He lay without moving, only just breathing, the darkness apparent through his eyelids. Good. Less chance of the person concerned seeing him.

He had no clear thoughts, no idea what he would do. An eternity ago, when he had first been brought there, he had been full of plans for ambushing and overpowering his guards one by one, disarming them and arresting them all. He had had commando training and could boast of being almost unbeatable in close combat, but ideas of that kind were now distant. He had been degraded and humbled, his perspectives narrowed to include nothing but what was closest. He was simply lying there feeling tingling satisfaction at for once being the one spying on *them*. That made him feel superior, though he did not dare open his eyes – yet. He heard a rustle over by his dish, then the mug being filled. The desire to steal a look, to be able to see his tormentor, became even stronger, overwhelming when he realized his visitor must be busy with his own tasks. He could feel cramp in his arms and legs and was unable to bear it any longer – he *had* to look.

In the semi-darkness he at first saw only an outline, apparently large, almost gigantic in this cramped space in which he had had no human dimensions other than his own. A man – a man bending over the dish. The man moved into the faint light from the half-open door, and Bean clearly saw the strong, shapely hands, the broad, barrel-shaped body, the ragged overall, a face . . . the face of an old man peering into the darkness through spectacles with thick lenses, his head wreathed in a mane of shoulder-length white hair. A half-blind, bowed ancient was in charge of him.

The old man stepped silently back through the door, closed it, the lock rattled and Bean was again in the darkness with his new sensational knowledge.

5

Naturally there were several of them. There *must* be several of them. On his own, the old man would have been incapable of lugging him to this place from the Dump (wherever 'this place' was). He had also heard voices, more than one, deep male voices. And the boy? What was he doing out here with an old man? There must be more of them, but the old man had been told to keep watch over him.

The thought excited Bean, even made him arrogant. He lay face down with his arms stretched ahead of him, pulling and tugging at the loose stone in the first grey light. He had planned it like this. One hour's hard work in first light, then back to the ordinary dull rhythm until the next morning. He had eaten the unappetizing gruel that had been poured into his dish. He had drunk the water. He persuaded himself he could feel his strength returning, but that was probably only an illusion created by his sudden optimism, the hope the discoveries of the last twenty-four hours had aroused in him.

He was breathing heavily as he worked, taking long rests with his head on his arms. He was no longer used to such effort, no longer in a state to keep his concentration fixed on any activity covering a longer period of time. Nevertheless it was relatively easy to loosen the stones sufficiently for them to be tipped away from the opening. On his hands and knees, he weighed up and calculated – it mustn't be so heavy that he couldn't manoeuvre it back into place. He mustn't make any blunders now that his goal seemed to be within his grasp. He must wait until he was sure.

But he dared, he *had* to dare. His fingers grasped, his muscles tensed. The stone rolled to one side and revealed a large gaping hole in the wall, big enough, although it did narrow off inwards – the wall was surprisingly thick – but a hole through which he thought he would easily be able to wriggle, as long as he could scrape away all the gravel and loose stones round the opening.

Streaks of daylight fell on to his hands as he persisted, the work laborious and unfamiliar, his hands voracious, like claws.

He persisted, urged on by his excitement. It was not so much gravel and stones as roots and low-hanging branches blocking the way out. He dug, cursing, thrusting his arm in right up to the shoulder, but it was difficult for him to see what he was doing, the opening smaller than he had first thought. He got his head and one arm through and could scarcely move, tearing out roots and coming up against more, thicker and tougher. His impatience made him gasp for air, air on his hands – he could feel it, fresh cool air from out *there*, but a thick mat was still blocking the opening, roots, branches, stalks, some as thick as lianas, intertwined like an elastic, living grating, agreeable but impenetrable. Freedom was within reach – but. . . .

He was feverishly jerking and tearing with both hands at the matted grid in the hole, which he had now made a little bigger. Part of him seemed to be acting on its own, in spite of the warning bells ringing in his mind – steady now, don't do anything rash, plan every move carefully. Suppose they are watching. . . .

A knife! If only he had a knife, anything sharp, even a nail-file. Exhausted, he lay with his face to the ground, trying to gather his wits. They were only roots, branches, plant fibres, not stone walls, iron or steel. Perhaps it wasn't going to be as easy as his first optimism had made him think, but it would work, it *had* to work – of course it would work. Branches could be cut through, broken off, torn off, gnawed off, of course it was *possible*. It was a matter of persistence, endurance. And if he had a tool. . . .

He looked round his prison again in the hope that there was something, *something or other* he could use, never mind what, which had escaped his notice. Eyes aching, he searched for a piece of metal, sharp stones, *something* . . . such concentration almost made him pass out. It seemed to him that his intense desire to escape prison must conjure up some means of help. His exaltation at that moment was so strong, he could see himself capable of black magic, reshaping his surroundings by sheer will-power. Then it happened. He saw something he had not seen before. He saw something he had not seen *in that way before*. He saw the round clay dish. It was breakable. It would cut.

He grabbed the dish and held it close to his face to examine it. Where should he hit it and how to get an effective shard as sharp as a knife? Doubts rose for a moment, his anxiety returning; it wouldn't work, it wouldn't cut properly, and by smashing the dish he would ruin his last chance needlessly. He sat paralysed under the weight of that possibility, then pulled himself together, found a stone that fitted well in his hand, and struck the base of the dish sharply. It broke into jagged pieces, leaving at least two large bits long enough to lie well in his hand and at the same time with an edge, rough as it was, but which seemed both hard and sharp enough to cut through tough fibres.

But even with these new tools, progress was too slow. If he were making any progress at all, it was scarcely noticeable. If he finally managed to cut through a root or a stalk, what was left seemed to be even thicker. His earthenware cutter also turned out to be far less effective than he had hoped, the edge brittle and small pieces breaking off when he made an extra effort. He filed and filed away on the thickest branch, the one he *had* to move if there were to be any hope of his getting through the opening, but to no avail. He achieved nothing but a few scars in the bark and some sap on his fingers. He was sweating. He chewed leaves to counteract his physical exhaustion, then tried again, persisting although he saw it was no use. It would take a long time, days, weeks. He realized that now. But . . .

His strength was ebbing, hope vanishing. He was aware of it and fought against it. But weariness overcame him and proved impossible to shake off, his despair at failing at this most decisive attempt draining him and becoming a dull pain far back in his mind. The unfamiliar strain had also reinforced his basic needs – thirst plagued him, and for the first time for ages he realized how terribly hungry he was. He hacked and slashed feebly at a small flexible branch with no visible effect. Would they be feeding him soon? No, now he remembered. They had given him something as long ago as yesterday – two or three days could go by . . . he groaned with dismay. Two days without food. He couldn't make it.

But if only he could get free now, it would be easy to get hold of something. . . .

As long as he wasn't caught again the moment he got out, pushed back in again and starved even more. Bean flinched. The opening he could just see behind the network of foliage had ceased to tempt him, and now fear seized him as he imagined escaping, crawling through the opening out into the unknown. If only he had some inkling of *where* he was – escaping from his pursuers without knowing in which direction rescue lay if it existed – hunted like an animal, a dog. . . .

Exhausted, he lay on the earth floor, sobbing for breath, tears running down his sunken, bearded cheeks. If only he had some water, something to eat and then be allowed to sleep. He had no desire to escape, no desire to be elsewhere, all he wanted was to sleep, sleep. . . .

His head resting on the floor, he lay as if lifeless, half-chewed leaves dribbling out of his open mouth as he lost consciousness, a few streaks of sunlight playing on his torn, blood-stained hands.

6

Hands were tugging and pulling at him. He was being carried away, half dragged, half lifted. He noticed it was colder. The sounds around him changed, the light flickering through his eyelids into his numb mind penetratingly sharp. Reluctantly he fought his way up to the surface of this nightmare, opened his eyes and saw the faces, closed his eyes tight again and curled up, waiting for the blows that didn't come. Then he heard voices, shrill and high, crude, incomprehensible, though he could make out individual words 'Done for.

Let him lie . . .', 'Some water. . . .' Someone laughed shrilly with a strange, crude heartiness.

His head was raised, something pressed against his mouth and he felt water against his lips. He drank thirstily, slurping it in until he started coughing, coughing and coughing. Then he threw up. They let him down to the floor again, where he lay gasping until he dared open his eyes and take a proper look at his tormentors.

There were four of them standing round him. The old man he had glimpsed that night – Bean realized it must be him from his flowing white hair – and a younger, thickset man with a dark look behind his wild hair and beard. Terrifying. Two were women, a large matron, dark as a mulatto, and a pale, thin girl. A naked child was crawling in the dust round the legs of the dark woman. That shocked him. For some reason he had not been able to imagine women – even infants – being involved in this, whatever 'this' was. And whatever it was, it frightened him. A glance at the silent figures round him confirmed his worst imaginings – dirty, messy, primitive savages, their clothes in rags, staring at him. As far as he could see in the sharp light making him blink, the room they were in was cramped and mean and filled with battered old furniture.

Voices again rose like thuds on his eardrums. Unused to any noise except his own breathing, his own suppressed whimpering, he curled up again at the racket.

'Get up!'

He at once understood what the dark solid man had said, but he was unaware that the words had been directed at him until someone grabbed him by the arm and jerked him to his feet. But his legs gave way and he fell, only to be caught by hard hands and pushed up against a wall.

'Stay up now. . . .'

An angry muttering, rather like a growl, as the large dark woman let out a peal of laughter. Not only hunger and exhaustion, but this sense of losing all grasp of reality made him stand there in a daze, face to face with these frightening creatures, quite alien to him, as if they had come from another world, a dream from which he couldn't wake up, couldn't bear. . . .

He peered, unable to see clearly, indifferent now. The terror that had tormented him all the time he had been shut in had grown into something more monstrous than his mind could take in and was now driving him into a sullen apathy. The dark woman's shrill laughter became indistinct. His head fell helplessly to one side. A firm hand was holding him upright. He saw his own feet, sockless and bootless, unrecognizable under the filth and grime, his trousers in rags round his ankles, colourless with earth and dust. His uniform jacket had lost buttons and had holes in the elbows. His hair hung over his eyes and itched down his neck. What on earth did he look like? A flash of clarity told him he looked like *them*, just like his tormentors, and he felt something warm and wet trickling down his thigh. The laughter rose to a shriek of primitive mirth and the others all joined in, nudging each other and pointing at him. He was pissing in his trousers, frightened out of the last remains of his self-respect. As he clamped his hands against the crooked wall to stop himself falling, the urine splashed down his legs into a pool on the dusty floorboards.

Bean tried to speak, to communicate with them. He was beginning to get the use of his senses back again, to look around and take note of simple things in a more systematic way. His head was aching, his eyes smarting and he kept turning dizzy as he took in the unfamiliar space around him, so much larger than the dungeon in which body and soul had been incarcerated for weeks, months. But he was not mad – his reason was still intact. He kept thinking, I am not mad, as if that were a vital invocation, his only guarantee against not *going* mad. Cautiously he moved his arms and legs – he *did* have control over his body as he obediently sat on a bench they had set out for him, watching what the others were doing, out in what he imagined was a yard he could just see through the open door, flooded with dazzling light.

What were they so busy at? They seemed to sharing out small heaps of grain or seeds on to various pieces of cloth. The old man was in charge, apparently supervising, now and again letting out some brief, incomprehensible exclamation. Bean couldn't decide whether it was advice, comment or orders. Otherwise they hardly exchanged a word. Nothing appeared to be directly threatening.

Once, the old man came quite close to where Bean was sitting, and Bean tried to attract his attention to make some contact. 'Where am I?' he said, startled by the sound of his own voice, now nothing but a hoarse whisper.

The old man turned his head and peered at him, shrugged his shoulders without answering and concentrated on what the girl was doing, helping her gather the grain or seeds, or whatever it was in the heaps, into the cloth and knotting the ends together to make a bag. His manner to her was friendly and considerate. That gave Bean renewed courage.

'What are you doing?'

His voice was nothing but a hoarse clearing of his throat. The old man turned his head again.

'Sorting seeds.'

Bean struggled to retrieve his powers of speech. The fact that he had been given an answer cheered him immensely. But he must not lose the thread now, must continue this 'conversation'.

'Why?'

His question received nothing but a shrug in reply, then they seemed to forget about him again, turning away and going on with their tasks. Bean sank back into his despair, again aware of his wretched state. He stank, his trousers were sticking to his legs, he was so hungry his head was spinning and he was aching all over. Worst of all was that he had to sit there (he couldn't trust his legs to bear him and hardly dared move) with these people – even if they were his guards and tormentors – around him, so close he could have touched them, and yet was not allowed to talk to them, or allowed to know anything, where he was, why he was there, what kind of people *they* were, their intentions, what (illegal – the policeman in him was still occasionally on guard) game they were playing with him. Everything he had imagined in his terror down in that cave now seemed to be on the verge of an explanation. A couple of concrete questions, a little information. . . .'

They pottered on in silence, apparently quite unaffected by his presence. An instant sentence to death would have been better, he thought; to be allowed to know everything, even the worst, to regain some kind of structure in this nightmare, even if it meant looking his downfall straight in the eye. Not knowing was the very worst of all.

'Where am I?'

His voice sounded more human now, a slight consolation, but the two people nearest to him paid no heed.

'Who are you?'

He didn't even try to keep back the note of strident hysteria that sharpened his voice.

They both looked at him.

'Take it easy,' said the old man impatiently, as if he were not used to having his work interrupted.

'But I *want* to know. I have a right to. . . .'

Bean was suddenly almost out of control, his cry loud in the cramped room. He scrambled to his feet and took a few unsteady steps. The dark man appeared in the doorway. The man grasped Bean by the arm. 'Now, just calm down,' he growled.

But Bean was in no state to calm down. Panic had overwhelmed him and, waving his arms about, he shouted: '*What do you want of me? Why are you keeping me here? Don't touch me! Keep away! Bloody filthy. . . .*'

He hit out blindly into the air around him, lost his balance and would have fallen if the dark man had not caught him and pressed him back down on to the bench.

'Bloody fool.'

But Bean did not give up, rose again and grabbed the arm of the man who had just saved him from falling, then sank his teeth deeply into the man's wrist. The man yelled, more from surprise than pain, and as if in a dream, Bean felt a couple of sharp blows before he fell.

He came to a moment or so later and stayed in a sobbing, moaning heap on the floor. No one took any notice of him. The dark man had gone out again, while the two others, the old man and the girl, were sitting close together on a ragged sofa, talking to each other in confidential, almost whispering tones. The old man had his arm round the girl, now and again patting her affectionately. She had her head on his shoulder. Bean couldn't help noticing the girl was probably older than he had at first thought. The old man's hands running over her thin, ragged clothing revealed she was adult, although Bean saw she had lost a tooth when she smiled at him like a schoolgirl. There was nothing importunate about the old man's affection, no lust or desire in the way he was stroking the thin body, and she pressed up against him with devotion, trusting, apparently quite without sensuality.

Bean was affected by this and sudden hot sexual urges ran through him, confusing him. He was lying so that he could see up the girl's skirt, right up her thin, dirty thighs, and he more than dimly perceived that this was a grown woman. But the old man just went on stroking her as if she were a child. Bean groaned and bent double with arousal; a hard-on would reveal what was the matter with him. That toothless smile. The wild, earth-coloured mane of hair. The pink thumb she kept putting to her mouth. And then those dark female loins he had glimpsed under the skirt. He had to fight a wild impulse to throw himself at her and sink his teeth into one of those thin, dirty thighs – Bean, who otherwise had been so proud of having his erotic impulses under complete control. He who had not wanted to sleep with Stella if she had not just had a bath and was newly powdered, newly oiled. He, who had loved her smell of soap perhaps more than anything else, was now lying on this filthy floor, in an agony of cramp, stinking, degraded, his ejaculation spurting seething warm sperm over his stomach as he rolled his eyes round to get a single look, be given one glorious chance of peeping at the loins of a poor ragged vagrant girl.

But it was not just her, it was the old man as well, what he was doing to her, or perhaps what he *wasn't* doing to her. It was probably the first time Jonathan Bean had ever seen people caressing each other with no other motives and making no demands, without either having to give or take anything. For perhaps the first time, Bean experienced the sensual delight in being *close* to someone, in this case two people who did not fear him or each other, and it was almost unbearable.

He groaned even louder. It sounded like a sob.

The two on the sofa looked across at him again. He was in such a state, he could not look them in the eye, but through waves of shame and ridiculous embarrassment he heard the old man's voice.

'You really are an idiot picking a fight with Allan. He saved your life. Run-Run wanted to finish you off there and then, but Allan stopped him. You should thank him instead of behaving like that. If you keep trying Allan, you'll not be much use out here.'

The dark man called Allan put him to work. Although it was simple, it seemed to him completely meaningless and so strenuous and enervating. Out of a buckled zinc bucket of rusty scrap-iron, he had to pick nuts and bolts, nails and screws, to sort out those usable according to size and then find nuts and bolts that fitted. It was slow work and he soon got bored, exhausted with hunger, tormented by his uncertainty, though to be entrusted with work, any work, was a consolation, if only because it seemed to mean he was not in any immediate danger. But his fingers were clumsy, unused as they were to such employment, his concentration soon wavering. The unreality of the whole situation paralysed all systematic thought, confused pictures coming and going in his head. He reacted impulsively, like a child, tears alternating with delight, every new perception wiping out all traces of those that had gone before.

The fact alone that these *creatures*, these bandits (his self-confidence still sharply differentiated between *them* and *him*, even if his mind told him that outwardly there was no difference between him and his guards at this moment), took such an interest in collecting bolts and screws, bewildered him. Old tools and rusty parts lay around in cases and boxes, on tables, on the floor or simply in heaps all over the room. What did they use them for? To him these people seemed to belong to some primitive tribe. It even seemed surprising that they knew how to use the more complicated tools. He could see that from the room, rickety furniture tied together with something that looked like rope. Was it plant fibre? Creepers were growing profusely, wildly all over the only window, making it impossible to see out. The ceiling was full of holes and half covered with a thick mat of interwoven creeper, much like some jungle hut. What kind of house was this?

He had noticed the way Allan and the old man had handled the scrap-metal, most of it rusty and defective, carefully and considerately, as if every useless twisted piece of metal represented something rare and valuable. What did it mean? *Where* was he? His uncertainty again overwhelmed him and the need to whimper, weep, give up, tightened his throat. The result of his meaningless labours lay in two or three heaps in front of him on the floor. His head spun.

'I'm hungry,' he almost shouted at the back of the old man, now mending some clothes.

The old man hardly turned his head as he answered.

'You'll have to wait.'

That brief and negative exchange of words, of human language, alone soon swamped Bean's mind in an avalanche of questions his reason demanded he should ask.

'I suppose you are aware you are holding a sergeant of the Force prisoner . . . that I will be missed and they will send out a search patrol . . . that the punishment for abduction is severe. . . .'

His agitation made him drip with sweat. He noticed he was incapable of articulating as he ought. Provided there was a little intelligence left in these creatures, they should be receptive to sensible arguments. But he simply could not grasp what madness had persuaded them to keep him prisoner. He *had* to be found. They *had* to be held responsible. That would mean severe punishment for them all, maybe even the death sentence in the present state of emergency, should anything happen to him . . . he wanted this expressed calmly and with conviction, penetrating their primitive ignorance and their certainty that the law and authority, the whole of civilization, of organized society, was on their side. But the words would not come or arrange themselves in proper sequence, and his superiority evaporated with the stench of his soiled clothing.

'What if I escape?' he cried out in despair. 'What if I get away and . . . *report* you?'

He thumped his fist on the floor so that the dust flew, defiant as a child.

The dark man was again in the doorway, looking at him and shaking his head disapprovingly.

'Bean . . .' he said.

Bean started. The man knew his name. Of course. They had taken his wallet, his identity card. But all the same, they knew more about him than he knew about them.

'No, Bean,' said the black-bearded Allan in a gentler, almost superior voice. 'You won't be going anywhere. You'll be staying here.'

He was given no food until it was dark. The old man gave him two slices of hard dry bread and water, and ate the same himself. The mulatto woman and the child had gone, in as much as he no longer heard or saw them. Allan came in and out, arranging the boxes of scrap-iron. In the course of the day, Bean had sorted two or three handfuls of serviceable nuts and bolts, that was all. He considered his contribution more than feeble, but neither Allan nor the old man seemed to mind. Who could guess what was going on – if anything – behind those expressionless faces? Bean had been tormented by hunger and thirst all day. Once or twice he had asked for water, but the old man had just shaken his head. When Bean had asked a second time, he had replied curtly, 'We have to save water.'

Bean had noticed the others neither drank nor ate anything, so he said nothing more.

Now they were munching on the dry bread together, except for the young girl, who had fallen asleep on the sofa, her thumb in her mouth. Bean could see the daylight fading, and fear overcame him again. What would happen at night? Again, he suddenly felt that longing to get out, to be free. He had not dared approach the door all day for fear of arousing their suspicions. Now his eyes settled on the square of trampled grass and gravel he could see through the doorway, trees just visible in the background. It was already dim inside the room.

'Where am I?'

He had asked before, begging for an answer, but had been met with nothing but a shrug, as if they did not really understand the question, or that it was of no interest to them. Perhaps it irritated them that he asked questions to which the answer was obvious.

The old man was now looking at him through those thick, dirty lenses with a resigned but not unfriendly gaze. 'The Dump,' he mumbled.

'Are we on the *Dump*?'

'Where else?'

The old man shook his head indulgently and turned his attention elsewhere.

'But. . . .' Bean could not stay silent. 'But there's grass here. And trees. And . . .'

'The Dump's bigger than you think,' said the old man, getting up from the table. 'Now we must see to it you're all fixed up for the night.'

At first Bean did not understand what he meant. That was the longest sentence he had heard from the old man all day, and he was still tasting the words when he suddenly felt his arm seized. He was dragged to his feet and shoved towards a small door at the far end of the room. He protested instinctively and tried to resist, but at the same time realized he hadn't a chance. Beyond this 'room' was an even smaller room like a bedroom, as it contained an old iron bedstead with some bedclothes on it, grey with months if not years of continuous use. The ceiling slanted steeply as if the external wall had once collapsed. The old man pushed him towards a kind of opening, a low door in this collapsed end of the little room, and he suddenly realized what was going to happen. He was to go back, down into that dungeon where they had kept him imprisoned. They were going to shut him in again. He let out a shriek and started struggling. The very thought of that stinking dungeon induced panic in him. He would say something to them, beg and beseech, plead with them not to shut him in, not there. He would promise them . . . he would agree to anything . . . he . . .

But only inarticulate sounds came out through his clenched teeth as they dragged him the short distance across to the opening, pushed open the door and flung him down on to the earth floor inside.

'Take it easy,' mumbled the old man, roughly pushing away Bean's hands clinging to the door-frame. 'It's only for one night.'

A shove sent him backwards into the darkness. He hit his head and shoulder against the wall where wall and ceiling had collapsed and become one. Then the door slammed and the lock rattled. Bean was alone again.

<h1 style="text-align:center">7</h1>

The person with whom Bean made best contact was the sodden wreck of a man called Smiley. Smiley understood what he said. Smiley talked so that Bean understood, said things with some meaning, and he had the impression Smiley actually liked talking to him, or rather, *at* him, when he chose not to reprove or simply torment him. In this respect, he was worse than any of the others. In that respect they looked down on Smiley, who talked so incomprehensibly, and this made Bean feel safer in his company. Anxiety was still the worst of his torments, worse than hunger and thirst, vermin and itching, and the terrible daytime heat which burnt out all his strength. At night his cramped dungeon turned into an unbearable oven in which he lay for hours struggling for breath, the sweat pouring out of every pore.

Smiley mocked him for his lack of stamina. 'Luxury guy, eh?' he spat, as Bean staggered along groaning under the weight of a cylinder block from some wreck of a car Old Doc had told them to fetch. 'You'll have to get used to a different life from trotting from air-conditioned office to air-conditioned car and driving home to an air-conditioned apartment. Eh?'

Bean clenched his teeth and struggled on through the piles of scrap-iron, stumbled, but managed to keep on his feet. His feet tolerated it all better now. The first weeks on the Dump with no shoes had turned the soles of his feet into painfully inflamed sores, and every evening Doc had tended them with green leaves under tight bandages, ignoring his feeble protests and prayers to have his boots back. Doc was merciless. 'Do you think we want you running about free out here?' he said brusquely. 'A fool like you might try escaping. . . . Anyhow, your boots have long since been sold,' he added when Bean, near to tears, promised vociferously and by all that is sacred that he would never dream of escaping, that he would never make the slightest attempt as long as he could have some shoes and escape this torture. The rags bound round his feet soon wore out and were little help, and his feet simply bled and ached. But Doc put on his green leaves and ignored his complaints.

The amazing thing was that this quack treatment seemed to work, not miraculously and not at once, but the swellings had anyhow usually gone down by the next morning, and the sores were not bad enough to prevent him standing up and walking. Then the natural hardening process did the rest.

He once asked what kind of leaves Doc used and the answer he was given was remarkable.

'Plantains. There'll be no more artificial medicaments left, so we'll have to turn to nature's own. Plantains. The best thing for sores ever to see the light of day. Didn't you play with plantains when you were little? Put them on your knees when you had grazed them? They grow everywhere, in town, too, between the paving-stones. No, you probably didn't. Yes, plantains . . . even the Romans had plantains for blisters. But you probably don't know who the Romans were?'

No, Bean did not know what 'the Romans' were. But his feet had gradually got better, the soles now as hard as bark.

'Hey, fool!' cried Smiley, struggling at the other end of the heavy piece of iron. 'Let's take a rest, shall we?'

Bean nodded thankfully and let go, then more or less collapsed and lay panting with his back against some large stones.

'I'm beginning to see the whites of your eyes,' said Smiley, grinning. He was also gasping and wiping away the sweat, but retained his superiority over the exhausted Bean. 'You aren't up to much, are you? I thought men like you were specially trained to stand anything. Anything, but not life without air-conditioning, eh?' He grinned. 'If it's any consolation, it'll be much worse later on in the summer, when there's less water, and what there is tastes bitterer than what you're getting now. More difficult to get food, too . . . if you haven't died by then.'

Bean did not answer. He could never find anything to say in response to Smiley's perpetual stream of malicious irony. The humiliation and rage which would normally have welled up in him at being treated like this became a dull unpleasantness at the back of his mind, not even an irritation. He found it difficult to find words, here where speech was so rarely used, then used in ways with which he was not familiar. The more he understood, guessed or somehow fathomed of their conditions and way of life, the more impossible it seemed to find adequate words, or to be able to define his own relations to the facts now dominating his life. He felt it must be worth while trying to find some expression for his amazement at being alive at all. Considering the way he lived, he had good reason to reflect. His days were filled with hard labour, largely out on the scorching Dump, exhausting him almost to unconsciousness, and his nights in the clammy dungeon were one long struggle against the heat and the panic that overwhelmed him in the darkness, the sense of having been dumped into an utterly alien and insane world, where nothing functioned as expected in relation to attitudes and rules he had learnt to respect.

During the first weeks he had been obsessed by the idea of escaping. Restless, impossible plans had spawned in his brain, as if contemplating escaping was his last shred of reason, a protest against the meaninglessness by which he seemed to be surrounded, threatening to send him out of his mind. The hopeless passivity that had recently paralysed him when he had been imprisoned for a short while had then been relieved by feverish speculations about escaping. Finally *seeing* the creatures who had imprisoned him, how degraded and down-and-out they were, the way they lived like rats on the garbage they found on the tip, had produced a flicker of his old sense of superiority. He was a sergeant in the Force, trained in anti-terrorist strategies. He would get himself out of this mess.

But his ruined feet had at first effectively put a stop to all attempts to escape, and as the weeks went by, day by day, in the heat, toil and inhuman monotony, he could feel his determination dulling, as if the very capacity for purposeful thought and action had slowly dissolved as a result of the shameful conditions in which he was living. Although no one directly maltreated him, his waking hours were one long torment. Scared, shouted at, he scuttled around like a slave, carrying out as best he could the often meaningless and degrading jobs they gave him, bemoaning his fate whenever he had a moment to himself. And yet, without their orders and commands, he would undoubtedly have abandoned himself to an apathy from which he could never have extracted himself without help. That is what his surroundings had done to him.

There were also the difficulties he had orientating. Although he could usually just glimpse either the bay on one side and the elevated motorway on the other, or both, he still had great trouble judging directions and distances in the peculiar landscape of the

Dump. The strip of sand they had to pass to get to Doc's ruin of a house seemed endless, and in Doc's jungle-like garden, where tall trees suddenly shut off the view, he completely lost his sense of direction.

He knew Sweetwater was furthest in in the bay and that it extended about ten to fifteen, at the most twenty kilometres, in reality not even that far, because building in the city also reached beyond the suburbs, almost all the way to the waste land out here. People who could help him must actually live only five or six kilometres away, if only he could at least get a message to them, a cry for help.

It was now a long time since his imagination had contained plans of that kind, a long time since he had felt anything that might give rise to spontaneous action, a plan for outmanoeuvring them and leading him to freedom. His degradation and dulled existence had sealed his self-confidence into a cocoon of anxiety, a terror of not having his most trivial desires satisfied, not being given food, water, time to rest, sleep; the terror of suffering injury, being hit or tormented.

But even in clearer moments when he saw what was happening to him, how feeble and oppressed and dependent he had become, this no longer produced a shower of bitter self-reproach. He had ceased to expect anything, his perspectives extending from sunrise to sunset. And if in the evening, before they shut him in, he even noticed the lights from Sweetwater, a dull yellowish reflection from a cloud of smog that always hung over the city, he felt nothing, or perhaps simply a distant, melancholy stab of loss, which would soon be replaced by bitterness, for instance, over not having had more to eat, or the sneaking fear of the unbearably lonely claustrophobia of the night.

To start with, they had kept an eye on him, and he knew it as he hobbled off, complaining, blood-stained rags round his feet and his head full of plans for escaping in an unguarded moment, hiding under a heap of garbage until dark, making his way to the gate, to the road, hailing a car. . . .

But recently they seemed to have realized that his decisiveness, even the world of his imagination, was crumbling in the conflict between the life he knew, where he belonged, traces of which he could no longer distinguish, and the alien reality surrounding him. They allowed him to operate more on his own, sent him on longer errands, out of sight. Theoretically the chances of his escaping were better than ever, if a chance arose for him to attempt it, especially now his feet were so much better and he could make his way everywhere with no difficulty. But the idea occurred to him more and more rarely. He thought they were keeping a wary eye on him so that he would not notice anything, to test him out, the tall, silent man and the little boy also visible everywhere, at all times. Nothing escaped their sharp senses.

He noticed he didn't really like moving too far away from the others. He gazed over the endless stretches of the mountain of garbage between him and a 'normal' life, which seemed more and more distant and unreal. The very thought of setting off out over that landscape, with its unfamiliar paths and directions, towards an uncertain goal on the other side, filled him with panic. His eyes sought those of the others working closest to him, usually one of them within sight, and the sight of a human being, although one of 'them', gave him a sense of contact, consolation and protection.

He had sunk that low.

In clear moments, his reason told him he was degenerating, losing his human dignity. He had read of similar cases and knew the symptoms from descriptions of victims of lengthy torture, brain-washing. He himself had not gone through anything that might be called torture or brainwashing, but he sensed that although he occasionally managed to keep an idea in his mind, his mental processes and morale had declined to the extent that they were approaching simply instincts, the primitive he had always despised – and all this had happened very quickly. How many weeks or months had he been out there? He had shown no particular resolution, no particular strength of mind, nor had he any strength or independence left to reproach himself. He was lost in a will-less chaos of fear and despair, binding him more and more firmly to his tormentors, and he registered this with sick resignation, with the perverse pleasure of debasement.

'Bean. Why did you come snooping out here?'

Smiley's insolent, teasing voice broke through the seething thoughts floating round Bean's numb brain. He recognized the question. He had been asked it several times before. It was Smiley's favourite question, as if he enjoyed knowing Bean would never really be able to explain properly how his brother had disappeared, the clues leading there, how important it was for him to clear his brother's name.

Once, it *had* seemed important.

As he struggled to find words to explain the disgrace of being suspected of desertion, he seemed to have difficulty keeping to abstract concepts such as 'duty' and 'honour', no doubt owing to his increasing uncertainty with words and the others' indifference to precise language. Nor had they time to listen to his elaborate attempts to give them an answer to what to them seemed a simple question.

'What brought you out to the Dump?'

Smiley's repeated question moved something inside him, as if something were driving him to try to put it into words yet again, at least to Smiley, who seemed to have some desire to improve his linguistic skills. Something told him that this was also essential in itself, to keep in mind that he had a mission, the goad of loyalty to his brother's reputation, to the principle of justice, even in the long run to law and order, to a just State. He felt this to be a last anchorage, the last shred of human dignity left in him. Without it he was nothing – an animal.

'It was my brother . . .' he began. 'Because of my brother Joseph. He disappeared. He was registered as a deserter. But he was no deserter!'

'How do you know?'

Smiley's question was put quietly, but the irony was sharp. Bean had a fleeting sense of being made a fool of, that Smiley had again asked the central question just to observe his efforts to find an answer and gloat over him. But, determinedly, he tried again.

'Joseph wasn't like that. He wasn't that *type*. He was doing his job. He was investigating some business about foreign workers when he disappeared. He mentioned the Dump in his reports . . .'

' . . . but his car was found in the multi-storey car-park at the East Terminal?'

'Yes . . . yes, that's right.'

Bean's brain struggled, painfully sluggish in the heat. Here was something, a detail that didn't fit. The policeman in him had got hold of something.

'Yes, but how do you know that?'

'You just said so.'

Smiley's grin was malicious, condescending, impossible to fathom.

'No . . . I? No, no . . .'

'Yes, you did.'

He was sure he had not mentioned what he read about his brother's car in the report. He still instinctively avoided anything to do with confidential information. But how otherwise would Smiley have known about? . . .'

'You shouldn't know about that!' he blurted out.

'The heat's gone to your head, my dear Bean,' said Smiley. 'Everyone knows Joseph Bean's official car was found stripped and abandoned on the top of the East Terminal multi-storey. Everything sellable had been taken. Only his notebook was found, wedged between the seat and the back.'

'How do you know that?'

Dismay had overcome Bean. Smiley's words affected him strangely, conjuring up a ghost of his intention to clear his brother's name, while they also made him feel more helpless than ever. Worst of all was that what he had said indicated that Smiley really knew *more* than he, Jonathan Bean, did, he who had sworn to solve the mystery, learn the truth and save his honour.

'You shouldn't know anything about that!'

The idea that this wreck of a man perhaps knew something about the truth for which he, Jonathan Bean, had sacrificed his job and professional prestige to ferret out, and for which now, every day, as if he were being punished for it, he had to work himself to death in grotesque circumstances, made him quite beside himself. Again it shot through him, what was left of him – his sense of duty, his pride, his insistent respect for law and order, civilized instincts that had lain dormant in the wretched shell of the man into which they had turned him.

'What do you know?' he shouted, a burning, fanatical glow from the past seizing him and shaking him through and through. *'What do you know about my brother?'*

Humiliation was one thing, but to be so near the truth he was seeking and then being made a fool of was more than he could bear. He had got half-way to his feet and was standing with his hands on his knees, trembling like an animal about to leap.

'So you came out here and rummaged around just to find out what happened to your brother?'

Smiley had not moved and was looking quite unaffected, his grin simply a trifle broader. Bean was incapable of replying, but simply stared at him, the other man, his prison guard, who had wrapped his thin arms round his knees, the malicious grin playing in the sparse, carroty beard.

'You could have asked, and you'd have been given an answer.'

His tormentor, so indispensable to him, was dwelling on it, savouring every word. Bean was about to answer, but his voice failed him. His throat was dry, his hands cold. Something had broken inside him and his field of vision blurred into waves of reddish-yellow sunlight as tears filled his eyes and ran down his cheeks. He fell back against the warm stones and lay there with one hand digging in stubborn rage into the dry sulphur-yellow earth.

'He's over there,' said Smiley, nodding indifferently at the low heap of stones propping up Bean.

Bean didn't take it in. 'There?' He didn't move. Turned his head. Sniffed. Waited for the next thing from his tormentor.

But Smiley had caught his audience and said nothing, just waited. When Bean at last understood and turned his head and saw the oblong contour of the cairn of stones he had been leaning against, he leapt to his feet as if he had been scalded. Smiley put his face down on his knees, gasping with crazy laughter.

'Fool! It's not true! You're lying, you damned. . . .'

Smiley could scarcely answer, he was so overcome with mirth.

'I . . . I really do think you should take the trouble to lift a few stones if you don't believe me. Since you're so full of energy after all. . . .'

He peered at the shattered Bean, who was limping round, wringing his hands in helpless impotence, whimpering incomprehensible, infantile abuse.

At long last he got back his power of speech, the words coming jerkily in a whisper, every syllable a torture.

'Who . . . did it?'

'Allan buried him so the corpse wouldn't infect us. Run-Run probably did him in . . . he got too nosy, you see, just like you. It must run in the family . . .'

'How do you know it was . . . him?'

'I've seen his ID card. Allan's got it. Otherwise there's not much left. He even sold his uniform buttons. We don't like snoopers out here.'

'I'll kill you! I'll kill Allan . . . Run-Run. . . .' Bean was almost inaudible.

'Now listen, Bean. Allan saved your life, don't forget that. He came just when Run-Run was about to cut your throat. It's because of Allan you're still alive. And you couldn't cope with Run-Run. No one can get the better of Run-Run. He sleeps with his eyes open.

He's quicker and stronger than any of us. And he's only waiting for an excuse. Haven't you thought about that?'

No, Bean had not thought about that. He sank to the ground and lay there twisting and turning, dust blinding him, earth grating between his teeth and Smiley's laughter ringing in his ears.

8

But when darkness had fallen and they were to eat, Bean sat there with his plate together with the others, slurping in whatever Allan dished out. They often ate together after days when they had all been searching the Dump for something edible or saleable. The only one not there was old Doc, who usually kept himself to himself, or was with the girl Bean had discovered was Allan's other wife. The girl, Lisa, pale and silent, was sitting close to Allan and the majestic mulatto woman, concentrating on what she was eating, and the naked girl-child kept crawling up and down on to her lap, whining until she was heard, and as usual got her way. With a sigh, Lisa pulled up her cotton jersey and let the child suck, sitting astride her lap while Lisa herself went on eating.

Bean no longer felt disgust at the sight. He had been confronted with it often enough and at first it had upset him. A girl feeding a half-grown, semi-wild child who could walk and run and even speak a few words. Then he had found out that the child, called Rain, really was Lisa's, Allan the father, and that the massive woman, Mary Diamond, mostly looked after it. And he found out more. That Mary Diamond had belonged to Smiley, but now lived in a camping van as Allan's wife. Also that Boy, the wild, dumb little boy, was the son of Allan and Lisa. That Lisa, who seemed turned in on herself, infantile and rarely participated very actively in their common chores, was under the protection of Doc, 'loaned out' to him, although his feelings for her were no more than grand-fatherly.

All this Bean had gradually found out, and the simplicity of their lives, as well as the wretchedness and toil, the stench and filth, the vermin and the whole degrading background of their primitive existence had appalled him and filled him with intense loathing – so much more despairing because he himself lived there with 'them' in exactly the same way, outwardly in no way different from them. The thought that he looked like 'them' and that it was only a matter of time – weeks? months? – before he would *become* like them, had tormented him until he had thought he would lose the last remains of his sanity.

But no longer. He sat leaning over the table, concentrating on the food on his plate, unable even to bother to eat slowly, savouring the food. His hands scrabbled and tore at the tough, rank dog-meat. He smacked his lips and licked his fingers, then stretched out a dirty, horny fist for more. Run-Run was sitting cross-legged and bolt upright beside him, eating as always with slow, deliberate, almost mechanical movements. It was he, the mute savage with such resourcefulness and skill with a knife, who had got them a dog that day. They did not often have meat. Bean grabbed the piece Allan handed him and stuffed it into his mouth, unable to control himself, although he knew he would not be given any more. The crisp, hard skin tasted burnt and next to the bone the meat was raw and tough, for they had been unable to wait for it to roast right through. Bean thought it tasted wonderful.

Nothing else existed for the moment. After the episode with Smiley that afternoon, he had been devastated. The incredible revelation about his brother's disappearance (it never occurred to him to doubt it was the truth), his *acceptance* of this truth, his complete powerlessness to do anything about it, his panicky dependence on his brother's murderer, all merged into a paralysing awareness of his own wretchedness. He had been given proof of how irretrievably low he had sunk, and that fact had been more than he could endure.

Hunger and thirst were something else. As the sun had gone down and it had grown darker, he had felt the pain beginning in his guts. He had staggered to his feet and dragged himself away from the place where Smiley had contemptuously left him, then headed for the camping van where he knew they would soon be eating.

Weakened, he had tried to orientate himself, to find his way through the garbage heaps round about the camping van, to the others. It had been slow going. A new fear had overcome him, the fear of being alone, to him synonymous with being lost on the Dump. Smiley had gone. The others had assembled somewhere in the hideous labyrinth of mounds of garbage. As he had walked, he had struggled to find landmarks, stumbling at every step, the landscape around him apparently increasingly unfamiliar and threatening. Once, he had thought he had lost his way, and he had fallen helplessly to his knees, cursing Smiley for leaving him alone.

Prostrate, he had ground his teeth and dug his nails into the earth as dry sobs were forced out of his throat, until hunger had driven him on again on his hands and knees.

In a clearer moment, he saw he had never had a better opportunity to escape than just then. They had never allowed him to roam that far before. He could turn back, head for the gate and get out on to the road. He knew the solution to the puzzle, he had proof and could avenge his brother's murder.

But fear and hunger wiped out all ideas of freedom, retribution or justice. He was sick with the fear of not finding his way to the camping van, back to the others. Hunger made him double up in pain as he stumbled on, searching for familiar objects, landmarks in this decay, the decay of his civilization, decay of his personal moral integrity, hoarse cries as if from a child suddenly coming from him because he couldn't find his way back to safety, to closeness, to the place where he had been taken, in the hope that it would appear behind the next wrecked car, the next mound of this stinking rotting culture of prosperity.

On that short trek from his brother's grave to Allan's camping van, something of great significance happened to Jonathan Bean. He gave up resisting, utterly and for good, resigning himself to his fate, to their common destiny, as if the strains of that afternoon had finally wrought havoc in his mind, destroying his sense of proportion, blinding him to all perspectives apart from seeking the security offered by what was nearest: filling his stomach.

He had reached the others exhausted, whimpering, with but one clear thought in his mind, to be given food, to be with them. Everything else, Sweetwater, his present existence, his brother, his desire to restore his honour, his own pride and self-assurance, were all driven to the innermost, deep and unconscious darkness from which he no longer had the ability to extract himself.

So he reached out his hand quite without thinking for a bone Run-Run had put down, as he tentatively sought the wild man's clear gaze to see if he would disapprove of his gnawing at what was left of the tough fibres on the white dog-bone. He did not think of the man from whom he was begging a bone as his brother's executioner, or else that thought no longer had any connection with anything real, here and now. On the contrary, he felt admiration for the man with the knife, his tracking ability, his patience in the hunt, his alert accuracy with his weapon, the same weapon he had used to murder his brother.

47

It wasn't that – it was to get food, to have enough to eat for yet another day, feel the cramp in his stomach let go and be replaced with a limpness resembling well-being; to feel tiredness settling on him after his hunger had been stilled; the thought of rest, of sleep.

Where Smiley got hold of the liquor was a mystery, but that evening he passed the bottle round and everyone drank, even the unfathomable Felix, always correct but steadily more threadbare. Felix, Run-Run's brother and his exact opposite, drank from the bottle and wiped his mouth with the back of his hand. Allan and Mary drank, she with one arm round his waist. Lisa took a sip and wrinkled her nose. Even Bean was given the bottle, put it to his mouth and took a long, stinging swig of the fiery liquid that tasted of yeast, nuts and petrol. Run-Run was sitting on his own, his eyes closed, ignoring their presence. The children were asleep, the boy curled up on some paper sacks half under the camping van, the little girl leaning against Lisa's thin chest with the nipple in her half-open mouth and a streak of bluish-white milk running down her chin.

The liquor caused a harsh, limited cheerfulness between them. Grimaces, gestures, peals of laughter dispersed the bleakness of their exhausting day, their struggle for survival, their masks of weariness, fear and alert suspicion. The liquor opened the sluice-gates of communication, changing it, because it was usually held in and so became notably abrupt, coarse and primitive now that it was at last released.

Bean felt nausea rising and his head spinning from the crude liquor, he himself sliding, sliding in towards the warm, guttural fellowship, merging into it. He had never really felt such *closeness* before, such harmony with other human beings. He had to admit that, although they looked like a flock of primeval creatures, just like himself.

But that meant far less now, now he had food inside him; at least his starved guts were no longer gnawing at him. The sun had gone down and the air from the bay cooled the waves of heat rising from the ground, the stored-up heat of the day from thousands of tons of disintegrating concrete, corroding metal, rotting wood, cartons, cardboard, paper and brackish soil.

A dog howled.

Bean suddenly thought he could see a new 'order' around him. The two or three shacks largely made of packing-cases and cardboard they had put up around the open space in front of the camping van looked almost like a kind of 'village' in which the primitive structures made by humans were so similar to the disorder around them that they more or less became one, the people themselves, their animal way of life, in a strange way harmonizing with their environment of garbage, decay and wretchedness. At that moment this unity with the 'landscape' became a confirmation of the security Bean was feeling, now he had at last given up resisting the fact that he lived there and lived together with them all, had abandoned his plans to escape and all hope of being rescued, abandoned memories of a definite order of things, cause and effect, the overriding system of logic and principle he had always called justice. Now that it was enough to feel satisfied after eating nauseating, semi-raw dog-meat, weariness after the day's toil, and the liquor. . . .

He slid, noticing he was sliding, and it felt good to slide into the dark, fuzzy fellowship he thought they must all be sharing, seeing the distance between them and him growing smaller, wishing for nothing more than to be allowed to sit like this, close to them, hearing their voices chattering in their fractured language, seeing their faces, their movements, the close contact of their hardened, unbeautiful bodies: Mary Diamond's broad hand on Allan's trousered thigh, on his stomach, on his chest, up into his armpit. She took another swig at the bottle, ruffled his hair and stroked him as if stroking a cat, lazily, hungrily, a streak of his saliva on her neck. She was celebrating him, and he her. Soon they would fall on each other and abandon themselves to the crude, unequivocal sexuality they practised together. Bean had seen it before and it had embarrassed him, though the woman's unconcealed desire had lit a spark in his dulled imagination.

He simply sat there watching them, feeling the warmth rising in him, as if the rough caresses they were exchanging also concerned him, and he felt another avalanche sliding free and rocking his ideas, his prejudices, his taboos, turning everything upside-down and taking him with it, just letting it happen. He let it happen as he sat watching them, so close to them that they could see him, with no thought that what he was doing might upset or offend the others, no feeling of distance or shame, not even when she, from whom warmth radiated more than any of the others, saw him, saw what he was doing and laughed.

'Just look at Bean! Sitting there wanking away like any old

monkey! Hah-ha! Ha-ha, ha-ha-ha-ha!'

But Bean was by then beyond hearing or seeing anything.

The liquor also loosened Smiley's tongue. He harangued and held forth, turning first to one, then the next, ending with Bean, who was the only one not asleep or busy with something else or who could be bothered to listen.

When Smiley talked, all his latent talents broke loose, as if he were the last human being with the use of his tongue, as if their wretched fates depended on him expressing what was churning round in his head. Bean had often been frightened and annoyed by his flow of words, but now he found he hardly understood, or perhaps couldn't be bothered to understand what the other man was talking about. He noticed it was getting dark, and thought dimly it would soon be time for them to shut him in. He shivered slightly, drew a deep breath and noticed he was sleepy. Lisa was propped against the camping van, asleep with thumb in mouth, the child pressed hard to her thin breast. Allan and Mary Diamond were snoring, intertwined on a heap of paper sacks a short distance away. Run-Run was sitting immobile as if in a trance, his eyes half-open and his gaze turned inwards, as if nothing on earth would get him out of that position. Felix was leafing through a notebook, making notes with a stump of a pencil, then going through the thin pages again and covering them with incomprehensible signs in curly handwriting.

'Surviving in this dump,' Smiley was saying. 'Living in other people's muck like bloody tapeworms. You're bloody satisfied because you manage to scrape together enough garbage to keep alive from one day to the next, aren't you? And how long do you think that can go on? For ever, or until everything seriously collapses in there?'

He was waving his arms about, staring around provocatively, ignored by them all except Bean, who was dozing, pleased no one was bothering about him, listening now and again, largely out of fear that Smiley would suddenly become angry and hit him, just because *everyone* was ignoring what he had to say.

'All right. You can lie there wallowing in your own filth. But what'll you do the day things break up for good in Sweetwater? The day it all collapses and suffocates them all in there? The day when no more muck is brought out to the Dump for the rat-pack hiding out here? Have you thought about that? Have you ever thought about us being dependent on things going all right for them in there? Have you thought about us being finished the moment they get what's coming to them? We can't cope on our own. We sponge off *them*, we do. We steal from them, we sell to them, and we eat their garbage. What are we going to do the day our supplies stop coming, when no one brings stuff out here any longer? That'll happen when *their* supplies dry up – and that day isn't far off. Have you thought about that?'

'Shut up now and let's get some sleep.'

Allan propped himself up on his elbow and peered round. Mary Diamond grunted and let out a thunderous fart, heaved over and went on sleeping.

'Oh yes, just shut up and dig yourself down into the muck and pretend things are good and it can go on like this for ever. . . .' The words poured out of Smiley as if Allan's angry outburst was the cue he had been waiting for before really getting going.

'But I'm telling you, our paradise out here is singing its last verse, even if you are too thick-headed to understand. There's nothing called equilibrium in a society like that one in there. If growth stops, that means stagnation, and stagnation means the same as collapse because the system is geared to growth. They've spent years trying to prop up the corpse by "strengthening the State's right to the distribution of goods and services", as they call it. They might as well call it bringing in dictatorship and a police state. People are kept down by pious exhortations and their own fear of "chaos" without understanding the "chaos" they're afraid of *is* already here, camouflaged by the State's attempts to direct, ration and administer. And how much longer do you think they'll manage to keep that circus going? Until the next drought crisis? Until the next epidemic? Until international trade relations collapse completely and people have to starve? Perhaps that would get them going a bit?'

Smiley went on talking feverishly, his words tumbling over each other. Bean was frightened out of his semi-slumber, registering that something was wrong. Smiley's aggression was no longer his usual sarcastic torrent of words. He was waving his arms at Allan, staring at him in a way that clearly showed his hatred and bitterness. Every word he spat out was directed at Allan, but behind the rancorous tone lay an anxiety even Bean could sense. It made him feel ill. The hate-filled agitation spoilt the sluggish mood into which he had sunk, now it was almost dark and they were all to sleep. He had to look at Smiley properly to try to comprehend what the matter was.

He saw Smiley staring steadily at Allan, now lying on his back in silence, his hands behind his head, his elbows pointing upwards and *his* eyes fixed on Smiley. Or was it not at Allan that Smiley was staring so fixedly? Was it perhaps the sleeping mountain of Mary Diamond he could not take his eyes off as he sat there, leaning forward, menacingly, bleating, mumbling? Was it Mary Diamond's slow, satisfied snoring making him let off steam like this? She had been his wife. Now she was Allan's. Allan, who had had a wife before, but who had taken Mary and was now lying there, idle, tired and sluggish after their recent uninhibited struggle.

'It's rather ironic, is it not?' Smiley went on. 'The social revolution all kinds of extremists and fanatics called for and dreamt about for decades, and now it's come all by itself without anyone lifting a finger, and after most political opposition has merged into a gigantic attempt to put a stop to it? It'll become a bit more sweeping than even the most extreme had ever thought, all right, from the tidy society of the petty bourgeoisie to the cave-dweller stage in next to no time. We've had a little taste of it out here – we're the avant garde, so to speak.'

'God, how you do go on, Smiley,' growled Allan. 'Fine words no one understands. That you can be bothered. You're out here and here you'll stay. Just like us. It's no use you babbling on like that. Wouldn't it be better if you shut up and let us get a bit of sleep?'

But Allan's condescending grunt simply upset Smiley even more.

'Stay out here, did you say! But that's the whole bloody point, my dear Neanderthal man. How long *can* we stay out here when everything else is coming to a full stop and we have no one left to sponge off any longer? What shall we do *then*? Change our eating habits? Turn to foam rubber and scrap-iron? Doc's kitchen garden would perhaps last a few weeks, but what would we do then?'

'Can't you bloody well shut up!' shouted Allan, sitting up. 'Otherwise I'll give you something else to think about.'

'All right, you just hit me . . .' squeaked Smiley, his voice fading. 'The strong-arm stuff, the surest argument of the intelligentsia.' His voice died away as Allan put his hand on the ground and half rose.

'You're a coward, Smiley,' Allan mumbled as he got to his feet, turned his back on them and staggered across to the camping van.

At that moment Felix slapped his notebook shut, got up and went over to Run-Run, who was still sitting where he had sat all evening, unmoving, cross-legged, his eyes closed. Felix struck him hard on the arm, neither kindly nor brutally and said 'Come on!' Curtly, like an order.

Run-Run opened his eyes, got up, pulled on his dark, loose-fitting coat, and with long, lithe steps obediently followed his short, corpulent brother. Bean watched them go until they vanished behind the mounds.

Smiley got the use of his tongue back. 'Off on "business",' he spat. 'Every evening off on "business". Before, it was drugs and spirits and bits of jewellery and other stolen goods. Now it's bad times for lighters and perfume and tomfoolery. Now they're shifting the road signs up on the motorway, fooling people into driving into ditches, then plundering their cars when they've gone off to get help. If they *can* go to get help, that is. If someone gets rubbed out, all the better, then they get a few watches and bracelets, or the occasional wallet . . . they'll get caught one day, that's for damned sure.'

Bean was only half listening. It was always impossible to guess how much of what Smiley was saying was true and how much invention. But he had heard their buyer, Dos Manos, who came to Doc from Sweetwater at regular intervals, the only definite contact the inhabitants of the Dump had with the outside world, had complained that sales were getting worse, that people were much more interested in food and medicine than screws, bolts, metal and spare parts. The politicians themselves had had to give up their great 'resource-friendly' programme with rewards for recycling, when it all turned into orgies of unmanageable bureaucracy which in its turn became a straight invitation to swindling on the part of the public, and also accumulated vast stores of useless scrap waiting to be repaired, or for 'refunctioning'. Dos Manos had his own channels – he got by, as yet. . . .

Lisa had also woken and was sitting propped up against the camping van, staring out at nothing in particular, the sleeping child in her arms. She suddenly said something, hesitantly, questioningly, as if talking to herself, but quite clearly so Bean heard every word.

'So few cars out there on the bridge. I remember when we sat here looking at the lights going to and fro, red and white, up and down – there's hardly any now.'

She sat staring vaguely over towards the narrow glint of water just visible behind the mounds and the top of the arch of the bridge, where the motorway wound its way across the bay and disappeared into the gathering darkness. A few points of light were dancing in the twilight, seeking, retreating, swinging away, a few individual motorists out despite price rises and petrol rationing, and a few convoys of trailers of foodstuffs for Sweetwater, links in the Government's inadequate supply programme, a mere shadow of the traffic which once not so long ago had flowed like a glittering Milky Way up and down the highways on that vast steel and concrete structure.

'We used to be able to hear that sound all the way from here when the wind was offshore, day and night, always the same, always that sound when the wind was offshore. Almost like a song.'

Lisa's clumsy, mindless sentences were the last thing he heard before sleep overtook him.

When he woke, he was cold and wondered where he was. Then he realized why he was cold, and why he immediately curled up with fear of the unknown. He was lying under the open sky! He hadn't been shut in. They had forgotten him. Or they had noticed the change in him, realized and accepted he had become like them, so it was no longer necessary to shut him in, that he *was* out on the Dump, just as they were.

In the north-east above the misty sky was a flaring, dull yellow gleam of light from Sweetwater, a magical, sparkling, dying city.

Smiley was sleeping heavily with his mouth open, crouched in the same position in which he had been sitting, only fallen over sideways. The others had gone.

Bean was so cold his teeth were chattering. Although the days were unbearably hot, the early hours of the morning could be bitterly cold. He had to find some shelter, something with which to cover himself. Some rags were overflowing out of a box of rotting clothes they had scraped together, but there were few left. He grabbed something like a blanket or a rug, stiff with age and dirt, pulled it out, shivering, wrapped it round him, then scrambled over to the heap of cardboard boxes and crates (fuel for the winter) to find a suitable sized box. COLUX SUPER it said on the outside in red, half-obliterated letters. It was snug inside.

He sensed more than he could actually see around him. Felix and Run-Run's low shack, the station-wagon Smiley lived in, a wreck that had been dragged as close to the camping van as possible, Allan's camping van, the centre, the open space in front of it with the hearth for their fire ... a rickety collection of dwellings an untrained eye (an *enemy*, as he now thought) would scarcely be able to distinguish from the innumerable other heaps and mounds and stacks of refuse and junk round about, but which to him had now become a framework round a kind of existence, even if it sickened and depressed him, an existence in which he still felt some kind of security, a crude, primitive closeness to these people whom only a month or two ago he had pursued in order to arrest and punish them, and whom he would in no way have regarded as fellow human beings.

There was a rustle to his right, somewhere near where the bones and other refuse from their meal had been left. Rats, he thought indifferently as he glanced in that direction. But it was a thin dog, its legs trembling as it guardedly watched him, its body straining towards the heap of refuse, hunger fighting with caution. Its pointed nose was turned towards the leftover food like a magnet needle, its body as tense as a violin string, its glowing eyes staring at him as if reading in his eyes the attack that had to come before it reached Bean's tired brain. But Bean did not attack. He thought dully that he ought to find a stone and throw it at the dog, injuring it so that he could catch it, kill it and provide food for them all for yet another meal, but he hadn't the energy. He closed his eyes, looked at the dog once more, and blinked sleepily.

The dog seemed to understand his lethargy. Quick as its own fear, it slunk across, snatched up a bone, slunk back and retreated half-way behind a mouldy mattress as it licked its prey, its eyes fixed on Bean.

Dog-bone, thought Bean.

Dog eating dog.

An echo of automatic revulsion for cannibalism he thought common to all, always and everywhere, raced through his mind. For a second, the sight of the wretched emaciated creature slobbering and snuffling, using its forepaws to help tear the last invisible shreds off the bone, already gnawed white, was indescribably repulsive to him. But even that affectation slid into oblivion as suddenly as it had arisen.

It's starving, he thought. Ravenous. Better chase it away. Not good to. . . .

Doc had warned them that dogs might be diseased, carrying infection with them. Better frighten the bastard . . .

A quick wave of the hand was enough. The dog evaporated. But he would never have got the better of it. If Run-Run had been there with his knife, then. . . .

The rustle of rats under the paper sacks was the only thing to break the stillness. Tomorrow he would have to find shelter, something stronger, more permanent. Maybe he could find some corrugated iron, or a crate he could use. But sleep first. Rest. . . .

He fell asleep before he could complete the thought.

PART TWO

9

Dogs had become a plague. While previously there had been the odd lone one roaming around, they were now hunting in packs all over the Dump. The greater the number, the braver they became. It was true they usually kept their distance, out of reach of Run-Run's knife and stones thrown at them, but their constant sneaking presence kept reminding all that there were now more to share the prey – anything edible in the tons of refuse still being taken out to the tip and emptied, to the accompaniment of shrieking crows. Late in the evenings the dogs wriggled their way right up to the fire where food was being prepared, to devour any remains, and they kept everyone awake late into the night with their howls.

In daylight, at first glance there was nothing frightening about these packs, seven or eight filthy, shaggy animals of various colours, shapes and breeds, keeping together, hunting in a pack. The larger muscular ones took the lead, some of the others, clearly originally pets, following as best they could on short, degenerate legs, mud and twigs hanging from their long, untrimmed coats.

'People are moving out,' Doc had said, when Allan once mentioned the plague of dogs. 'They're moving away from Sweetwater and leaving their pets behind. Most don't survive and die after a few days, but those strong enough make their way out here. That can be dangerous, because if they fight the rats they could be infected with rabies.'

But the dogs had also become a welcome addition to their food supply as access to other edibles had steadily grown more limited.

Their trade was also stagnating, ordinary foodstuffs soon not available for barter, and the refuse itself no longer contained much that was edible. The truck-drivers picked out everything useful they could find and traded it on the black market. Dos Manos, their dealer, had told them all this.

So Run-Run's sharp eye and long knife assured them dog-meat when there was nothing else to be had. Other game was also around, the rabbits increasing in numbers in the undergrowth between Doc's overgrown garden and the elevated motorway, and birds and lizards. But the dogs also hunted them, and humans were not always the ones to take home the best prey.

The drought was also threatening Doc's kitchen garden, which had expanded each year and into which they now put a huge amount of work. The flow of water to his well was sinking year by year and it tasted more and more brackish, almost so that they might just as well slake their thirst in the bay. But Doc warned them not to, despite the fact that on the Sargossa Peninsula, the activities of Sweetwater's industrial area, now dark and deserted like a ghost city directly across the narrow bay, its black chimneys and empty office buildings reflected in the oily water, were but a small fraction of what they had been in the city's days of prosperity, so the poisonous effluents had been reduced.

When there was nothing else to do, Run-Run went fishing. Day in and day out he could be seen down on the shore with his home-made rod, patiently waiting, although everyone tried to explain to him that all life out in the bay had died several years earlier. He also put out traps and lines, equipment he had carefully made himself, knotting it in the evenings out of nylon thread he had found and unravelled into single threads. None of the others had ever seen such fishing-tackle before, and no one knew where he had learnt these arts. If they asked Felix, he just shook his head. 'My brother has always been able to do such things,' he said.

Then one day Run-Run came back with a fish he had caught.

It was a very strange fish, long and narrow like an eel, with a small pointed head, gaping mouth, no teeth, and blind, overgrown eyes. Run-Run was grinning broadly, dangling the fish in front of them. He was right, there *was* life in the bay. That was a good sign, although the fish certainly looked deformed and none of them had ever seen anything like it before. Run-Run lit a fire, boiled some water and put the fish into the pan. It was so long there was scarcely room for it and the water overflowed and hissed on the embers. While it was cooking, a thick, greenish scum formed along the bulging edge of the pan. But when Run-Run had cut it up, cleaned it and offered everyone a piece – he himself took the head and entrails – they had to admit the white flesh tasted good, almost like lizard, but not so sweet, and less oily.

From then on, Run-Run quite often caught one of these blind, eel-like fish in his nets, though they never saw any other sign of life in the waters of Paradise Bay, and one single fish occasionally was not enough to improve their steadily worsening food situation.

One night they caught Smiley stealing water from the well.

Doc stood shaking with agitation in the semi-darkness. He had pulled his dungarees up as far as his waist, his braces dragging along behind him in the stiff grass, his feet gnarled and dirty white against the dark ground and the lights from Sweetwater glinting in his glasses.

Allan was standing below the tall poplar, silent, shaking his clenched fists, Lisa whimpering in the darkness behind him. She had been with Doc and had heard the sound of footsteps before his old ears had noticed anything, so she had slipped out, run across the shore to the camping van and woken Allan. They did not know who the thief was, so best to be several of them, just in case. . . .

Felix and Run-Run had also been woken and came creeping after them, followed by Mary with Rain in a bundle on her back. Before she had left, she had thumped on the wall of Bean's rickety shack and called out to him: 'Come on, Bean, over to Doc's. This is something you should be in on.'

The sinner was sitting on the ground, peering rather uncertainly up at the figures standing round him, as if hoping his self-contempt would somehow wipe out the blunder he had made. But this was no blunder. He had committed a crime, the faces told him that, as did Allan's clenched fists and Run-Run's immobility, Run-Run's long knife, which he feared most of all.

Creeping terror and his hangover made it impossible for Smiley to speak and surprise them with his sarcasm, witticisms and self-irony. Nor would that have helped him, not this time, the way they were looking.

'He was lying face down slurping it into him,' said Doc. 'Digging down in the well with his hands, muddying it. I had to pull him away. Why did you do it, Smiley? What made you think of doing such a thing?' The old man was trembling with furious reproaches. 'Stealing water!'

'I was so bloody thirsty.' Smiley grinned, trying to smile in his old mocking way, but it became nothing but a harsh clearing of his throat.

'You don't know what you've done,' said Doc.

'*Done*? Jesus, all I've done is drink a little water! If you'd been as hungover as I am . . .'

'None of us has ever been as hungover as you are,' Allan exclaimed at last. He took a few steps forward, then stopped, breathing as if it were an effort for him not to hurl himself at Smiley and kick the life out of him.

'Bloody thieving bastard! We trusted you.'

That was Doc, Doc losing his temper and rushing forward to aim a clumsy kick at Smiley's knee, almost losing his balance, but kicking again, feebly, awkwardly, without injuring or even troubling him.

'You louse . . .!'

Doc gasped it out as he hitched up his trousers, exhausted by all this agitation.

'Now, now, Doc,' said Smiley. 'Your boxing days are over. Don't take it so badly.'

Doc's feeble attack seemed to have given him back a little of his self-confidence. He started getting up.

Then Allan intervened, grabbed him by the shoulder and yanked him to his feet.

'Hey, now, what's this. King Kong himself,' Smiley managed to say before Allan's fist crashed into his face.

The blow thudded against the eardrums of those standing looking on, not moving, silent, almost invisible in the darkness. Bean had collapsed and was sitting on the ground, the intensity of the scene in front of him frightening and draining him, but at the same time, amazingly, he had an erection and was wishing Allan would hit Smiley again. Again and again.

Smiley was flat on his back. For a moment everything was completely still, as if they were all holding their breath, as if they realized that what had happened was something quite different and would cause a decisive change in their lives, a tightening of the conditions under which they lived. This was not just about Smiley stealing water and Allan thrashing him. This was about rules they had to follow, about punishment. Allan's merciless blows were not his rage running away with him, but a demonstration to them all, emphasizing that this was about life itself, more absolute and merciless than they perhaps usually thought of it. Time passed, life went on, from one day to the next, even if water had to be rationed, shared out sparingly in small mouthfuls after sunset. Some days there was little or nothing to eat, other days sufficient for the worst of their hunger to be stilled. But they did not complain, just went on living like that, their ideas settling around that and that alone – finding food so that they could sleep more or less satisfied. An existence of this kind was static, containing neither anxiety nor hope.

But this dull, nauseating sound of blows was emphasizing something immensely important they had hitherto only sensed. There had been less food recently and what they needed from outside was now more difficult to acquire. They had to struggle harder for less in exchange. Little by little, their life had become an almost continuous state of emergency which nothing they did could truly change. That made demands on them, demands to which they all had to bow, cruel demands requiring cruel punishments if not fulfilled.

So they were all quite still, intently occupied, watching without compassion as Allan yanked Smiley to his feet to hit him again and again, up again, down again, and yet again, ostentatiously, almost mechanically, as if this were a drama being played out for them in the semi-darkness of Doc's scorched yard. The blows and Allan's deep grunts, Smiley's howls and groans, the blood flowing thickly on Smiley's face and Allan's hands, were all dialogue, sound effects and props in the performance, in this lesson on crime and punishment.

When Allan had finished and his victim lay senseless on the ground, no longer whimpering or whining, he looked round and fixed his eyes on Doc. 'You've got a gun,' he said. 'If you catch him thieving here again, shoot him. Got it?'

It had been said and it was unanswerable.

10

Allan was often very low at this time. All autumn it had become more and more difficult for them to support themselves on the Dump. There was practically nothing edible in the garbage brought out, and the trucks came less and less regularly. The packs of dogs had grown increasingly timid, so it was more difficult to lure them close enough to catch them, or tempt them into the traps Run-Run set up. The lizards were hibernating now, and Run-Run managed only rarely to catch one of his strange blind eels. The garden they cultivated at Doc's helped a little, but it wouldn't keep them through the winter, and on the black market along the motorway and in the city prices were rising impossibly now the laws against illegal trading had been tightened. Even Felix, who always seemed to have innumerable ideas when it came to bartering goods, had become rather passive in recent months. On evenings when he and Run-Run took the path up to the motorway, a kind of shudder of distaste seemed to go through them all. No one *knew* what the two of them got up to on nights they were 'out' operating.

Mary had also recently begun to make her way again up to the motorway occasionally, preferably towards evening, and from the path she could see the dark arch of the bridge, dominating and enormous in its high, rigid curve over the bay. Was she watching the lights of the traffic and weighing up her chances? The traffic had previously flowed along like broad bands of light to and from the busy city, and the girls had stood close together waiting for customers at every exit road, drifting in packs through the supermarkets and filling stations of the many service areas. Now, only a few lights were streaking up and down the useless great curve of concrete, and motorway prostitution had as good as died out. Mary might return the same evening with her task unfulfilled, but usually she was away until morning, when she came trudging back, pale, exhausted, sometimes half drunk, to go straight to bed and sleep until evening, no one daring to disturb her.

Allan's face hardened when she went off like this, but he could not deny they needed sugar, coffee substitute, liquor, lard, tobacco and the rare rations she brought back with her. Now and again she even managed to get hold of a little fresh milk for the smallest one, Rain.

If he had said anything, he knew it would be a waste of breath, for nothing could stop Mary doing what she considered necessary. He could perhaps have punished her physically, but he could never persuade her or exercise authority over her once she had decided to do something. She had once been a passive, painted whore, oppressed and exploited by Smiley, and now she was a bundle of determination. Conditions on the Dump had changed her. She had found in herself resources she did not know were there, vital to both herself and the others, the child, for instance, Lisa had been incapable of looking after. So she had moved in with Allan.

Allan had perhaps expected other things of her, but reason and his sense of proportion told him it was right she did as she liked when she contributed so much to their common good. She worked as hard as he did, and there were many things he could not teach her. Her influence was great, with or without Allan. It had turned out that they both undertook the provision of their common meals, so she also became involved in deciding what was most important – food they managed to get hold of. There had never been any kind of concrete agreement over housekeeping. The system they practised had developed out of sheer necessity as it had become impossible for individuals to acquire sufficient to eat to keep themselves alive for any length of time. So they had had to share what they had and concoct some kind of common plan for what they lacked most, what was most important to provide.

Mary kneaded dough in her buckled washing-bowl and fried solid maize cakes on the metal plate over the fire, although she said she couldn't be bothered with cooking and handed most of it over to Allan. A hunk of maize bread each, as big as a hand, only one, even if there were several left, and when she said they could have no more of what they had in the casserole, no one protested, even if they still felt hunger after the meagre meal.

Run-Run was the one who lived most outside the community. He seldom ate with them, and whenever he did, he usually preferred what the others left. He liked eating entrails of the animals they killed, and chewing plant stalks or leaves he found round the Dump or nearby. He could be seen picking up small objects on the shore and putting them into his mouth. He could also drink small mouthfuls of water from the bay without becoming ill. But what he liked was a small portion of tasteless vegetable soup, squatting down with the bowl between his hands and drinking with tiny sips, slowly, his expression blank, his eyes closed. He could sit like that without moving, a bowl of soup and an untouched piece of maize bread in front of him, utterly oblivious of his surroundings, long after the others had eaten every crumb of the rations they had been given and had crept into the shack to rest, or just rolled over with exhaustion there by the fire and fallen asleep.

Contrary to expectations, the children seemed to enjoy life, even if the food situation was poor and conditions otherwise pitiful. Boy mostly stayed with Run-Run, learning what he could from the mute wild man, knowing how to make use of what he learnt with astonishing skill and cleverness, and practically never speaking. Boy often caught birds for them in ingenious traps he rigged up all over the Dump, mostly crows, dishevelled and stinking. They roasted them whole on the embers before devouring the bitter flesh after plucking off the scorched feathers. Everything they couldn't eat they collected up and put in special places to tempt the dogs.

Boy turned to Lisa more often than he did to his father. Sometimes he almost forced himself on to her, demanding milk off her although his small sister Rain needed all the milk Lisa could force out of her breasts. Whenever he got his own way, he would fall asleep in Lisa's arms after having suckled for a few moments, as trusting as an infant. Otherwise he slept like an animal, guardedly, alert, always ready to leap up and attack or flee. He was usually up and away before the others had woken, appearing first long into the day and usually bringing some prize or other with him, an animal or a bird he had caught, or something that might be useful as a tool or for bartering. He was moody and surly towards his father, his thin body tense as if with innate rage whenever they got too close to each other. Although only eight, he was incredibly strong and lithe, as tireless as any of the adults.

Little Rain grew and developed, a calm, composed, apparently contented child, whether toddling around where they lived or securely bound to Mary Diamond's broad back whenever her large stepmother had to work a little way away and couldn't keep an eye on her every moment. As they lived now, there was little time left over to pay small children much attention, but Rain was also quite happy in her own company. Although it was hard to believe that the abrupt forms of communication between the adults would stimulate the three-year-old's power of speech, she had learnt a great many words and sentences, and when she was alone, as she mostly was, she would repeat the words she had learnt like a game with herself — so the words became a rhythm, a kind of song with or without content which she went around mumbling and humming as she found things to play with from the junk lying around.

She was most like Lisa with her broad, untroubled forehead, her bright eyes, blonde hair in a curly cloud round her open face, on those rare occasions when it was not stiff with dirt. But she was big and robust, with large, strong hands she may have inherited from Allan. She shared her affections equally between her 'mothers' and seemed to have no difficulty spending time with them both, looked after by one or the other according to the circumstances. Physically, she was still dependent on Lisa, as she still suckled from her, and Lisa always received her with that accepting, passive lack of expression that had become a form of self-defence with which to face life.

Very occasionally, she would smile at Rain and play with her when they walked together along the strip of shore to Doc's house and Rain found stones or shells she picked up to show Lisa. Lisa would kneel down beside her and start a long conversation with her child. About what? No one knew for certain, for they kept themselves well out of earshot of the others on those occasions. When there were several of them together, Lisa was nearly always silent and distant.

She spent more and more time with Doc, watching him pottering round the house, working in the garden or sorting or mending things he brought back from the Dump. Doc never lost his faith in that everything would come in useful sooner or later, nor his conviction that 'common sense', as he called it, would eventually be the solution to the problems of human beings. So he answered her childish questions as thoroughly and extensively as he was able, explaining the connection between things as *he* understood them, a connection necessary for him to understand, as that was what enabled him to continue this pitiful existence in the hope of something better.

Lisa mostly just sat watching him or playing with stones, glass beads or other things he hid in drawers and boxes. Whenever he had finished whatever he was doing, he gave her something extra good, perhaps a piece of sugar cane, a rare sweetmeat, or he sat down and told her stories until she fell asleep, and through her sleep she could feel hands covering her with a car rug which always lay neatly folded over the arm of the plush-covered sofa.

She spent whole days and nights away with Doc, keeping him company, helping a little as best she could, then fell asleep in his arms in the evening, to wake beside him in the night in the narrow bed and hear his whistling breath, or when he coughed or whimpered in his restless old man's sleep.

11

Two things happened almost simultaneously in Sweetwater that autumn to emphasize the extent to which conditions were worsening, for those on the Dump as well as those who lived outside in the rapidly disintegrating city.

The first was the shipwreck.

The second was the outbreak of yet another epidemic of influenza.

Together, the two events triggered off all the destructive tensions that had built up in that doomed city.

A large merchant ship went aground on a sandbank a kilometre or so out in the approach from the sea. They could see the ship quite clearly, keeling over on one of the shallows below the Sargossa Peninsula, her long, rusty black hull leaning a few degrees towards the mainland. For a while her funnel spewed out black clouds of smoke, but then nothing else could be seen through the mist except a thin, smoky, grey trickle.

The weather had been bad that night, stormy and – wonder of wonders – a downpour which sent water splashing through leaking cardboard walls and pouring down corrugated iron, filling their invisible pathways with turbulent streams, turning their fireplace into a bog, a shapeless, bottomless muddy hole, their cooking utensils and other possessions floating around in it like driftwood. But they had shrieked and laughed and danced about, ripping off their clothes and letting the pouring rain spill over their bodies and splash into their open mouths, revelling in this wonderful water that simply kept on coming down in swirling gusts. Their shacks could be put up again in a day. More important was that a cloudburst of this kind meant sufficient supplies of water for weeks and weeks. Even after they had used up what had been collected in buckets and bowls, there would be enough in hidden reservoirs all over the Dump, empty oil drums and defective hot-water tanks (the copper elements removed for scrap), a plugged wash-basin, a stained toilet bowl, a deep, rust-brown source where buckled corrugated iron had formed itself into a funnel, even in the twisted hollows of loose car bumpers.

The next morning there was the stranded ship, waves breaking over the long hull, her cranes and containers, and tugboats bustling round her. The ship stayed that day and the next, clouds of smoke coming out of her funnel at irregular intervals and tugboats and salvage craft dashing to and fro.

They all climbed out on to the steep cliff of garbage that ran down into the water, clinging on and gazing over the bay for hours out at the grounded ship, like monkeys on the edge of a precipice. The days went by and the ship could not get off. A ship in the bay was in itself no minor event, since shipping in Sweetwater harbour had declined; a ship run aground set all kinds of speculations in motion. Where had she come from? What was she carrying? And how could it be that she had run aground on a sandbank?

Doc was able to tell them the cause was sure to be the quantities of sand the river had brought down and spread out into the shallow bay. The constant dredging, previously carried out to keep the channels clear, had been neglected like all other public works during the economic crisis, and bad weather, particularly in the six winter months, could displace the growing sandbanks. That, possibly combined with faulty navigating in the storm, meant it would probably be impossible to shift the ship. The sea-bed had clearly become so difficult, larger boats could not manoeuvre close to the bank, so it was a slow and elaborate business getting the ship free and salvaging the cargo ashore.

They sat out there on the cliffs of the Dump, day after day, following the salvage work, their eyes half closed against the sulphurous sun.

In Sweetwater, rumour spread that the ship was loaded with food-stuffs for the city, a rumour neither denied nor confirmed from official quarters, but every small freighter of cargo brought into harbour from the grounded ship was strictly guarded. That did not stop increasingly large crowds of curious spectators going down to the quay area to look on, perhaps also in the hopes of stealing something should some of the cargo be exposed to an industrial accident. But the hundreds of curious people who gathered every day were kept firmly at a distance by members of the Peacekeeping Force.

No concrete information about the grounded ship or her cargo emerged, but none the less, or perhaps just because of that, interest simply increased. The thought of a whole ship's cargo of something mysterious they took to be food lying in the bay, and the secret cargo allowed to be brought ashore only in expensively and strictly guarded small loads, seemed to set minds moving in a strange way. The curious poured in in greater and greater numbers, gradually creating chaos in the harbour area. Reinforcements had to be called in to ensure free passage for the transports. For the first time for months, perhaps for years, people were drawn out of their state of apathy, standing in their hundreds, at times in their thousands, gazing at the unmarked crates, boxes and casks being shifted from the Force's small boats scuttling to and fro like freighters, then transferred on to covered trucks, to be driven away. They stood there patiently, solemnly, watching the work, as if with their reserve and good behaviour they would contribute to easing the work on this important cargo, thus hastening the distribution process, the distribution of food for them all.

That was the obvious response to the assurances of the State-controlled mass media that the supply situation had the highest priority and that all efforts were being made to ensure access to these vital goods.

For the first few days everything ran smoothly, as if the sight of tons of crated foodstuffs being unloaded from the small boats, reloaded on to trucks and driven away in an orderly, continuous, almost unbroken rhythm, had put the spectators into a kind of trance of a hopeful goodwill which gave them a sense of at least passively participating in the work of salvaging ton after ton of tempting sustenance from the wreck.

For people still had a spark of hope in them and they were not the ordinary black-market sharks, the fortune-hunters of times of emergency constantly sniffing around anything that 'happened'. They were Sweetwater citizens, the sensation of the grounded ship jerking them out of their isolation and giving them a chance to see for *themselves* a whole ship loaded with food, food for *them*, and in that way for a moment take a direct part in contributing to the bringing of supplies to the strictly rationed community.

It was Dos Manos the scrap-dealer who told them all about the situation in the city. Doc's radio was remarkably silent when it came to news about the salvaging of foodstuffs and the people gathering in the harbour area. Instead, a series of reports were broadcast on the storm damage plus exhortations to people to be careful with the use of water, to boil their drinking water and stay indoors to await messages from loudspeaker vans.

Dos Manos had contacts and was able to tell them the truth. The crowds down by the quays grew larger, some people spending the whole day there, as if watching the secret transports and speculating and commenting with everyone else had become a necessity. Naturally, the discussion on what kind of foodstuffs this delivery really contained was liveliest. Was it canned goods of the same kind that came on the trailers? Or was it frozen fish, meat, *real* meat? And those casks, what did they contain? Oil? Lard? Grain or flour? Dried fruit? No one knew, but everyone had a guess.

For long, sultry evenings, groups sat round talking about it, a subject that deeply concerned them all and would be vital to their own destinies as well as that of the city – discussions of that kind were preferable to retreating into isolation in apartments where the only contact with real events was through the media, and they broadcast only comforting entertainment programmes, propaganda urging moderation, and slogans, while suppressing important news.

Some people came long distances, all the way from the north-western zones. Some lit bonfires and heated up their rations or water for coffee substitute. The flames from the bonfires flickered along the quays in the misty twilight, blackening the stripped walls below the tall warehouses. People sat talking and imagining a better and fairer distribution. This ship must be the first. More would come, a whole fleet, an unbroken supply of necessary foodstuffs, meat, dairy products, a ton of flour for every household. The flickering fires competed with the sweeping spotlights of the guards.

But when a patrol arrived, the fires had to be put out, for open fires were forbidden. The storm had destroyed a great many water mains and the danger of fire was a problem in the older parts of the city. The bonfires were stamped out, then lit again the moment the rear lights of the patrol cars had disappeared round the corners of the harbour buildings.

The Force accepted their failure mildly. The harbour area ought really to have been closed off to people after dark, but it proved to be almost impossible to drive a crowd of hundreds, at times thousands, of people away from the area at particular times. So they contented themselves with reinforcing the guard and patrolling, as any fierce reactions might ignite the tension in the air. Their strategy was clear. In great numbers, the Force kept watchfully in the background, content to keep an eye on the situation, instructing the men and waiting in the hope that an explosion would be avoided.

Smiley had his own interpretation. 'A pirate ship, as sure as hell,' he said. 'A black-market shipping magnate with a cargo of canned food. Profiteers buying up wherever there are surplus stores and the Government is sufficiently corrupt, purchasing and smuggling out goods offered to the highest bidder – that is, countries with supply problems. That's why nothing can be made public. Our authorities mustn't get involved, no contracts, no accounts. International black-market trade. We are directly and indirectly at war with a whole series of producer countries, don't forget, a war of supplies, a war of food. A grain boat is just as important as a gunboat. Look at that hulk out there. They sail a scrapyard wreck bought for nothing, do a couple of trips and then it sinks. Massive profits for the cheating shippers, perhaps an insurance profit added. Another storm and it'll give up the ghost, believe you me.'

Smiley had sprained his ankle and was walking badly, his hollow cheeks glistening with sweat and his eyes glowing. After the water affair, he seemed to have deliberately retreated and in some indefinable way had also been placed outside their community, his bad foot adding to it. He could no longer work as before. He complained that Allan was the cause of his misery, that he had sprained his ankle in the struggle that fateful night. 'That Neanderthal stood on my foot and hit me at the same time,' he complained to anyone who would listen. 'He did it deliberately, although he knew it'd injure me. Nor is it getting better. I bet something's broken.'

The others found less and less time to listen to him, though that did not stop him making observations. 'The story of the last days of Sweetwater', as he called his lectures, but they fell on deaf ears. Nothing could impair Smiley's powers of speech and need to inform, particularly after he had difficulty moving freely around. Although he took his time, it was not that simple to get around the Dump propped up on a home-made crutch. So he spent most of his time lying on some sacks in the station-wagon's spacious luggage compartment, doomsday prophecies and acid comments on anyone nearby pouring out of him, his sunken face and burning eyes more and more clearly reflecting their common condition.

<h1 style="text-align:center">12</h1>

As time went by, impatience began to be apparent in the harbour area. Unloading was continuing just as slowly. No news of what they were most concerned with had trickled out, what kind of food it was, or where the goods were to be distributed. The relatively disciplined expectation in the thousands of people faithfully attending the unloading from morning to night, began occasionally, then steadily more often, becoming a distrustful uneasiness. The authorities had declared they had done their best to solve the supply crisis. Why then this silence now their efforts had produced results? The only answer to this and other burning questions was the tight security surrounding the unloading and transport of goods. And as if the authorities themselves noticed the restlessness beginning to sharpen, perhaps becoming dangerous, that the situation in the harbour might possibly suddenly develop in a perhaps uncontrollable direction, the unloading was speeded up, the work going on after dark in the light of powerful spotlights. Security was again reinforced. People crowded together in larger numbers than before. What was this? A new plan, a new strategy – why was this necessary? But there was no explanation for the new move, a remarkable move, like a *counter-move* against something . . . against *them*?

The harbour area was now a seething mass of people, standing and sitting in groups of three or four, in large crowds, or drifting about on their own or in company. Most of them were perfectly ordinary people, ordinarily dressed, many young, but most middle-aged people to whom the perspectives of what was happening appeared momentous, as if their experience was the only thing that could give these events their right depth. They were representatives of a population subdued for years by an authoritarian political plot that came to be called 'community government', with steadily more restrictive legislation and increased security, with no systematic political opposition since a leftist movement had splintered ten years earlier into factions squabbling among themselves and exhausting each other, so easy prey for security forces when demands for 'lawful democracy' increased. They were representatives of a population subdued by hopelessness about their actual conditions and by an even greater fear for the future, who had handed over their right to a share in decision-making, and with that their vitality to their rulers as if concluding a deal. If you gain power, do you promise to save us from chaos? Will we be given stability and supplies of the necessities of life in exchange?

The idea that perhaps their trading partner, those in power, would not keep their side of the bargain, had at last begun to grow. The spark struck, the thought caught on and spread, almost before it was articulated, burning low under the discipline that had become a habit, like a fire that glows beneath heathland in times of drought and spreads incredibly rapidly, just as news does in times of crisis. They still hesitated to act, but for how long?

In the grey light of one cold morning, the fifth day after the grounding, something happened.

One or two people got hold of a boat and set off across the water. Then others with the same idea followed suit, and soon the long washes of four or five little boats were swinging across the quicksilver, smooth water in the direction of the dark hull, now just visible in the distance through the mist. Some were busy tying planks to empty oil drums, a raft, their first whole-hearted contribution to piracy, although the thought of stealing and black market was never very far away in some these days. They were the vanguard, reconnoitring. Keep the ship in sight, see what there is to find out, where she comes from, what she is loaded with. Simple questions it seemed quite natural to ask. Why had they not been answered?

The leading boats were nothing but distant dots when the counter-offensive started. Foam shot up in great fountains from the bows of the slender harbour patrol boats, their course cutting off the small boats' progress. From the quay it was impossible to see in detail what was happening, but the four or five little boats soon reappeared again – on their way back. Had they been threatened and frightened into turning back? The dots grew larger and larger, testifying to resignation, the hopelessness of all personal initiative.

But this reminder, the disappointment usually enough to put a damper on excitement and desire for action, suddenly brought about the reverse. Even before the returning boats had reached the harbour basin, the first boats of another and larger batch were already on their way out. The news had got around that morning and resulted in an astonishing assembly of craft bobbing along the quay, everything from barges and home-made canoes to old pleasure-boats and cabin cruisers, buckled, spotted, discarded since the glorious days of water sports, but afloat, at a pinch usable. Someone boarded a moored barge and, amid cheerful shouts, got the engine going. As she set off, others jumped down on to her deck from the edge of the quay. A ripple seemed to have become a wave that rose and then kept on swelling and swelling. A seething mass of boats in the harbour basin, the barge setting course across the water towards the wreck, a trail of small boats behind her, outside them all the patrol boats cruising back and forth, waiting.

All this time, crates of food were being unloaded from the salvage vessels and transferred to trucks, the circle of security guards slowly tightening. But now the spectators' attention was turned in another direction, out on the bay where the patrol boats were approaching

Sweetwater's own improvised armada. Suddenly puffs of smoke appeared in a line above the deck of one of the patrol boats. Then the sound from the salvo reached the quays and echoed round the streets of the city.

The cry went up: 'They're shooting!'

The first shots were simply to frighten them off, but the formation of little boats did not change course. The crowd could just see the barge ahead of her little fleet through a pair of binoculars passed from hand to hand, but still on an outward course, the patrol boats swinging round in wide circles. Could they give up? A question that was never openly asked among the crowds on the quay, though felt by them all. They soon had an answer.

Another few puffs of smoke, thick and white, sharply outlined through the greyish yellow mist. Then the shots, reverberating across the lifeless water. Only two this time, with a gap between them. Two short, ominous bangs . . . then a cloud of smoke, black and greasy, billowing up in the colourless morning light. They could see it from the quay, but even with binoculars it was impossible to decide just *what* had been hit. The dots were rocking on the surface of the water, the cloud of smoke thickening above them, the wind drawing a mourning veil over the bay.

Then another shot, a sharp flash, the slow boom of an explosion, and more smoke.

'*They're shooting at them!*'

There was no doubt about it now. The unloading stopped. Everyone was staring at this manifestation of what they had known, but nevertheless . . . again came a flash and a roar like an unnecessary confirmation.

'*They're sinking them all!*'

'*The swine!*'

The movement for action now grew into a roar, an avalanche impossible to stop, until that moment directed at the ship, but shifting direction now that confrontation was obvious. The guards drew even closer together on the unloading pier, putting on helmets, tightening their belts, fingering buckles, straps and batons – a silent packed line at the ready. But nothing could stop the movement; people flocked together, their minds fixed on the stacks of food crates and those who stood between them, stopping them. Now! At last they were going to help themselves.

The élite troops of the Riot Squad of the Force were shoulder to shoulder, helmets with transparent visors, glinting plastic shields, and combat suits of hardened synthetic hide, batons, gas-guns, hand-guns, ammunition belts, knives. Black gloves up to their elbows. Face to face with the approaching human wall, apparently about to tip the Force straight into the sea. An order, a warning came through the loudspeakers, then a couple of warning shots, then gas. No effect. The crowd was there, pressing against the barriers. The Force could not use gas now without crippling themselves. Some commandos were already on the ground, coughing and writhing. Their anti-gas gear had not been designed for hand-to-hand fighting. An almost silent, determined rough-and-tumble was developing. Feet stumbled, soles slipped on the concrete. Blows fell on living flesh with sickening thuds. Cries were quelled in throats, screams bitten off. A few insane seconds of fighting, man to man, on every inch of the quay.

Then a shot, several shots, scattered and nervous, then more intense. Killing now. Someone screamed. Someone fell. The loudspeakers rattled again, drowned by the roar.

'They're shooting at us!'

More fell, others treading on them as people stormed on. The sharpshooters crawled into position behind the crates, pulling down as many as they could before the crowd was on to them, brushing them aside, hitting and kicking, hurling many into the sea. And then – the line wavered, a break in the iron ring, and a woman climbed up on to the stacks, grabbed one of the crates, struggling with the unfamiliar weight, scrabbling at the lid and tearing her nails on the strong metal fittings, then losing her grip and letting her prize fall with a splintering crash on to the asphalt. Those closest ran slap into the confusion, while a fierce struggle was being concluded on the outside. Here at last was what they had been waiting for, patiently, gullibly like cattle. Fumbling among broken crates, then an amazed outburst rising to a shout. A man stood up with a piece of metal raised high up above his head, black, gleaming. A gun!

The crates were full of *arms*.

The supplies they had been waiting for so long, so loyally, were arms for the Force.

Uprising.

Rage – simply increasing in strength. Crowds in a blind leap at the enemy in helmets and uniforms. Fifty or so, perhaps a hundred killed and injured lying about on the dirty grey asphalt. Blood glistening around them in the dust, one person kneeling, trying to help among all those running people. Uniforms and plastic helmets hunted down like wild animals, caught, struck and dying, trampled on again and again by hundreds of feet heading for the next one. Outrages committed in a flash, for there is no time to lose. A chorus of sirens in the distance. The Riot Squad have managed to call up the Force before being overrun.

More people seemed to be arriving, although no one is in control now, no one has any clear idea of what is really happening except quite close to them. Nothing but movement, excitement, shrieks, screams of pain, of anguish, of triumph, movement which makes people run in confusion in the opposite direction, behave mindlessly, and rise up in the exultation of despair, ordinary people, not trouble-makers or rebels. They are people from the labour exchange, people from the bread queues, people who against all odds have insisted on a normal existence in the disintegrating city of Sweetwater. People tempted out on to the street in the hope of relief in the precarious food situation; now racing, howling and shouting round each other, giving their disappointment free rein.

In the course of a few minutes, their rage starts clamouring for weapons. Crates are tipped off narrow ledges and smashed to pieces. Gleaming automatic arms are passed from hand to hand, useless; where's the ammunition? There! Crates and boxes of it, cartridges in clips and long belts. But which goes where? The mob press on, as starved of arms as a few moments ago they were starved of the tempting, imagined food. Guns are eagerly handed out, brand-new, gleaming and useless, barrels and muzzles blocked with grease. Two men with military experience, their faces scarlet, try to explain, try to curb the most eager, shouting in order to make themselves heard, the veins in their necks swelling. Some go their own way. It is urgent, the sirens getting closer, and that can mean only one thing: Fight! Open warfare! Stop them! Barricade the streets! But how?

Unimaginable bedlam.

Shouts and questions, people running about aimlessly in all directions, the dead on the ground, some in sleeping positions, others ripped open by bullets, by nails, unimaginably battered by kicks. Unimaginable. The blood darkening in the dust. Unimaginable, dead everywhere and left lying, sirens wailing and the crowd simply running, leaving the dead lying, some hand-to-hand fighting among small groups. The few men with experience, knowing what it is all about, get the guns ready, as many as they can, choosing pistols and light rifles, the simplest to handle, abandoning the heavier equipment. The sirens are wailing down in the harbour now, too late to stop them. The crowd swings in another direction, raging blindly straight *at* the wailing armoured vehicles just appearing in sight, firing and shouting, not running away or taking over.

Human beings against motor vehicles. The first ploughs into the crowd, is forced to stop in a nightmare of bodies and screams, is overturned and set on fire. The thick, stinging smell of smoke excites the raging mob even more and shots are already coming from the next vehicle as it races forward. In a moment that, too, will be charging straight into the crowd. Some try to get out of the way. The few with guns that function blaze wildly away at this screaming, swerving death — the Force's arms against the Force. Then something unexpected happens — an explosion behind the second vehicle, powerful enough to lift it up from behind and hurl it on to its side the moment the petrol tank explodes. The crowd flees from the flames, howling, jubilant. Then another explosion like the first, which stops a third vehicle before it is able to swing out on to the quay and open fire, transforming it into a hissing, glowing wreck in the narrow passage behind two warehouses. Flames roar upwards, shrapnel flies — hand-grenades exploding, crates of hand-grenades appearing, some people throwing them as if in panic in the direction of even more sirens wailing, the resulting explosions greeted by yells of victory. A warehouse is burning now, more wounded screaming, smoke pouring over the whole area.

A shout goes up to take the fight into the streets. Hundreds are still refusing to give in, riding high on the thirst for blood the excitement has now become, racing to confront this superior force — determined, bare-headed men, mostly men, but a few women among them, young and not so young, some not altogether steady on their pins, some with no shoes, their clothes and hair in disorder, panting, running, burdened with whatever arms they have been able to lay their hands on. Inexperienced hands cling to gleaming rifle-butts, smooth pistol-stocks. Arms mean power. Ordinary people have long since been prohibited from possessing arms. The guns, even with no ammunition and useless, stoke this madness, the reason why they go on charging against the impossible.

Those left on the quay have set fire to the transport truck, now encircled, ammunition exploding inside it in the smoke, ammunition for which no one thinks there is any use, ammunition which nevertheless could not have helped a leaderless rebellion against the authorities.

Sirens wailing from all directions now, fires raging where arsonists have been, smoke suffocatingly thick over the quay, where only the dead and the seriously wounded are left.

Barely half an hour has passed since the first salvo was fired far out in the bay.

13

Dos Manos told them. He had been there. He had seen most of it, had been one of those to get away. The rebellion had soon been put down, but it had taken time to stamp out the sparks. The guns had been passed round too many hands, and suppressed discontent exploded into assaults, plundering, wanton destruction and looting. The many killed had enraged people, bitter anger driving small groups and individuals to desperate actions, but they were faced with a powerful enemy who put them down without mercy. The Force surrounded the parts of the city where there was still unrest and systematically fine-combed every quarter, searching houses and rousing families in the middle of the night.

Stamping out the last remains of the rebellion was not done in the twinkling of an eye, although all available mobile forces were called out. The size of the city centre was in itself a problem. Hundreds of older and irregular small blocks huddled between the great avenues running lengthwise and crosswise. The number of police required to achieve an effective blockade of a whole area of the city was enormous, nor could the spread of unrest to more distant zones be halted. The half-suppressed cries of the rebellion seemed to have rung from one part of the city to the next faster than the Force could even set up a communication network. New fires flared up all the following night like red claws against the smoke-filled sky. The sirens shrilled, the shortage of water making the Fire Service's efforts ineffective, so fires often gained ground.

The unrest ebbed away the following night, and on the third night the city was quiet, apart from the sound of armoured vehicles roaring through the streets with patrols searching for 'suspects', whom they arrested and took away during a series of random razzias. The more unobtrusive search-parties operated from house to house, from quarter to quarter in areas where the bitterest fighting had been.

Dos Manos made it all come alive to them. He had been there. He had seen and heard. He had his contacts. He told them about the wild exultation of the first few hours, the crowds of young and old had stormed through the almost deserted commercial areas, smashing the vast plate-glass windows, helping themselves freely from the window displays, hauling counters and fixtures out on to the pavements, barricading the streets with wrecked cars . . . he told them about people who downed tools and joined the crowd, people who ran out of their houses and joined the trouble-makers, ordinary people suddenly running in the streets, shouting, yelling, threatening and swinging weapons.

A rebellion by whom and against what? No one was quite sure. Only the few who had been down on the quay during the battle had a pretty good idea, and they were the most savage, the most bitter, for they had been face to face with the authorities and seen people fall screaming to the ground, seen the blood on the ground. They knew they had little more than half an hour, so they had run fastest, shouted loudest and ravaged most wildly as they raced on, looting and plundering at random in the stores as the wailing sirens came closer and closer.

Only very few had an overall view of what had happened, but the rage from the quay burnt in them all. The battle-cry Arms for Food! ran from mouth to mouth. What treachery! So they smashed, they plundered, making the most of it, although they knew there would be reprisals, although they feared oppression would be even harsher afterwards, for what they were doing would not change anything, would be of no importance; a disturbance, minor looting. They were too few and what they did too insignificant, their opponents too powerful. For every soul who ran with them, hundreds remained behind locked doors, refusing to open up, refusing to listen to anything except the television accounts of what was happening outside, out on the streets, bowing their heads obediently to proclamations on curfews during the state of emergency, while waiting for the promised afternoon programme of a parade of the stars.

Then came the cleaning-up operations, the arrests, the deportations. Whole quarters were cleared, the inhabitants interned 'until further notice' under the emergency regulations, the Force patrolling the central areas day and night. House searches, arrests of random 'suspects' were common, and, as if the disorders were a welcome reason for the departments to tighten the screws yet again, food·rationing was soon made even more severe and the Force took over the distribution of all vital provisions with immediate effect. From then on, goods such as meat substitutes, bread, protein flour, sweeteners, coffee substitute, canned fruit and dried vegetables could be found only in supply centres divided into zones under the administration of the Force and only against the production of identity and ration cards.

Queues for food had long been the order of the day in Sweetwater, but now became the dominating factor in many lives, for most private traders who had hitherto somehow managed to keep going now had to close because most of their diminishing stores had been confiscated. People had to make their way to one of the official supply depots almost regardless of what kind of food they were trying to lay their hands on. In the depots, the tempo was sluggish, essential goods often lacking, the queues winding their way along the filthy pavements, block after block. But people seemed to comply with this too. Now the unrest had been put down and the whole matter belittled in all the official media, people seemed to be turning away and simply complying.

Patrol cars were still roaring through the deserted streets day and night, the curfew was eased, but not totally lifted, and surveillance was markedly tightened.

Dos Manos told them all this, as pale, thin and pursed he sat in Doc's room every time he came out to the Dump, describing recent events in a warm and lively voice, in marked contrast to his usual tones. This priest turned scrap-dealer and more recently a black-market wholesaler – to 'help people', as he always said, 'to help poor wretches by getting hold of what they need' – Dos Manos, told them about the tightening up of regulations for what was called illegal trading. He himself risked prison for his activities. Nevertheless he carried on.

'Why, I no longer really know,' he complained. 'I've barely any clothes on my back. The petrol ration gets smaller and smaller and every day I risk being stopped at a checkpoint and having the van searched.'

But there were still things on the Dump he could barter with in the city – clothes and shoes, for instance, which were becoming unavailable in Sweetwater.

Warm, practical clothes and thick, strong shoes would obviously be what was most in demand in the autumn, with winter approaching, but that was not so.

On the contrary, finery, party clothes, preferably in old styles long since out of production, were much in demand, and high-heeled shoes of multicoloured leather, the kind that had not been available for several years but could often be found in boxes and cases out on the Dump. And decorative items, knick-knacks, rubbishy articles no longer available, had suddenly become very popular. Changing atmospheres in the city were producing amazing manifestations.

The paralysis following the now acute crisis may have seemed only apparent. In the central commercial and office areas, activity was certainly a small fraction of what it had been in normal times. Almost all the shops and stores were closed, the great central cafés shut and their terraces empty, and in what had been entertainment districts, dance-halls stood with gaping, broken windows and smashed juke-boxes. Amusement arcades – where videos and cassette automats had provided sound-and-light shows – were now deserted, their equipment smashed and machinery destroyed, no longer reassurances to their dazed and brainwashed audiences.

Some people felt the need to find other means of getting together, and collected in groups, in private homes, grubby cafés on the outskirts or in basement premises, all under cover, in secret, though such meetings were not forbidden. No great demands were made on the premises, a few benches and tables, a few chairs, a serving counter where the Government's economy policies considered enjoyment to be mainly chemical beer and synthetic tobacco, and where it was possible to get home-brewed liquor on the black market, apparently always if the right places were frequented, despite prohibitions and difficulties with access to raw materials.

This form of contact was gradually becoming quite usual, Dos Manos told them, particularly after the rebellion had been suppressed and surveillance by the Force had been tightened up. The need to be with others, to sit and talk, perhaps over a glass or at a dance, seemed to become so great, people found a kind of halting fellowship, fumbling but close, experimental, honest, as if the city's entertainment centres with their juke-boxes and 'amusement arcades' had never existed.

At these gatherings, clubs, 'societies' as some people called them, a market for peculiar clothes gradually emerged, garb that would emphasize the need for freer forms this new kind of togetherness brought with it. The satisfaction felt by getting together in this way seemed to have to strike out into a new, almost desperate abandonment, singling out individuals and groups who entertained others, at first spontaneously, spurred on by the moment and the atmosphere, then later becoming regular elements of these places. Although most of this entertainment was crude and amateurish, individual performances could give rise to excesses among both audience and performers, as if the intimacy, the directness made it possible for them to experience their own selves, a *togetherness*, which dissolved inhibitions and extended all boundaries. Dressing up in old-fashioned clothes, or following up other bizarre fashions was an expression of a new experience of the body's possibilities, encouraging a desire to try *everything*, seek out the whole spectrum . . . since freedom for them, this powerless minority which had not lost its ability to see what was really happening around them, had defined itself by examining all aspects of the sensual. No other opportunities existed for the inhabitants of Sweetwater.

A new kind of life was seeking expression in small groups in the battered communal rooms in tower blocks, in private apartments, in basements or abandoned shops that had stood empty along the endless straight streets of older properties, where all maintenance had been neglected over recent decades, so they had soon reverted to slums. Small, handwritten notices could be seen there, pinned to doors, stuck on window-panes, informing people of performances, meetings, dances. That was where they suddenly found a new form of display for people who had previously had to be passive consumers of increasingly extreme forms of audio-visual aphrodisiacs, the distribution of which over the years had developed into a gigantic industry, the State extracting its share in fierce taxation and instituting a – totally illusory – censorship and approval authority.

This was where, in small, forgotten corners of this great metropolis, that the new, rather perishable forms of community first arose, striking root and flourishing, briefly, from one week to the next, withering and dying from one week to the next. The pressure was far too great, and the need for freedom so immeasurable, attempts at liberation carried excess within them. Sensuality had been re-· leased, but it had no direction, nor could it find one in such circumstances, so simply circled round itself. So the result had to be dissolution, resignation and defeat.

Dos Manos had seen most of it all, experienced the excesses, the exaggerations. He had picked senseless people up off the pavements and tried to bring them back to life, those for whom there was still hope. Suicide raced at regular intervals like an epidemic through certain city zones. He had seen 'Sodom and Gomorrah', as he put it. He was expecting the crash. Even his old contacts were beginning to fail him. People moved, packed up and left. Like a mania, an apartment house or an individual street might suddenly become as good as deserted. People saved precious rations of petrol for months to have fuel for at least a part of the journey – to where? To another city where circumstances were the same? To a smaller place, another country town where there was neither housing nor work?

'Sodom and Gomorrah,' mumbled the scrap-dealer priest as he sat crouching in Doc's room, talking to those silent heads all round him, and they sat listening, following attentively, as if they all knew *their* part of the story, and were now waiting for the parts to be put together into the saga of which they all feared the end.

A week or two after the episode out in the bay when police boats opened fire on the fleet of small boats on their way out to the wreck and sank many of them, three bodies floated ashore by the tip.

Allan came back and told them. Run-Run got up to join in the investigation. Allan fetched Bean, and together they set off across the garbage heaps.

The bodies were lying on the edge of the water, shapeless, a dull wave washing them out and back across the slippery stones on the shore, garbage, semi-dissolved cartons and oily slush floating all round them. Their dead skin gleamed bluish-white, on the verge of dissolution, beneath the filthy water, their coagulated eyeballs protruding dully and blindly out of hollow eye-sockets. Finer facial features had already been washed out, fingertips dissolved, gnawed off . . . three men, identically dead, identical in their rotting, scarcely recognizable caricature of human form.

Allan wound a piece of sacking round his right hand, waded out into the slimy sludge of the layer of yellowish-grey mud, and hauled one of the corpses ashore. Run-Run then did the same with corpse number two. Bean refused until he realized what was expected of him. He forced himself to take two or three steps out into the cold water, groaned when the cold bit into his legs, and approached the last corpse. A hand on his shoulder from behind almost tipped him over. Allan's grating voice: 'Put something on your hands, fool! Do you want to get infected?'

As Bean stumbled back ashore, Allan hauled in the last corpse. Run-Run was already squatting down examining the dead men. Slowly and methodically, he started pulling the clothes off one of the corpses, first the jacket, then the boots, the trousers . . . Allan did the same, very carefully, not touching the dead skin with his bare hands. The clothes were eased off, the shoes twisted and turned, weighed up and evaluated. Bean wanted to try, too, but as he approached the bodies, such a nauseating smell of decay rose towards him he had to turn away in disgust. Allan pushed him roughly aside as he bent double, hands pressed to his stomach, then set about the third body himself. The dead men's clothes were soon lying in a heap. Run-Run put a rope round them and slung the bundle over his shoulder. Without a sign, he started off back and, when Bean made to follow, Allan called him back with a grunt.

'We must cover the bodies with stones.'

They worked for several hours humping stones over the dead men, Bean almost collapsing each time he lifted one, but he did not dare give in as long as he was working beside Allan. They were both working in a slow, even rhythm to conserve their energy. Bean had also learnt that. Although exhausted, he had to work from when it turned light until darkness fell now it was autumn and no longer so suffocatingly hot in the middle of the day. He was surprised he didn't simply fall down and remain lying, but the even working rhythm helped his body to perform, to put one foot forward, walk stiffly and slowly away with his burden, not hurry, not reduce speed, even when his legs seemed no longer able to bear him. His body reacted more willingly when it was able to decide its own pace for itself. Bean was always amazed how much work – according to his own befogged mind – it was possible to get out of the thin caricature of a human being he had become.

A dog appeared, then vanished again, appeared again and stood uncertainly at a safe distance, sniffing at them, attracted by the smell. Allan stopped, motioning to Bean not to move. They stood perfectly still for minute after minute, waiting for the dog to dare come a little closer, and then a little more, until it was so near, Allan could hurl the stone he had in his hand. The dog, a slim spotted mongrel, sharp and thin-legged, leapt aside as it scented danger, but the heavy stone struck the thin body on the back with a loud thump, followed by the dog's piercing squeal. Its hind legs stiffened, paralysed by the fierce blow. As Allan ran up, he seized another stone and threw it with all his might at the scarlet jaw glistening at him with bared fangs. The stone struck the dog on the head, crushing its skull, the trembling body immediately slackening, paws quivering. Allan drew his knife and slit the dog's throat, then hoisted the corpse up by the hind legs and let the blood run out of his prey.

Bean watched with silent satisfaction. They would have meat that evening.

14

Bean fell ill at this time. An epidemic had already been raging in Sweetwater for several weeks.

They had heard about it but had taken little notice, because almost every year some kind of pernicious influenza struck and raced through the city, leaving the health authorities helpless with insufficient vaccine, no staff or organization that could effectively be put in action in an emergency situation. Sweetwater's epidemics, however, never reached them out at the Dump. Their daily familiarity with the city's garbage and the physically demanding life they lived had apparently made them immune.

But Bean had fallen ill and was lying babbling in a fog of high fever, shouting and raging. At first Mary tried to force a little soup into him, but he resisted, and if he managed to get any down, it soon came up again in clumps of slimy, blood-spotted vomit. So she finally had to give up, for there was no point in wasting food. Bean lay there on a heap of ragged blankets in the squat, derelict shack, whimpering and shuddering as nightmares rode him and woke him up out of his unconscious, deathlike state.

'If he gets through the ninth day, there's some hope for him. That's what they used to say in the old days.' Doc worriedly shook his head, for there was nothing he could do. Drugs such as penicillin, for instance, were impossible to get hold of. Even Dos Manos with all his contacts couldn't get any. Doc could only look on while fever racked Bean's thin body, and shake his head and hope. . . .

Meanwhile the epidemic was raging in Sweetwater, causing hundreds of deaths every week. Nor did it give way, but grew worse. It was soon clear this epidemic was of a more dangerous type than any before. Appeals were sent out for people to stay indoors as much as possible, to avoid contact with the sick, take care with hygiene and so on, but thousands succumbed all the same. The hospitals were soon full and the attempt to set up a peripatetic health service with first aid for the sick was hopelessly ineffective. Victims were usually left helpless in their apartments with no hope of medical help, and most died after three or four days, dehydrated by fever, coughing and vomiting blood. Decently disposing of the dead soon became a problem as great as distributing insufficient stocks of the ineffective medicine that existed.

After four weeks of rising numbers of sick, increasing deaths, and panic and chaos in the population as well as in the administration – now more or less paralysed – the authorities were forced to declare Sweetwater a disaster area. The city was put under military control and the administration moved to provisional premises outside the city. Military units were sent in to transport the bodies, while the sick were evacuated to large field hospitals hastily erected on the outskirts of the city. The worst affected parts of the city were experimentally barricaded off and put in quarantine to stop the steadily growing desire to escape. Distribution of necessities was taken over by the Army in co-operation with the Peacekeeping Force, and the curfew was enforced for twelve hours a day. Sirens could be heard day and night from patrol vehicles and wailing ambulances under police escort. The numbers of dead kept steadily rising and news bulletins broadcast misleading figures in the hope of avoiding panic. But once a death was reported, a patrol with chemical sprays disinfected the victim's apartment and relatives were put in quarantine. Whole apartment blocks were sprayed in the worst afflicted areas. People lived like prisoners with no chance of getting out. Breaches of quarantine and curfew regulations were mercilessly punished and police surveillance had never been stricter, although the epidemic had also made great inroads into the forces, both the Army and the Peacekeeping Force. Morale was low.

With wailing sirens accompanying the roar of convoys of military vehicles taking supplies to the food depots, or the sick and dying to the hospital camps outside the city, military checkpoints were set up in all central parts of the city and mobile riot patrols made ready to intervene at the least sign of panic or unrest, the last shreds of human civilization in Sweetwater seemed to have collapsed and a monstrous automatic machine taken over. Loudspeaker vans echoed through the deserted streets, information and warnings bouncing off cold walls, blank façades, dark windows, placards and directives scattered all over the streets and blown about with waste paper and the other rubbish no longer collected.

Dos Manos still seemed able to move around fairly freely. In the November darkness, he sat with them in the glow from the hearth and told them what was happening in the city, the looting, robberies and suicides. The Force dealt with the looting, while riot squads came down mercilessly on the gangs and hunted them from one part of the city to another. Anyone found with arms was shot on the spot, in accordance with emergency regulations. In some places, open conflict had arisen between the Force and Army units over the organization of evacuation and food distribution.

He also told them about the crowds of refugees on all the main roads leading out of the city, bewildered, desperate people mostly escaped from quarantined parts of the city, who had never before set foot outside the boundaries of Sweetwater but were now fleeing in huge numbers, carrying whatever they could manage of their belongings, disorientated, terrified, with neither hope nor sensible plans, many of them already sick.

Added to the terror of catching the deadly virus and dying helplessly in enclosed residential complexes inside the city were the first gusts of autumn cold which had made many people leave. The shortage of fuel oil was so acute, whole residential areas could not be heated. While people sat behind closed doors, as if imprisoned, listening to the exhortations on the radio and television, boiling their water, holding sterilized towels over their mouths and noses whenever they dared to go out on to the street to try their luck in one of the long queues at the food depots, the cold slowly crept in through the concrete walls, making life increasingly unbearable. When electricity was rationed and oil almost unobtainable, the armed forces had requisitioned all stores on the authority of the emergency regulations – city dwellers were cut off from all sources of warmth, their apartments becoming shivering concrete tombs, condensation flowing down the walls. Out in the open, they could at least gather round something combustible, light a bonfire!

Dos Manos had seen refugees, individually and in groups, being stopped by patrols, then forced up into open trucks and taken to tented camps. This mass exit of people with no hope of coping on their own without supplies or anywhere to live simply had to be stopped. In addition, refugees might be heading for other cities in no better a situation than Sweetwater. No city was in a position to receive the torrent of frightened, helpless people already amounting to tens of thousands and whose numbers would in all likelihood soon be doubled.

A gust of desolation swept round them as Dos Manos told his story by the light of their fire. The influenza for which the health authorities had no advice, together with the sudden autumn cold, had started up this movement towards chaos. The foundations of this had been the political and economic crisis of recent years. The latent collapse lying in wait, which had become reality for a moment in the brief but savage uprising in and around the harbour area early in the autumn, was now an obvious political factor that could no longer be rewritten or covered up. In a few weeks, Sweetwater had been transformed into a jungle in which brute force ruled over desperate need.

Dos Manos still had his licence permitting him to move around relatively freely, as well as a bundle of coupons that could be exchanged for fuel for his old van, and he still went round his many contacts, bartering, buying and selling what could still be bought and sold, so he heard everything and remembered everything. Individual destinies concerned him most – he had kept contact with *individual* Sweetwater, with people who had made attempts to live humanly beneath the weight of the inhumanity of the city. Now he saw even those running aground. He had seen people who had previously sought each other's company in the clubs robbing and stealing from each other before escaping, or seeking death together in orgies of alcohol and drugs. He had seen suicides lying in the streets with their wrists slashed, insane men and women setting fire to their apartments and themselves. He told of the hundred who had drowned themselves in the drinking-water tanks, mad with hatred and the desire for revenge.

He reckoned this was the last time he would be able to get to them. Checkpoints had been set up on all the main roads out of town, and it was uncertain how long his licence would be accepted by the guards. The petrol coupons would presumably be confiscated at the first checkpoint, if he wasn't to fall victim to a mob and be robbed, or even killed. Dos Manos sat there, slowly telling them in detail and with emphasis as if reading the last pages of the history of civilization, as if he were the last human being to pass on the

continuity in the collapse of Sweetwater, the swan-song of techno-
logical culture before all darkness fell. From now on there would
be violent, fragmented images, tumult, cries, gunfire, occasional
screams – then stillness.

Their faces were sombre as they sat listening to him, to the
incomprehensible savagery in his story, as distant as a mysterious
adventure, yet none the less so close that signs and echoes of it
reached them every day, each day becoming more and more difficult for them to survive. Tipping had already ceased several weeks
ago and the packs of dogs had retreated. They could see naked
death in each other's faces. They caught rats and chewed bark.

It was dark and cold despite the fire, a few stars winking through
the mist above them. In the north-east a veil of smoke absorbed and
reflected scattered points of light from the city. They all felt hunger
gnawing at them, uncertain as to whether they would find anything
edible the next day. They would soon have to raid the store Doc
administered, small bundles of seed-corn, root crops intended for
the very worst winter months. And when the winter months
came. . . ?

Bean lay there crying and whimpering on the sixth day of his
delirium.

It was almost midnight before Dos Manos left. All he had to offer
them in exchange for the goods he took with him was a few boxes of
cooking fat from a military camp. They were carefully put in a case
and stored away.

It was so still, they heard his van starting up over on the service
road. They followed the whirring, complaining sound until it disappeared, then all they could hear was the howling from packs of
dogs and the hiss of the fire. And a sleepy mumble from a child
curling up and shuddering against the cold under its ragged
blanket.

15

Mary scented danger, turned round and saw the four intruders
standing a little way away, watching her. She froze. They were
standing completely still, staring at her with tense, anxious faces
and alert expressions, like deer frightened at their peaceful grazing
by a predator. And the distance between them was no more than
thirty or forty metres.

Their total immobility lasted only a second. She saw the tall man hunching down ready to leap, and she at once gathered up her things and ran, sprinting for her life along the water's edge, muddy water splashing up her legs. Although she did not turn round, she sensed they were following her and she had to use all her strength and concentration to shake them off. But it was heavy going. She had Rain on her back and a sack containing the precious tins under one arm. She was strong and knew the terrain of the tip like the back of her hand. In normal circumstances, she could outrun any-one, but the child and the heavy bundle were a hindrance, and she realized they were catching her up. In between the mounds — perhaps she could escape them there!

But no, she could hear them and, when she glanced back, she saw the man towering behind her, his unhealthily yellow face a distorted mask of desperate determination. He was breathing heavily, but his legs were long and though Mary's pace was quick, the three-year-old and the sack weighed her down and she knew he was gaining on her. The other three had already fallen behind, but the tall man was getting closer. Panic flashed through her as she ran, making her put on a spurt, but through her terror she noticed how exhausted she was. Had she been alone, she could have stopped and taken up the fight. She was as large and heavy as an average man, and growing up in the Palisade in the red-light district of Sweetwater had taught her a trick or two, but with a child tied to her back, she was as good as helpless. She raced over the heaps of loose, yellow soil and scrap-iron, then darted in behind a burnt-out bus, so perhaps. . . . But he was close, soon just behind her. She could heard his wheez-ing, whimpering gasps, far too close, so close she caught the sour smell of him.

Then she stumbled and, as she flung out an arm, she grabbed at a piece of piping protruding over the invisible path she knew so well. She noticed how it gave way as she regained her balance, took in its length, its weight, heard her pursuer's cry of triumph and knew that now, and with this weapon, it had to happen. *Now*, while she was still moving. She grasped the piping with both hands, still running, and yanked it free, then whirled round with such force and speed as if the whole momentum of her wild flight lay behind it and struck the man on the side of the head, sending him flying forwards towards her, tumbling into her outstretched arms. Still holding the piping, she tried to grab him and protect herself against this body hurtling at her, threatening to knock her down and crush her beneath its weight. For a moment she stood with him in her arms, as if embracing a dead man, but she let him go with a scream of fear and disgust – he fell face down at her feet, the blood from the blow on his temple seeping into the greyish soil.

Then she was aware of Rain wailing and remembered that there were three more of them. The moment she remembered, she heard them, shouting and yelling quite nearby. They sounded as if they had given up the chase and were now calling out to the man, clearly their leader. Like lightning, Mary got the child off her back, covered her mouth with her hand as she clutched the terrified child as close to her as she could while running for shelter behind some crates, then waiting, her cheek pressed to the child's face. The closeness calmed Rain, and she stopped wriggling, as if her stepmother's tense stillness had infected her. She lay quite still with her face pressed to Mary's as the voices came closer and closer.

Then they came, a grey, lolloping group suddenly appearing behind the wrecked bus, two adults, a man and a woman, and a youth, a boy hobbling and grimacing at every step. They were thin and filthy, moving heavily and laboriously – unnecessarily noisily, stumbling awkwardly over the inevitable heaps of garbage. There was a loud scream – one of them, the woman, had spotted the lifeless body of their leader and they gathered round him. From their exclamations, Mary could tell they thought the man was dead. She had hit him as hard as she could with the piece of piping, had felt bones cracking and seen a dazed veil kill the glint in his eyes . . . but if he were dead, she did not care. She had acted as she had had to. It had been him or her. The sight of the three intruders no longer frightened her. She could see their helplessness as they stood round the lifeless man and hear their wailing, anguished cries. They started glancing fearfully round as if expecting an attack, and after an agitated exchange of curses and accusations, they soon retreated in the direction they had come from, now lost, occasionally glancing back as if expecting to be followed.

They never even took with them the clothes and shoes of their leader.

Mary looked at what she had found floating at the water's edge. Most of the tins had lost their labels, and the surviving labels were printed in a language she did not know. She realized the tins were supplies from the ship still on the sandbank, a wreck now, covered with water after the recent storms. They had found flotsam earlier on, once a whole keg of cooking fat, a stroke of good fortune that had helped them through this difficult autumn. And now tins, hidden stores missed by wreck-robbers, those from the Force as well as those defying the prohibition, going out in small boats, preferably after dark, giving themselves away with their lights bobbing on the waves, and pale lanterns fumbling over the rusty hull.

Mary was worn out. Her flight from the intruders had drained all her energy. There was no one in their living quarters. All of them were out looking for something to eat. Even poor Bean had survived his crisis as if by a miracle and was now on the road to recovery, so had to be up and away.

She had put Rain down on the foam rubber mattress and tried to calm her, get her to sleep. She even gave her some hard maize bread to suck on from the remains of a small pile later to go into the soup. She sat down on the steps and studied the cylindrical tins, soiled and soaked by sea water and mud. She weighed them in her hands and tried to guess what was inside them. On a couple of the surviving labels, the printed words were illegible, but she recognized a picture of ham in tempting slices.

The weight of all that food lying in her hands!

She stroked the can, an unusual attack of weakness in her. She knew she had to watch herself. If their community cracked, if either she or Doc or Allan, or for that matter Felix and Run-Run, was disloyal, what would happen to them? What would happen if they all began to think only about themselves? Every man for himself out here on the Dump – how would that go? Who would kill whom? In the end, who would be left? It was not often Mary felt fear, but the idea frightened her.

None the less she sat there stroking the tin of ham as if she simply could not put it down, as if every moment she sat there, she had to resist an impulse to sink her strong teeth into the thin metal and suck the contents into her, sucking new strength into her. She could feel how weak she was, the way running had affected her. She had always been able to rely on her strength before, but now she was trembling with exhaustion.

Those damned tins!

They had had only four meals that week, meagre meals that had simply emphasized how hungry they were. The children, even the tough, resistant Boy, had gone to bed shivering, clutching hard pieces of bread in their hands to console them. Lisa's milk had dried up and she had grown noticeably thinner. How long could they hold out like this?

Thoughts of this kind were new to Mary. All the time they had been on the Dump, her attitude had been that they had to adapt to circumstances, make do with what they had, making the best. of everything. They were at least better off than the poor wretches in the city. But now. . . ?

With a swift glance around, she took eight of the tins, wrapped them in a piece of cloth and packed the bundle away under the camping van in among the garbage and scrap. The four tins left would be enough for a reasonable meal for all of them. But doubts assailed her. She knew she was doing wrong. Though something else, a vague certainty that a change was coming, made her act as she did, like a sleepwalker, instinctively sure. She hid the eight tins because something told her she *had* to.

By the fireplace she found a burnt crust of bread that had escaped everyone's notice and put it in her mouth. As she chewed slowly on it, she squatted down and half-heartedly tried to light the fire that had gone out while she had been away. Sometimes she glanced impatiently round for the others. She was waiting for Allan to appear. Insight grew in her with a determination that almost frightened her.

16

'Are you sure he was dead?'

'No, not entirely . . .'

'If he's dead, we must cover him with stones, or we might get typhus out here, too.'

'Wait. . . .'

He was half-way to his feet, but she held him back. She could see how tired he was. All day out on the Dump without finding anything, deep furrows etched into his weather-beaten skin, his heavy features, the fingers of the hand under hers hard, short and blunt, the nails ruined by working on the scrap-iron and garbage.

'Wait,' she said again. 'There's something I. . . .'

He looked up, alert. It was rare for her to restrain him with arguments. They seldom sat talking together like this. Words had become strange to them both.

She struggled to express what she thought to this dark, almost suspicious face.

'Maybe there's no need . . . I mean, whatever happens, it's not going to work out any longer.'

Did he understand? Nothing told her he had heard or understood what she was saying.

'There's no food left,' she went on. 'We've no stores any more. We eat everything the moment we find it. It's not even proper winter yet, and even so we're scarcely managing. You've found nothing today, have you? The others have found nothing. I found those tins. . . .'

They had feasted on three of the tins. The fourth turned out to have a hole in it, so the contents were ruined but could perhaps be used to lure a roaming dog?

Darkness fell early now. The others had retreated to sleep, for once without hunger gnawing at them. Only Smiley was still sitting by the fire, his head hanging and a sullen expression as he rubbed his injured ankle, still badly swollen and showing no sign of getting better. He despised old strips of cloth Doc had bandaged round it, for they kept falling off as he humped round on his home-made crutch, hurling abuse at everyone and everything, life unbearable since it had become difficult to get liquor from the city.

'I know,' said Allan, staring straight ahead.

The long day's search for something to eat with no result had left him in a gloomy mood. It had always been a struggle to survive on the Dump, a struggle against the mean, dead landscape, the seasons, the climate, the wind and weather, but it had largely been a struggle to *secure* themselves a life, to make the most of the circumstances, to make use of their labours so they produced most for them all. . . . But now, every day had become a struggle to find something to put into their mouths, a struggle from hour to hour against hunger and despair, on top of their doubts as to whether it was any use going on at all. Until now, Allan had managed to push the decision to the back of his mind. There had always been *something* to find, and with their joint efforts they had survived, but for how much longer?

'Even the dogs have gone!' he mumbled gloomily.

'Yes,' she said. 'It's not going to work out, Allan. . . .'

The decision grew in him, the one *she* had taken that same afternoon. 'We must leave,' he said curtly, and the connection between thought and action was so direct, he was at once on his feet.

'Yes, but *where* to?'

'Back to Sweetwater.'

'But. . . .' She was uncertain now. 'The city is blocked off – what about the epidemic? How can we . . .?'

An unhealthy grey of exhaustion lay beneath her dark skin, her eyes glowing like coals with fatigue and anxiety over the unknown consequences this decision might have.

'Where else can we go?' he said briefly. 'It's just as bad in other cities – even if we could get there. We wouldn't stand a chance out in the wilderness in winter. No, Sweetwater is our only hope. The epidemic is dying out. The disease won't spread so much in the winter cold. Anyhow, there'll soon be no one left there.'

She knew he was right.

'We must take the kids with us,' she whispered, glancing through the van door at the sleeping Rain.

He nodded. 'We'll talk about that.'

He was on his way.

'Where are you going?'

'Over to Doc to arrange something.'

'But . . .'

'It won't take long. Go to bed and sleep. Get some rest.'

Smiley came to life over by the fire. He grabbed at Allan as he passed.

'I heard what you were talking about all right!'

Allan stopped and looked contemptuously at him, but he said nothing.

'You're going, leaving the rest of us to rot here.'

'*You*'ll rot whether we're here or not!' Allan snapped.

Smiley got to his feet and came humping over to him.

'You mustn't do it, Allan. We couldn't cope. You must take us with you – you've got to take *me* with you!'

'Give me one good reason why I should keep you alive any longer.'

'Intelligence, you know, wits . . . you can't let that go under. And you need mental stimulation.'

He tapped his forehead with his finger and grinned. He seemed to like this role, denigrating himself to a helpless, babbling beggar, although it was now quite clear he was really scared.

'Poor fool,' mumbled Allan and strode away.

'Wait!' cried Smiley, limping after him, but Allan had already vanished behind the nearest heap.

'Wait for me!' cried Smiley, this time real fear in his voice.

But in the darkness only a dog howled and a dirty grey moon hung low over the Sargossa industrial area.

Lisa was asleep. Doc had just heaved himself on to the sofa and spread the car rug over them both when Allan opened the door and came in. 'I must talk to you,' he said into the darkness.

'Yes, yes . . . just don't make so much noise,' whispered Doc, hauling himself up and fumbling over the table for matches to light a candle. 'What is it?' He peered uneasily at Allan in the doorway. Although it was accepted as fact — by Allan, too — that Lisa occasionally slept with him, he disliked anyone coming when she was there.

'What do you want?'

'Talk to you, I told you.'

'What about?'

Doc had sat down on one of the wooden chairs, shivering.

'We're leaving,' said Allan.

At first Doc did not react, but then he nodded quietly, as if what Allan said confirmed what he had known — or at least had considered for a long time.

'As soon as possible,' Allan went on, as if trying to make the old man react.

Doc nodded again. 'Yes, yes, but where to?'

'Back.'

'To the *city*?'

He nodded almost imperceptibly to the north-west. 'Yes.'

'How will you manage?'

'Don't know. It's our only chance. We'll starve to death here.'

Doc paused, thinking, anxiety in his dim eyes. 'Oh, we'll get through this winter as well . . .'

'I don't think so. We're leaving. It's decided. When we go, there'll be more for the rest of you.'

'How . . . how many of you are going?'

The old man was looking down, his voice trembling. 'Mary and I . . . and the kids.'

The pale, almost blind eyes flickered at Allan again. 'No one . . . else?'

'No.'

Doc was struggling now, his Adam's apple bobbing, one hand on his forehead, his breathing fast and wheezing. Then it came.

95

'What about Lisa? Er . . . she's your wife, Allan . . .'

'I came to talk about your gun,' Allan broke in.

'My *gun?*'

'Yes, I need it. The situation in Sweetwater being what it is, I must have a gun. Will you sell it to me?'

'But I need it myself. It wasn't entirely safe out here before, and it's worse now . . .'

'No one one will find you here.'

'Don't say that. Everyone who can, gets out of Sweetwater because he thinks it's easier to save his skin somewhere else. They'll come here, too, I'm sure of it. And if they get this far, they'll be desperate.'

'I *must* have the gun.'

'What shall I have to defend myself – ourselves – with, then?'

Doc's eyes flickered helplessly towards the sofa. Allan glanced at Lisa and saw she was lying quite still with her eyes wide open.

'If I have the gun, you can have her,' he said, nodding towards Lisa.

The Adam's apple leapt again. 'But . . . but you said only you . . . and Mary . . .'

'If I can't have the gun, I'll take Lisa with me.'

'*No!*'

Lisa cried out in anguish, staring at Doc. Doc clenched and unclenched his hands on the table.

'But Allan – you can't . . . you don't mean it . . .'

'Yes, he means it! But I don't want to go, not with him. You mustn't let him do it, Doc!' Lisa was weeping, her eyes wide open, mouth gaping, her voice unrecognizable, as if she were incapable of controlling herself.

'Allan, you can't . . .'

'Yes, I can,' interrupted Allan, without moving. 'You can have her, if I can have the gun. If not, I'll take her with me. That's my right. I'm married to her.'

'Perhaps I should . . .' mumbled Doc, scarcely audibly. 'Perhaps I should let her go with you? Perhaps she would have a better chance with you than staying with me. You're strong, Allan. You'll survive . . . I'm old. Perhaps it would be for the best. . . .'

He bowed his head and for a moment he seemed to be asleep. Lisa was sobbing in his arms, her thin shoulders shaking helplessly, the back of her neck scrawny and dirty. Doc's gnarled hands kept stroking her unkempt mane of hair. Apart from Lisa's weeping, it was quite quiet. Then Doc whispered: 'All right, you can have it.'

'Cartridges, too.'

'Whatever you like. Whatever you like . . .'

'Wise of you.'

'You're hard. I hope you're not *too* hard.'

'I'll get by. Just hand over the gun and you'll be rid of me.'

'All right, all right. Since you're in such a hurry.'

Doc got up and took Lisa over to the sofa, speaking quietly to her in a childish voice. Then he went over to a cupboard and took out two boxes. He put them down side by side on the table, took the lid off one of them and slowly unwrapped the gun from the oily cloth in which it had been wrapped. Allan held out his hand before he was ready, but Doc ignored it. 'It isn't loaded, you needn't worry,' he said quietly, putting the weapon down on the table. 'I hadn't thought of doing anything. I'm too old to escape my destiny.'

'Cartridges, too,' said Allan curtly, snatching up the gun, weighing it in his hand and examining it. His hand was trembling, although he was doing his best to conceal his excitement. 'You must show me how to put . . .'

Doc took the other lid off and extracted two smaller boxes, opening one. Two or three cartridges fell out and rolled across the table. 'Look,' he said, picking up one of them and holding out his hand for Allan to give him back the gun, but Allan jerked the gun back and held it close to his body.

'No, I'll do it myself. Just tell me how . . .'

'For God's sake, Allan.' Doc looked appealingly at him and shook his head. 'Have things gone *that* far?'

'Don't waste time,' said Allan sharply. 'It's late. Let's get this over and done with, then I'll go.'

Doc sighed, then slowly began to explain in almost a whisper: 'Press that button on the top by the stock there, then the magazine springs out. . . .'

Allan grabbed two cartridges before doing what Doc had told him. The magazine came out and fell into the palm of his hand.

'Then insert the cartridges,' Doc went on in a scarcely audible voice.

Allan did so at once, concentrating intently.

Then Doc broke. 'My God, I should never have done it! I should never have allowed you to sell her! You've turned into an animal. A *monster*! And me, too, who could *buy*. . . .' He wept. 'It wouldn't have made any difference what I'd said . . . if I'd refused, you would have taken both – wouldn't you? *Wouldn't you?* He stared at Allan, a wild look of despair, not hatred, directed at the man on the other side of the table concentrating on the gun in his hand. '*Wouldn't you?*'

Allan looked up. 'Yes, I would,' he said. '*You*'re old and you don't need it.' The gun barrel drew a semicircle between them. 'I am young. I'm going to live, and I need a gun.'

Lisa held out her hand and touched Doc – to console him? To seek some security against what was so terrifying in Allan? Doc responded by squeezing her thin hand.

Allan saw this and barked quickly and impatiently, 'Hurry now and tell me how to do this. We haven't much time.'

17

They were all there when he got back. Smiley must have spread the news. Mary Diamond was in front of the camping van as if on guard, the others in a semicircle. They had put wood on the fire, so it was burning brightly. Uneasiness could be seen on all their faces. The children were also awake, Rain whimpering in Mary's arms and Boy standing beside Run-Run.

Allan stopped by the fire and looked at them, saying nothing. It was up to them to say something. He tried to catch Smiley's eye, then Felix's, but their eyes flickered away. Only Run-Run was staring straight at him, a hint of a grin on his lips.

Finally Felix spoke. 'We hear you're leaving?'

'Yes.'

'Just you alone . . .'

'Yes. Mary and I and the kids.'

As Allan said 'kids', something flashed through Boy. He stood there tensely, every muscle trembling, almost baring his teeth at his father.

'Why are you going?'

'We can't cope out here any longer.'

'Why just you?'

'I think the fewer we are the better our chances, the situation in the city being what it is.'

'It'll be hard for the rest of us – losing two who can work.'

'There'll be more for each of you when we've gone.'

'But it'll be more difficult for us to get anything . . .'

'We have to do it this way – a whole bunch of us wouldn't have a chance in Sweetwater. We wouldn't even get into the city.'

'But it'll be worse for us.'

Smiley could contain himself no longer. 'You're not going to get away with it!' he shouted, humping a few steps forward on his crutch. 'Now listen . . . we'll make sure you don't get away. Going off and leaving us . . .'

'You go,' said Allan contemptuously. 'Just go wherever you want to. No one's stopping you. Go off to the city and see if you can find someone who'll stuff food into your mouth. But you're not coming with us.'

'And you're not going anywhere if we don't want you to. We're four against one,' shouted Smiley, limping another couple of steps towards Allan and grabbing his arm, holding tight on to his tattered sleeve as if trying to stop him moving away from the spot. Allan struck out at him. The hard backhander smashed across Smiley's cheek and his babbling mouth. He lost his balance and fell head-long, landing at Allan's feet.

The others did not move but stood looking on, the firelight gleaming in their eyes, their breath white in the cold of the autumn night. Rain had fallen asleep again and was lying with her head dangling over Mary's shoulder.

Allan stepped over Smiley's body and went and stood in front of Felix. 'There's no other way out,' he said in a quiet voice. 'I've been thinking about it for a long time and I've tried to think of alternatives. There are none. I don't know how we'll get by in the city, but we'll be destroyed out here, that's for sure. They're not even tipping out here any longer. Even the dogs. . . .' He kicked the ground angrily.

'But what if we refuse?'

Felix was standing like a statue, imperturbable in his aura of correctness, his frayed cuffs flapping round his wrists, one trouser-leg split up to the knee and his white shirt the greyish-yellow colour all cloth gradually acquired on the Dump.

'Shit to that!'

'But we are many against one.' Felix issued the threat in measured, almost benevolent tones.

'Not another word!' Allan's voice roared out of his black beard.

Felix immediately fell silent, but his stance remained unchanged, distinguished, a trifle exultant.

Allan was breathing as if he had run all the way back from Doc's house.

'First of all, I won't be alone. . . .' He glanced at Mary, still standing there with the child on her arm, guarding the entrance to the camping van. 'Secondly. . . .' He thrust his hand inside his shirt. 'I'm . . . I'm not so stupid as to go to Sweetwater empty-handed.' He let Felix stare for a long time into the barrel of the black gun. 'And it's loaded!' he snarled into the dead silence that had fallen over them as he had pulled out the gun.

The shot went straight up into the air, as if the noise was intended to split their eardrums. The flame from the barrel exploded into their eyes, cordite stinging their nostrils, suffocating and sharp. They all stared at Allan as if hypnotized. Bean sank to his knees with a moan, but the others took no notice of him.

Even Felix's eyes widened. 'Where did you get hold of *that*?' he managed to say.

Allan shrugged and thrust the gun into the belt inside his shirt. 'That's worth anything in Sweetwater, meat, oil, forged papers. . . .'

Felix's eyes gleamed. 'Even the Force have very few firearms. Their losses have been enormous. The officers have looted the stores and sold them on the black market! Have you got cartridges, too?'

'Two boxes. Eighty.' Allan patted his pocket.

'What did you have to give for it?'

Allan did not answer.

'You could get enough food to keep us for most of the winter for that.'

'It's going to get Mary and me to Sweetwater.'

'What about Lisa?'

'Doc's going to look after Lisa.'

Allan's tone of voice ended the conversation. Felix understood and looked down.

Allan half turned to Mary. 'We must start packing and get away as soon as possible.'

They had to go that night – it was no longer safe for them there.

Then Run-Run leapt up and stood, almost bent double, in front of Allan, his lips drawn right back from his fine white teeth, his arm out, trembling like a violin string, his finger directed at the shapeless figure of Bean on the ground, lying there without moving. A few seconds went by before Allan understood.

Meanwhile Felix had drawn breath, summed up the situation and the explanation came laconically: 'He means, what shall we do with Bean?'

'Well, what shall we do with him?' said Allan, always rather ill at ease in the presence of the wild man.

Run-Run grimaced and pointed, at Allan, at Bean, back again at Allan, then waved his arm over to the north-west sky, now brooding darkly, no lights flickering from the city.

Allan understood.

'He means you must take him with you.'

Felix's bleating voice in the background sounded like a provocation.

'What the hell do we want with him?'

'What do *we* want with him?'

Then Smiley came to life. He had sat up and was waving his crutch about.

'You saved him, didn't you? When Run-Run here wanted to finish him off. So he's your responsibility, you see? You can't unload him on to us. You must take him with you. That's the only real, the most *just* solution, don't you see?'

'Smiley's right,' said Felix. 'Bean is a sick man. He can't work. He's just a nuisance here. You were his guardian angel – take him with you.'

Run-Run looked from one to the other, his eyes glinting. Then he drew his knife and held it out to Allan, pointed at Bean lying curled up and groaning on the ground. Then Run-Run drew his forefinger across his throat and squatted down again with a wide, expectant grin.

Felix's flat voice once again expressed what they all understood: 'If you don't want him, then finish him off yourself.'

Allan was in a dilemma. He had no fondness for Bean, now on top of everything else a sick man scarcely able to stand upright. When he had stopped Run-Run killing Bean, he had acted intuitively, in automatic protest against the wild man's mindless desire to kill, which filled him with a fear of the law of the jungle, of the anarchy of the desire to kill. What if they all . . .? He had stopped Run-Run to protect himself and all of them from uncontrollable blood-lust, not because he felt any special responsibility for Bean – an officer in the Peacekeeping Force, to boot. But to kill him now in cold blood because he would be a burden on them in Sweetwater? Could he do that?

He was tempted. What did a miserable cop matter? He was mostly a burden to them. The enemy in one person? As the situation was now, both here and in Sweetwater, it *was* the law of the jungle, every man for himself, and the weakest, the most stupid and most unfortunate had to take the hindmost. Only a few would survive. He thought he had a chance of being one of those who would . . .

survival entailed being able to sum up a situation, act quickly and resolutely, forestalling everyone else. He had faith in his ability; his physique was intact and so was his instinct for self-preservation. He was better equipped for the struggle to come than the wrecks of civilization in Sweetwater. He would make it. He and Mary. For Mary was strong. She had survived harsh conditions before and knew what to do in tricky situations.

But a helpless policeman, dazed with fear and fever? What would happen if he came? Would he be more than just a hindrance? Perhaps even a danger to them? Of course, he would undoubtedly be nothing but danger to them! So why didn't he act?

Allan was still hesitating, Run-Run's knife in his hand. He couldn't make himself go over and simply execute the wretch. A spark of compassion in him made him abandon the idea. He couldn't just kill a human being. In a man-to-man fight, a life for a life, perhaps yes, but not like this, for the sake of convenience.

Logic told him he had to cut Bean's throat. Avoiding the decision and letting him stay here to try his luck with the others was the same as killing him here and now. Then he looked into Run-Run's eyes. The logic of the situation was so clear to him that the hand holding the knife seemed to twitch, but just as clearly he knew there were limits, for him anyhow. He could *not* commit a deliberate murder of a defenceless wretch who was only indirectly a threat to their chances. He flung the knife to the ground, went over to Bean, lying there rigid with terror as he had gradually become aware of what they were all talking about, grabbed his arm and hauled him to his feet. 'Come on,' he said darkly. 'Come with us.'

Bean was shaking so badly, he could scarcely stand.

'Pull yourself together,' growled Allan. 'We must be off soon.'

Mary had gone into the van to gather up their things into the car rug she had spread out on the floor.

Allan turned to Boy. 'Go and help her,' he said curtly. 'The sooner we get away, the better. We must go while it's dark.'

But Boy just glanced at him and did not move from the spot, half hidden behind Run-Run. When Allan made an impatient movement, as if about to go over and fetch him out by force, Boy let out a shrill scream, half in terror, half defiant, swung round and disappeared like lightning into the darkness.

Bean collapsed again, so Allan had to grab him before he fell. Smiley giggled shrilly.

'Damn me, he's going to be quite a burden to you! Why don't you chop off his head and leave the body here, so we've got something for the dogs?'

With icy calm, Allan turned to Bean.

'You heard what Sir Intelligence said, didn't you? You must pull yourself together now, or you'll end up as dog-meat. Come on, we've a long way to go. . . .' With one arm round Bean's shoulder, he half supported him as he dragged him over to his cardboard shed. 'Collect the things you want to take with you, but remember you must carry them yourself. We've quite enough of our own.'

In his words was a warning that it would be up to Bean to keep up with them on the long trip.

Out in the darkness, they could hear the rustling and squealing of rats fighting over the leftovers, another reminder of the way things would end for anyone unable to keep up.

The big gate had been taken off its hinges and lay rusting and half-buried in the mud, bent and buckled by wheels of heavy vehicles. The high wire netting was down, a bare fencing-post jutting up here and there. The tracks made by wheels out to the tipping place were there as always, full of evil-smelling mire, though the paths down to the inhabited part of the Dump were no longer visible even to the few who knew where they were.

It was difficult for them to make their way over the heaps, now soaked by the heavy autumn rains. At the gate they stopped for a breather and looked at each other, their faces drawn in the early grey light, the bay behind them like a sheet of polished metal. Mary put down her pack and handed Rain, asleep and bundled in a shawl, over to Allan. Then they turned to see Bean humping twenty or thirty metres behind them, a bundle on his back and a rolled blanket under his arm. They had no need to call out to him. When he saw they had stopped, he tried to move faster, his hoarse breathing slicing through the morning stillness.

'We'll take the service road for a little way,' Allan said. He had spoken quietly to Mary, but it was so still even for out there, his voice carried a long way. 'We can get under the motorway up on the ridge and shelter there until it gets dark.'

He had decided to try the motorway, to follow it as far as they could, then they would be certain to get themselves in towards the city. In the unplanned jumble of streets in the southern parts of the East Zone they would have to go through if they chose the ordinary highway, and, for instance, tried to follow the route the bus used to take out there, he was afraid they would lose their way and become an easier prey for patrols of the Force or mobs operating in the suburbs. So he had decided on the motorway, although it was wide and open, the danger being observed from the air, for instance. He knew helicopters were occasionally used in the hunt for refugees.

'About how far is it?' asked Mary.

'I don't remember. Maybe a night or two's walking.'

Bean had caught up with them and was sitting gasping and wiping his face. Allan tied Rain firmly to himself, then heaved his pack up on to his back. Mary did the same. She was strong, carrying as much weight as he was. They would make it, he thought, as he headed along the overgrown service road, now nothing but a quagmire in the dying vegetation, over to the place where it was best to start the climb up the side of the ridge towards the broad columns where it was possible to shelter under the massive concrete roof formed where the motorway lanes cut into the ridge, just below the monastery which had given Abbott Hill its name. They would be able to sleep there as long as they liked, then wait for darkness to fall. Wait before setting about the long march back.

PART THREE

18

Up in the 'roof', the uneven grey underside of the motorway where the girder system joined to bear the weight in a variety of angles, ledges and niches, spaces behind rusting joints were concealed in dark crevices. In places, Allan could just see collections of brushwood and dry grass which seemed obtrusive in all that concrete, untidily breaking through the layers of powdery dust that had swirled up and settled on the motorway landscape over the years. At the time, traffic had been constantly on the increase, so the motorway and the countryside around seemed as if they were being preserved, deposited under a thin shell of ultra-fine, weightless dust that would harden over the years until it finally became stone.

Allan was awake, staring up at the concrete arch at those amazing clumps of tangled twigs and brushwood, wondering what they were. Then it dawned on him. 'Birds!' he exclaimed, so loudly his voice echoed under the arch.

Of course, they were nests. When he thought about it, he knew there had been large numbers of predatory birds along the motorway, often waiting side by side along the verges, undisturbed by the traffic thundering past, waiting for smaller birds or mammals to be run over. For them, the overcrowded years of traffic in and out of Sweetwater had been years of plenty. Their nests were still there under the arched bridges, several generations of them, now abandoned, collapsing and being scattered by wind and weather. Had their inhabitants retreated to better hunting grounds after the decline and now almost total cessation of traffic? Or had they been exterminated by the air pollution, the lead and mercury in the flattened prey they had taken in such numbers along the motorway?

Allan was lying on a bed of leaves and twigs, fully clothed and wrapped in a rug, staring at the last remains of wildlife along the motorway. Mary was beside him with Rain pressed close to her, both sound asleep. Bean was snoring a little way away.

Allan had been awake for an hour, thinking about the best route to take and then how to get into the city, now guarded almost like a fortress to stop refugees running amok and swarming out on to the roads. He had heard that they had stopped the forced evacuation of residential areas, and the city there was as good as deserted. But might that be just rumour?

He lay staring at where there had once been a mass of predatory birds. He had seen them, hawks and falcons, sweeping elegantly down over the asphalt, snatching up some unfortunate mouse or crushed small mammal without stopping in flight, silent, swift dives down between the roaring cars. Perhaps he could learn something from them?

Fatigue came over him and his thoughts raced. The hollow ache in his stomach was unpleasant, but he had decided they must save the little food they had until the evening, when they were to start walking. Only Rain had had a piece of bread to suck and a little water mixed with dried milk from the last box Dos Manos had sold them.

The pale autumn sun also took the edge off the cold where they were lying in the shadows. Allan felt the tension in his body giving way. The last thing he took in before falling asleep was the roar of a vehicle racing along above their heads, undoubtedly a military vehicle. He listened to the sound, a jeep, presumably on road patrol. That was the first that day. So they did not come out all that often. They probably had to save fuel in the present situation. His thoughts flew again: to strike like a hawk on to a patrol of that kind.

Then he fell asleep.

At dusk, they scrambled up the last steep ridge, climbed over the low wall and up on to the motorway itself. The road to Sweetwater lay before them, incredibly wide, incredibly flat, unfamiliar smooth, hard asphalt beneath their feet. The low bank disturbed their equilibrium, making them dizzy, so now and again they had to wave their arms about to keep their balance. It was unusual for them to be moving in completely open surroundings. They trudged on without apparently moving, horizons gradually retreating as they slowly moved along the vast concrete plain.

None the less walking there did not seem unnatural, as it would have done only a few years ago. Allan's thoughts turned to the days when the black-market had flourished, when the parking lots off the motorway had sometimes become market-places. He had quite often gone up there himself to sell or buy or exchange something from those who travelled along the motorway with goods on offer. At the time, these surroundings, this concrete construction bearing its strange noisy life-style, the impregnable *greatness* of this machine carrying people and vehicles back and forth, had seemed threatening to him, unnatural, something he had to resist. The years out on the Dump had made him think like that, *he*, who as a boy had sat by the window of his room and stared as if possessed at the lights on the petrol station changing colours in the darkness, thinking it beautiful, the most beautiful thing he could imagine.

It was quite different up there now.

First of all, the emptiness, the stillness, the absence of traffic. They were walking along the wide straight road, their steps resounding on the asphalt, the echo striking back from the walled edges on both sides. The sound of cars they had always associated with this road, a sound they were soon able to recall whenever the word 'motorway' was mentioned, had been silenced and replaced by the ringing sounds of human feet. The brutal movement associated with sounds from up there, the roar of powerful engines approaching and disappearing at high speed, the scream of tyres flayed along the hot surface – now the only moving things were three slow, burdened figures trudging towards the city, across an endless desert, shimmering wherever it caught and reflected the last of the evening light.

Other things had also changed. The recent decline in traffic, particularly over the last year when ordinary traffic had finally ceased altogether, had created a connection between the motorway and the landscape that had not been there before. In its newly found stillness, the surrounding countryside had crept up to subdue the contrasts, softening conflicts between nature and what had been created by man. The vegetation on the banks had grown and thickened into jungle in some places, small trees, bushes and climbing plants creeping up here and there on to the asphalt and hanging low over their heads where the road ran through a cutting. On the central reservations, the same kind of lushness had run wild. Although most of the vegetation was dry and dead now in late

107

autumn, they could see how flourishing bushes had scattered their leaves over the roadway and creepers had sent out runners as if to close the nearest lanes to all traffic. The vegetation in some places was so tall, they could only just glimpse the road surface on the other side, the parallel lanes which before had carried the noisy traffic in the opposite direction. Edging stones had tipped over where roots had forced their way through. Strong green grass was growing out of cracks in the surface, steadily becoming bigger as repairs were not carried out. Nature herself was blunting the edge of destruction, laying a sheen of indulgence over the memory of man's miracles, of a crumbling pride, a civilization that had at last been allowed to collapse.

They were walking steadily, although Bean kept complaining he was hungry and that his feet hurt. They ignored him. Bean's communication with the world around him consisted largely of a perpetual whine, whether there was any reason for it or not. He was a dog always grovelling around with his tail between his legs, waiting to be kicked and beaten. But it turned out he could keep up when he had to. They had eaten before they had left, a piece of bread each, spread with a thick layer of cooking fat from one of the tins Mary had hidden away. They still had water in two plastic bottles, at least enough until the next day.

As it grew darker, the going became more difficult. Bean in particular kept stumbling over plants growing across the motorway. With no lights or fixed points except glimpses of asphalt two or three steps ahead, moving along this inhospitable surface apparently extending into infinity was like balancing on the edge of something threatening, a precipice, an eternal vacuum.

They slowed down. Allan had fixed his eyes on a point of light some way ahead and stuck to it as if he needed an anchorage for his eyes in order not to stay marching on the spot in one place. Only a year earlier, the whole of the sky ahead of them would have been a sparkling fog of lights above Sweetwater. Now only feeble individual flickering points of light reached them from the blacked-out city, no stronger than the stars above their heads winking behind a veil of mist.

Allan stuck to his navigation point and tried to increase their pace. He hadn't reckoned on its being so difficult to walk in the dark. He sensed they were walking far too slowly and it worried him. They had not meant to use up their resources on the way into the city. He kept feeling as if he were about to fall. He regained his balance, fixed his eyes on the light again, but found he was swerving to the right. What was this? *The light* was moving! At the same moment they heard a sound like a distant roar.

'Listen!' cried Mary behind him.

They stood quite still and listened to the sound, now rapidly increasing in strength, a menacing, alien sound after they had got used to hearing nothing but their own breathing and their steps on the asphalt. The light was slowly swinging regularly from side to side ahead of them. The sound came nearer.

Suddenly Allan realized what was happening. 'A car!' he cried. 'A car's coming. Take cover!'

He ran over to the edge of the motorway, fumbling in his pocket, then lit a precious match and stared over the edge, trying to fathom out how steep it was and how far down . . . but there was no time for such thoughts.

'Come on!' he barked, leaping over the wall first and sliding down the gravel and dust. Mary was soon behind him, Bean whimpering in the background. They were lucky. The bank was not high. They landed in some bushes a little way down where the bank stopped. Crouching, they stared up at the approaching light, the sound of the engine now much louder. A puff and a roar and it had passed. The noise retreated, the light vanishing.

'A jeep,' mumbled Allan as he sat on his heels, rubbing his sore hands against his thighs. He was thinking. Again he saw in front of him the swift hawk waiting by the roadside until the mouse was squashed, and swish! – diving out and securing its prey. Then there was nothing else to think about except going on.

19

They had passed large numbers of wrecked cars and saw even more the nearer they came to the city. Some looked as if they had been there a long while, total wrecks, rusty and testimony to the times when multiple crashes were the order of the day on the motorway. Others seemed to be of more recent date, relatively new and fairly intact, as if the owners had fallen out of them on the roadside and then abandoned them. But flat tyres, gaping bonnets and open boots bore witness to the fact that most of them had been there for quite a while, probably remnants left from the first wave of refugees trying to get out of the city and abandoned when they had run out of petrol or had engine trouble. Or when they had been stopped by a highway patrol, arrested and held in internment camps.

In the grey light, these silent wrecks along the roadside, here and there with quite short distances between them, looked ghostly.

When it grew light, they found a place where they could crawl in and rest, even get a little sleep. Allan had been careful with his choice of resting-place. They were getting closer to the city now, and this was clear from the area all round them, a wilderness of sandy soil and stones and gravel churned up by heavy machines, one or two machines left behind to rust away. In three or four places vast foundations had been completed and the beginnings of a wall raised. A resplendent hoarding, now leaning precariously, announced *Silverdale Company* . . . the rest gone. The area had once been designated as yet another building zone 'in quiet surroundings of natural beauty, far from the clamour of the city', as it also stated on the hoarding.

A dried-up drainage trench ran under the motorway through a man-high concrete pipe, and that seemed ideal, the motorway curving a few hundred metres away, so suiting Allan's plans perfectly. But first they had to get some rest. Rain was tired and unwell after a hard night with so little sleep. She was fretting, so was given a piece of cane sugar from Doc's garden to suck. They still had some left of their share of the year's lean crop, the last of which had been harvested a few days before they had left.

In the evening, they climbed up on to the motorway again, and Allan started putting his plan into action. Not far away stood two abandoned cars. With Bean's and Mary's help, they pushed them out into the motorway, one after the other, so that they blocked most of it just beyond the curve.

'Now all we have to do is to wait,' he said.

'What for?'

'The patrol.'

'Are you going to kill them?' she said, grinning as she smashed her clenched fist into her palm as if to illustrate the inevitable collision.

'No, just get them to stop,' he replied.

Bean said nothing, but his eyes flickered.

So they went back into the concrete pipe, lay down and waited. Allan knew they would be very lucky if his plan was going to work, but it was worth trying. He could see no better method of getting safely into Sweetwater. What worried him most was the possibility of *no* patrol coming along that night. No vehicles had passed them all day long, and the day before he had twice heard jeeps racing south – perhaps they did not patrol according to a fixed schedule?

The day had been still and endlessly long. He had been so occupied with his plan that he had not slept. A rabbit had scurried along the bottom of the ditch, hopped over towards them and come so close he had been able to kill it with a stone. So they had food, but he didn't dare light a fire for fear the smoke would be seen. He had skinned and cleaned the rabbit in a few minutes, wrapped it up in a dusty newspaper he had found in the ditch and tucked it into his bundle. Food would have to wait. What lay ahead of them now was more important.

An infinity went by before darkness fell again.

'Something coming!'

Mary's hoarse whisper woke him. He had dozed off, but for how long? It was pitch-dark outside.

'Sounds like a car!'

She had the sharpest senses. She could hear a lizard dragging its scaly belly across stones and she could smell a dog as it approached.

The sound was more distinct now, the roar of an engine approaching fast from the direction of the city. Perhaps they would succeed after all?

Allan crawled up the bank to keep a look-out. He could just see his barricade in the dark. The sound of the engine was coming steadily nearer, lights sweeping over the few trees remaining on the bank ('surroundings of natural beauty'). The car would soon be in sight, roaring round the slow bend. . . . Allan ducked and closed his eyes tight, blinded by the light suddenly coming straight at him. The military vehicle was travelling at an insane speed, its engine roaring so loudly he had to cover his ears. The wrecks they had dragged out on to the motorway could be seen in clear outline. But the vehicle carried on without braking – hadn't the driver seen anything? Then there was a scream of rubber against asphalt – too late! They would never manage to stop at that distance. A collision was inevitable.

It came.

The driver managed to wrench the vehicle over into the left-hand lane, the one not blocked by the wrecks, but was unable to clear them. The vehicle swerved into the far end of Allan's road-block, taking a mudguard and a bumper with it, then swerved on along the wall towards the central reservation with a splintering screech.

One of the tyres exploded with a loud bang. For some reason — perhaps the driver was desperately trying to regain control — the vehicle suddenly swung right across the motorway, crashed into the outer edge of the wall and at last came to a stop, tipped at a dangerous angle with the front part hanging over the remains of the wire-netting fence. Then — not a sound. Nothing. Just the lights shining on trenches and heaps of gravel.

Allan scrambled up on to the road, fumbling inside his shirt and pulling out the gun as he ran over to the crashed vehicle. His plan had failed. The vehicle was wrecked. Well, there was still time to make the best of it. As he got closer, he noticed a movement inside the back window facing him; so someone was still alive. Then the door sprang open and a figure more less fell out on to the motorway, heaved himself up and remained seated propped up against the back wheel, rocking back and forth making clucking noises halfway between groaning and laughter, paying no attention to Allan, who had stopped some way away. The man pulled himself together sufficiently to be able to speak, turned his head and shouted something into the car behind him.

'Christ, that was bit of a circus! What the hell was that in the way, Stan? I thought they'd cleared away all that stuff.'

The man laughed foolishly, his voice blurred, and to his astonishment, Allan realized the man was dead drunk. The voice babbled on.

'Hey, you, Stan, how're we going to go on now? In this heap of scrap? Stan? Hey, Stan!'

He was trying to attract his companion's attention by shouting louder, twisting round and sticking his head in through the car door opening, but he collapsed again, cursing and groaning.

'Christ, my side hurts! Stan! How's it with you? I'm feeling dead rotten, I. . . .' He put his head down between his knees and vomited. 'Christ! That stuff they get now is bloody poison.'

He threw up again, coughing and spitting and swearing.

Allan took his chance, moving in swiftly, and struck the man on the back of his neck with the butt of the gun. The soldier collapsed with a sigh. Allan glanced into the car. The other man was quite still in the front seat, leaning over the wheel, blood all over his face. Allan leant through the open door, grabbed his shoulder and shoved him back upright. He could feel the man was not dead the moment he started going through his pockets. Not much joy there, identity papers, keys, money, a small pouch of tobacco. He extracted a powerful gun out of the man's holster, then, gripping him under each arm, he hauled him out of the car on to the ground by his companion, by which time Mary and Bean had appeared.

'Are they dead?'

The question came in a sober tone as she looked down at the two figures.

'No, only passed out.'

The two were in military uniform but none the less looked unkempt and slovenly, their jackets unbuttoned, belts and straps unbuckled, and one of them had no shirt on. They looked as if they had not been out of their clothes for several days and both had a week's growth of beard. A frightening thought struck Allan — supposing they weren't a patrol, but two drunken soldiers out on the razzle? Or two deserters? In that case, a regular patrol might appear at any moment. He would have to act quickly if they were not to be caught in their own trap!

'Pull them over to the side of the road so they're not in the way here.'

Allan got into the car again, fumbled on the dashboard shelf and found a long, cold metal cylinder — a torch! At last something useful. In its powerful beam he examined the wrecked vehicle — a covered jeep. The left side had struck the central reservation and was badly damaged, the door off and mudguards wrecked, but the lights were intact, though the left front tyre was flat. Otherwise things seemed mostly in order, apart from possible damage to the front from the collision. As the vehicle at the moment had its front tipped up against the wreckage of wire-netting, that was difficult to confirm. Allan leant inside and tried the steering-wheel, but nothing happened. Perhaps the right front wheel was jammed against a fencing-post? After fumbling around for a while, he found the switch which turned off the lights.

'Come on,' he said. 'We must get it down on to the road again.'

After heaving away for a while, they got the front off the edge of the wall. Allan found a tool-box between the seats, hauled it out, discovered the jack clamped under the chassis and started taking off the punctured front wheel, while Bean got the spare wheel out of the back. Bean appeared to be more interested in the two men lying unconscious on the roadside, he who otherwise hardly ever showed any interest in anything. With an inquisitive eagerness almost amounting to voracity he squatted down and stared at them, at their faces and uniforms, and could hardly be persuaded away when Allan needed him for something.

20

Changing the wheel did not take long. Allan had not lost his skill as a mechanic. The front of the car seemed to be all right. He got in behind the wheel and switched on. The engine started. He found reverse and backed a little way, changed gear, accelerated and drove the jeep round in a wide sweep until its battered front was facing the way it had come. The wheels obeyed and, despite the wrecked body, the vehicle was roadworthy. Allan stopped and jumped out.

'Bean!'

Bean leapt to his feet at the sound of his name, then hurried across to Allan.

'Your turn now, Bean.' Allan's voice was urgent.

'What?' Bean sounded scared stiff.

'To contribute something. Come on. . . .'

With one hand on his shoulder, Allan half dragged, half shoved Bean over to the two unconscious men. 'Let's see now,' he said, turning the torch on them. 'Which is the tallest? I think we'll try this one. Get his clothes off.'

'What?'

'I said get the clothes off the one on the right, and be quick about it! We haven't got all night.'

'But . . .'

'Christ, you fool. Get his boots and trousers off and I'll do the tunic.'

Allan started pulling off the tunic and Bean at last understood, grabbed one of the boots and in a few minutes they had stripped the man.

'See how they fit,' Allan said to Bean, who was standing there fingering the shoulder-strap.

'What?'

'For God's sake, man! Get those rags off and put these on. A disguise. We're going to go behind enemy lines. Don't you understand?'

Bean was still hesitating, an ungainly, emaciated figure in torn overalls and tattered rubber boots, his grimy, bearded face a parody of the purposeful police officer he had been a year ago. Not until Allan flung the tunic at him so fiercely he almost lost his balance, and only then, was he able to pull himself together sufficiently to do what he was told.

Meanwhile Allan removed the other man's clothes, stripped off his own clothes and started getting into the uniform.

When they were both ready, Bean looked at Allan in dismay.

'Do you mean we're to . . .?'

'Yes. We'll drive the jeep back as if we'd been on patrol. If these guys really *were* on patrol . . .'

'It won't work.'

'There's a chance. His identity card's in the top pocket. I've got mine here . . .'

'But it's nothing like me,' said Bean, staring at the photo on the card in the light of the torch.

'Look at him. Is it anything like him?' growled Allan. It was true, the photo was of a smooth-shaven young recruit and in no way resembled the man lying on the ground in front of them.

'But . . .'

Despite the querulous voice, a change had come over Bean the moment he had put on the uniform. Although crumpled and dirty, it fitted him fairly well and he seemed to straighten up a little in the unfamiliar garments, his stride longer and firmer in his new boots. With the uniform cap on his head – the only one they found in the vehicle – he looked considerably taller than the other two, and the shoulder-strap made him straighten his back and puff out his chest. He ran his hands ran over the familiar material, the buckles and rivets of the belt and shoulder-strap, then stopped at the empty holster.

'Maybe you think something's missing?' Allan's tone was spiteful. 'But I don't think this is the moment to equip you with a gun. You might "desert", eh?'

Bean vigorously shook his head, his manner as cowed as before, but a small flame had begun to flicker inside him. The feeling of the uniform, snug round his body, as if propping him up, had given him back some of his identity and self-confidence. He suddenly felt like a human being, self-sufficient and not dependent on the other two. For the first time, he realized the *extent* of the fact that they were on their way back to Sweetwater – the consequences, the *possibilities* it entailed.

'Get in! You drive.'

Bean flinched out of habit.

'I can't . . .'

'Of course you can. Everyone in the Force can drive. Get in now. Less chance of you thinking up some tomfoolery that way.'

Bean obediently got into the driver's seat.

Mary was giving Rain something to eat and drink. She pointed back into the darkness where the stripped white figures of the two men could just be seen.

'What are we going to do with *them*?'

'Leave them there. They'll make their way back into the city when they come round again. And if they don't. . . .' Allan shrugged his shoulders.

Mary got into the back of the jeep with Rain in her arms. Allan handed her one of the guns. 'Take this and keep an eye on our driver here,' he said. 'If he gets up to anything, just shoot him. OK?'

She nodded.

'Did you hear that, Bean? You're under surveillance. Mary here has got you in her sights. Think about that as you drive.'

Bean nodded, his eyes flickering. But once he had got the engine running and found all the various switches, his movements became surer and calmer. He had been a good driver and he knew it. Top marks in the police driving course. This light jeep was child's play. He felt his skill coming back as he let the jeep bowl along close to the central reservation to manoeuvre it past the two wrecks. He was exhausted, but felt amazing satisfaction that his body was functioning.

'We must get over on to the other side,' growled Allan. 'We're on the wrong side. Supposing someone saw us.' It seemed meaningless to talk about 'sides' when the entire motorway was deserted both ways. But he was right. The Force sometimes sent a helicopter out — or they might meet another patrol. In any case, driving the wrong way would arouse suspicion. A little further along, a piece of the central wall had collapsed, so it was easy to manoeuvre the four-wheel-drive vehicle through the forest of bushes between the road-ways, then down the other side. Once there, Bean stepped on the accelerator and the battered jeep roared away, the wind icy as it whistled in where the door had been and swirled round their ears.

'Slow down now,' said Allan.

Bean obeyed.

For the last ten minutes the motorway had been swooping through Sweetwater's south-eastern outskirts, dark and gloomy on both sides, only the odd light here and there. Although they saw no destroyed buildings, the area all round was like a city in ruins. In the distance, a stronger light suddenly flared up, reddish and flickering, increasing in strength, a fire, a building, perhaps a whole quarter alight?

'First turning off,' said Allan.

He had his plan quite clear now. He would take them to the district round Abbott Hill Road. He was familiar with it after having worked at the PAC station out there for two or three years. The buildings in the area, once one of Sweetwater's pleasanter suburbs, were mixed, older – often derelict now – rows of houses and smaller apartment houses from before the days of building satellite city-complexes. There were still trees and greenery round a few of the houses, and back gardens . . . also the Park, the overgrown recreation ground surrounded by allotments now gone quite wild after so long without any attention. From the East Terminal, he would easily find his way. That meant heading straight for the place decided on; as the situation was now, bumbling round in the city at random would be lunacy.

'Watch out for the turning. Here it is!'

'Where do you want to go? I don't know this part of the city,' Bean protested weakly. The indefinable sense of hope in him at the thought that they had escaped the Dump and were nearing the city where there would be dozens of possibilities to . . . he hardly dared think the thought through, threatened by this blacked-out, unrecognizable mass in all directions around them, no landmarks or signs, just flames burning higher and redder as they approached.

In his dazed mind, Bean had fastened on an image of Sweetwater as he had known it, districts where he had lived, gone to school, to work: buildings, streets and parts of the city he knew well. But this . . . he looked around and saw the flames growing higher and more frightening every minute (wasn't the Fire Service there to bring it under control?), glimpses of other lights, here and there isolated street lights in random rows strung up like temporary lighting. What had become of the city he had known? Of course he knew it was there, but . . . it is never really dark in a city of a million people. Not *that* dark. For the first time he had some idea of the extent of the destruction that had hit Sweetwater. The fact almost paralysed him, the darkness enveloping everything he associated with civilization – more frightening to him than the darkness that had oppressed them all out at the Dump.

'Follow the directions to the East Terminal,' said Allan. 'Just do as I say. When we get to the terminal, I'll know where I am. Here's the turning now – turn off, man!'

Bean had been staring as if hypnotized at the fire, fear rising in him, a reluctance to leave the smooth, level motorway where for the moment he at least felt safe, the swift, even movement ahead, the sound of the engine, the effort of having walked so far, the lack of food and rest almost lulling him to sleep.

Allan's shout brought him out of his trance, but by then the wheel had already been jerked out of his hands, the jeep swerved over to the right, brushed a row of kerbstones and almost went into a spin. Allan was only just able to straighten it out so they did not crash head on into the railings on the opposite side.

'Brake, for Christ's sake, man!' yelled Allan as the vehicle lurched along the exit road.

At last Bean seemed to come to his senses and slow down. Allan let go the wheel and sank back in his seat with an ominous snarl.

'Good Christ, man, you can't fall asleep when you're driving.'

They drove slowly down the exit road off the motorway in wide curves above the rooftops. In a few minutes they would be down in the city itself. Bean was again filled with terror as he looked around at this place which he knew and yet didn't know. Then he noticed Allan straightening up and staring intently at a point ahead of them.

'Look there. . . .' He pointed. 'It couldn't be . . . it couldn't . . . the bastards!'

Bean stared and thought he could see something out by the edge of the road a little further ahead, some construction, in front of it a kind of fence stretched across the roadway, and he thought he could also see a vehicle.

'A checkpoint,' hissed Allan. 'They've barricaded off the exit roads. I thought . . .'

'Shall we turn back?' Bean had almost to shout to drown the sound of the engine.

'Are you mad? There's no one else on the road! They've heard us coming for ten minutes, you fool.'

'But what shall we. . . .'

It *was* a road-block. As they came nearer, they could see every detail. Behind the barriers was a bank of sandbags, and in the background what looked like a guardhouse or hut and a patrol car in the Force's colours. The opening in the barricade was just wide enough for a vehicle to get through and a single spotlight on a mast illuminated the whole arrangement. Not a human being in sight.

'But what if . . .?' Bean was overcome with icy panic.

Allan grabbed his shoulder and shook him. 'Take it easy now, that's what we're going to do. We've been on a road patrol and picked up these two here. . . .' He nodded back at where Mary, drooping and half-asleep, was holding on to Rain. 'Can you remember that?'

Bean tried to nod, but his chin was trembling. They were approaching the barricade, and still no one was visible.

'Listen now, Bean!' yelled Allan, on the verge of losing his own composure. 'I'll do the talking. Just drive on and keep your mouth shut and we'll be all right. You've got your identity card if anyone asks for it. We're the *Force*, you see. We're the military. Maybe they won't bother about us at all. Just drive quite normally and stop when they signal, but not before. Do you understand what I'm saying?'

Bean nodded again, apparently calmer. Some of the words Allan had shouted at him had stuck in his mind and were churning round and round in his head, about to turn the whole situation round for him: *'We're the Force . . . We're the Force . . . We're the Force. . . .'* Of course! The Peacekeeping Force was in charge of order within the city. The Force! *His* service. His corps and mates! When they were stopped, all he had to do. . . . He remembered Mary Diamond's gun, but a glance in the mirror confirmed that she was exhausted, her eyes drooping.

A hundred or so metres left. Allan was far from calm, remembering Dos Manos's stories of rivalry between the Army and the Force. He cleared his throat and sat up straight in his seat. Bean was sitting as if on the point of leaping, clutching the wheel. The grey and blue paintwork of the patrol vehicle behind the barrier seemed be signalling '*home*' to him, the Force's colours. He had driven innumerable miles in vehicles of that colour and now found it difficult to control his excitement and exhilaration.

'Take it easy!' said Allan, no doubt thinking Bean was still out of his mind with terror, but Bean could have laughed aloud he was so excited. He was aching to see uniforms, the grey uniforms of the Force, a lot of them, swarming round their vehicle. The jeep had no door on his side. Once they had stopped, all he had to do was to wait for an unguarded moment, and then dash out. He could. . . .

Still no one in sight down by the barricade.

Seventy-five metres left.

Still no one. Bean and Allan were both staring as if transfixed by the barrier under the glaring light, where nothing moved. Mary had shaken off her sleepiness and was leaning over to see better. Allan pushed her back.

'You're our prisoner, don't forget.'

Thirty metres left.

'Just drive on.' Allan jerked the words through his clenched teeth. 'Don't stop . . . until the swine. . . .'

Bean's uncertain mood changed again as he suddenly saw his life was in danger, caught as he was in an impossible situation together with two other people, essentially his enemies. If the men from the Force were lying there under cover behind the sandbags ready to open fire, how would he get a signal to them? Make his presence known? He would be massacred with Allan and Mary and the child, and no would ever know. . . .

He fought down a wild impulse to shout, yell loudly, use the horn, anything to get them, his friends, his brothers-in-arms to realize that. . . . Meanwhile the wall of of threatening sandbags seemed be looming towards them, white in the light of the headlights. Involuntarily, he headed for the small opening where rescue was at hand . . . where death lay in wait. . . .

'Go on! Just keep driving,' hissed Allan almost inaudibly. He had got out his gun and was sitting low down in his seat, tense as an animal, obsessed by the thought of striking before 'they' hit him, his eyes dancing from point to point ahead to find anything possible, a shadow, a small movement that might give him some idea of what to expect behind the barrier, an excuse to act.

'Lie down.'

Mary crouched behind the front seats, hugging Rain to her.

By this time Bean was hardly aware he was steering the jeep any longer, the confused thoughts racing through his mind now replaced by paralysis. He was lost, in a death trap without being able to lift a finger. As if in a dream, he watched the menacing opening coming closer and closer until it was no longer possible to avoid. The sound of the engine echoed back off the sandbags like a barrage. As they passed the barrier, Bean ducked his head, shut his eyes tight and waited for the firing to start, for the explosion, half in despair, half curious. For a tenth of a second it flashed through his mind that he could jump out, hoping not to be hit, hoping to be allowed to live until he could tell them who he was and why he had arrived in this way. But his panic locked his hands on to what was there to hold, the wheel his last straw, the only fixed point able to stop his body from falling apart. It was coming now. Now! His flesh crept as he waited for what was unthinkable, indescribable, the projectiles, points of glowing hot metal slicing into his body. . . . Now. *Now*!

But nothing happened.

He heard Allan exclaiming in amazement and he opened his eyes, then felt Allan's hands over his on the wheel.

'Look out! What are you doing?'

Bean straightened up the jeep as it started towards the side of the road. His thoughts elsewhere, his eyes tried to take in what they saw. Not a person in sight. Nor inside the barrier. Nothing moving, no one coming out of the makeshift guardhouse. No light, apart from the spotlight. Everything apparently dead, like the rest of the city.

'Not a soul.'

Allan was peering from side to side with tense attention.

'Where the hell have they all got to?'

Bean could see other things now, the door of the guardhouse swinging on one hinge, the window broken, a patrol car leaning heavily over two punctured tyres, its grey and blue paintwork cracked and bubbled round a badly burnt patch on one side – after an explosion? He could see two smashed spotlights dangling from the top of the mast alongside the one still alight.

'Someone's cleared the place out.' Allan's voice was full of amazement.

In less than a minute, the barricade, guardhouse and the wrecked patrol car were all behind them. Allan was still peering watchfully around, but now with an expression of relief.

'Not a soul.'

Bean could not believe it. To have been so close to rescue and now . . .'

'Get a move on, man! No point in dossing down here, eh! Ha ha.'

Allan laughed hilariously and slapped Bean on the back. Then they both saw something lying in the road, something round and metallic. A bomb, thought Bean. They've got us after all. Almost with relief, he saw a collision with the object was inevitable.

But Allan shouted. 'Look at that! A helmet. They must have been routed.'

The left front wheel struck the shiny helmet – equipment for hand-to-hand fighting against urban guerrillas. Bean recognized it at once. It rattled ahead of them, a harmless symbol of defeat. No, thought Bean. It can't be over. They're sure to come back. If we wait a while . . . if we're unlucky and drive off the road. . . .

He pressed the accelerator and the jeep speeded up. He dimly realized that he wanted to perish with them, be wounded, even killed, but that seemed not at all frightening, not now, not so frightening as having to go into this dark, hostile city – then a new thought occurred to him, even more frightening, this empty and deserted city.

They were driving towards a tunnel, walls looming on both sides. Bean took a decision and turned the wheel. But Allan was on to him before the jeep went into a skid, jerking the wheel out of his hands, at the same time striking Bean a crashing blow in the face with his elbow. Stars spun in front of his eyes and blood spurted thick and warm down his mouth and chin. With a kick, Allan knocked Bean's foot off the accelerator and pulled on the hand-brake. The jeep slowed and Bean caught a glimpse of steel before he felt the cold muzzle against his temple.

'Now just drive nice and calmly where I tell you to. Got it?'

Bean's eyes were full of tears, the road ahead floating together. He made an effort and managed to nod.

'I ought to shoot him,' mumbled Allan darkly to Mary. 'But I'm damned if I'm going to waste a bullet on the bastard. For Christ's sake, look where you're going.'

A blow made Bean's already spinning head ring. A road sign ahead of them, amazingly bright and intact, showed the way into the city centre, the harbour and the East Terminal. They were out of the tunnel. Bean concentrated on selecting the right lane. It was amazingly difficult, almost nightmarish in these vast streets with no traffic. City buildings towered above them on both sides, dark, apparently empty, so even more threatening to the terrified Bean. Not a light to be seen apart from the jeep's headlights, not a sound penetrating through the noise of the engine. He saw cars, numerous cars, but they were all standing still, abandoned in parking-places, along edges of pavements, some burnt out, some stripped down to rusty bodies, some with flat tyres, with neither bonnets nor doors, some apparently still roadworthy, others simply heaps of scrap-iron, all according to when they had been abandoned and how long they had stood there. Only a year ago there had been a black market for spare parts despite petrol rationing. But with the cessation of oil deliveries and official requisitions of stores, the car had suddenly become an utterly useless, meaningless appliance, a waste product like everything else, surplus and unusable.

The streets were strewn with refuse, cardboard containers, scrap, bits of smashed furniture, loose paper, paper swirling up as the jeep went on. To Bean, the wrecks of cars lining the street on both sides seemed to be grinning at him like death's heads, the decapitated crania of mechanized civilization.

21

The house was old, a two-storey brick villa set a little way back from the street, a burnt-out, four-storey apartment house on one side, on the other an empty plot stacked with materials and heaps of soil and stones. In the dark it was impossible to see whether there had been a house there which had been demolished, or whether the material was for a new house to be built.

The fence along the pavement had been torn down, leaving only the low wall foundation. There had once been lights on the gate-posts, but they were now smashed. Inside the gateway were two tree stumps, one on each side of the gravel path, gleaming white, splin-tered and gaping. The original trees had clearly been felled fairly recently and in a very crude way, presumably by people needing firewood — there must still be older houses and apartments in which the old heating systems had not been modernized and replaced by district heating fuelled by massive, oil-driven heating works, now cold and inactive.

The garage built on the side was empty and gaping towards the street, wrecks of cars on the road everywhere, just as elsewhere.

Windows blinded by the dark. Front door half-open — *someone* had been there . . . was the house inhabited, or had it just been looted?

Allan decided. 'We'll try here,' he said quietly, glancing at Mary, who had also been scanning the house and surroundings.

She nodded.

Allan went up the gravel path first, gun in hand, Rain on his arm. Then came Bean, staggering under the weight of his own bundle as well as Allan's, and finally Mary keeping a watchful eye on Bean, but he was now beyond all thought of escaping and rejoining the Force and was stumbling exhausted behind Allan with only one idea in his head, to get to some place of safety away from the dangers threatening them, to be allowed to lie down and sleep.

The jeep had run out of petrol a few minutes after they had passed the East Terminal, so after stripping the vehicle of everything of value, including the Army radio receiver, they had had to walk a stretch which had seemed an infinity, heading in the direction Allan had thought would lead to Abbott Hill Road.

They had kept close together as they walked, unnerved by the unnatural stillness, keeping to the pavements out of habit, as if the notion that the people had all gone, anyhow out of sight, and all traffic had ceased, was too much to take in. It had been strange and frightening, walking along deserted streets lined with wrecks, the buildings on both sides dark and desolate, although they couldn't all be completely empty of people. It was just that there was no sound, not a glint of light indicating life anywhere in the blocks along the narrow lanes of the East Zone, where they tried to subdue the ringing sound of their own footsteps and struggled to keep on a more or less southerly course. Here and there a stretch of road was lit by a single light, insanely winking, or the ghostly light from a shop window that had escaped plundering. In other streets, the electricity supply appeared to be cut off completely. The acrid smell of smoke hung in the air and mingled with the sweetish stench of garbage they knew so well from the Dump.

The first living creatures they saw in Sweetwater were rats, rats scurrying across the cracked asphalt from heaps of refuse on the pavements, through gateways and down into cellars, frightened by their footsteps. They also saw a lone dog or two, and a cat creeping like a snake along the walls and vanishing through a half-open street door. They heard the first sounds of human beings as they approached what Allan thought was Abbott Hill Road – a shot rang out, then a few screams, then the sound of running feet . . . they stood breathlessly listening in a gateway. What was happening? A minute or so later everything was quiet again and they went on. The sky in the north-west was a veil of smoky red from the fire, which must have spread, but the stillness did not bring with it the familiar wail of fire sirens, only the sound of occasional distant thuds, as if from explosions.

Allan signalled them to stop. Mary took over Rain, then Allan cautiously pushed open the door. Nothing happened. He stepped inside and stood in the pitch-dark trying to sense any possible danger. Not a sound. He switched on the torch and saw that he was in an outer passage with an open door leading into a hall. He could just see stairs up to another floor. He waved to the others and went into the hall. Two doors, one on the left, the other on the right, were closed, an open door straight ahead, to the right of the stairs. Allan turned the torch in that direction – a corner of a table, a couple of tubular chairs, a saucepan, a broken cup on the floor, half buried in some white powder scattered about. The kitchen.

A rapid inspection produced the expected result. The rooms to right and left were almost empty. Some furniture remained, open cupboards and contents strewn about, but nothing of interest, nothing edible. But there were possibilities in the kitchen. The looters had been in a hurry and had obviously found a store cupboard and hastened to take their loot to safety. Two bags of flour lay split open on the floor, their contents scattered. Mary was at once down on her knees sweeping up the precious flour with her large, strong hands and tipping it into a saucepan. There were signs of rats and mice everywhere. Bean had collapsed on to a kitchen chair and propped his head in his hands. Allan screened the torch with his hand as he walked round opening cupboards and drawers. No point in advertising the fact that they had taken possession of the house.

Upstairs were three bedrooms and a bathroom. They chose the largest of the rooms, with two windows, one facing the back garden, the size and extent of which it was just possible to make out under the greying sky announcing that the night would soon be over, the other facing the burnt-out building where they could also glimpse the road. From there, they could keep a look-out to some extent, and the room also faced on to the back, so protected them from observation from the street.

Most of the bedclothes had gone, but two beds still had mattresses, and Allan found a pile of damp quilts in a cubby-hole. Together with the rugs they had with them, they were able make fairly comfortable sleeping arrangements. They dragged a mattress in for Bean; as a matter of course, they all slept in the same room.

Rain was still sound asleep, full of a gruel of flour Allan had stirred together with the last of the water they had brought with them. Nothing but hissing, gurgling sounds came from the taps in the kitchen, so finding water would be their first problem. Naturally the electricity was not working, and to his disappointment Allan discovered the old-fashioned central heating he had expected to find (perhaps reinforced with a stove or two) had been replaced with a modern but useless district-heating apparatus. So it was going to be difficult to keep warm, although the house was old enough to have chimneys – perhaps that held possibilities?

His preliminary inspection of the kitchen had produced meagre results – a few forgotten packs of dried vegetables and half a bottle of rancid oil. The haste with which the looters had plundered the house gave him hope of finding more after a more thorough search.

'We must keep watch,' he said to Mary, who had just fixed beds for them. 'I'll stay up until sunrise, then you can take over for a few hours. Keep a special eye on our lodger here. . . .' He nodded at Bean, now lying on the mattress, shuddering under the covers.

If Allan thought Bean was lying there planning another attempt to escape, he could have spared himself the worry. The last bit of their drive and the long march through the dark, silent streets had dispersed any remnants of hope of his being able to intervene and get free of his captors. The sight of the city as it had become had appalled him beyond belief. He had heard news of crises, epidemics, mass flights and forced evacuations, but in his depressed state he had been unable to associate them with anything real. Now he had reverted back to the same state again after the brief blossoming of initiative and self-reliance the uniform had given him, and when he had recognized barriers like those used by the Force and the Force's colours on the patrol vehicle. But the very sight of the deserted checkpoint now kept haunting him, the ruined guardhouse, the smashed vehicle, the helmet rolling in the beam of the headlights, shining, rattling, empty. . . .

Bean was shaking all over, his legs drawn up underneath him, and his arms folded over them. The coarse material of his tunic still provided him with a spark of warmth and consolation, but his courage had failed him. As he lay there, he could only put his trust in Allan and Mary, their physical strength and endurance, their quick command of the situation and sense of judgement, their determination to cope, to *survive*. Bean was at their mercy again.

22

Mary Diamond sat by the window watching the dark clouds gathering above the sooty black rooftops. Rain, she thought with satisfaction. Rain meant water. Acquiring water was going to be their first major problem. They had food for a few days, perhaps a week, and they were used to managing on very little. But water . . . she gazed across the neglected garden, all dead weeds and refuse for a stretch behind the house, ending in a high wooden fence concealing one of the yards at the rear of the dismal row of low apartment houses shutting off the view. She thought she could see someone moving behind one of the dark windows, but she was not sure. The gun on her lap, she sat looking out over the neighbouring buildings, trying to make out whether they were inhabited and, if so, what kind of people would be living there. She was neither scared nor shaken by the thought that perhaps they had neighbours. She was actually far less uneasy than Allan and Bean. She had grown up in the Palisade and knew the bitter poverty of the slums. She had lived for several years as a cheap prostitute on the streets, selling herself for a roof over her head or a meal. That was before she met Smiley, who had seen the possibilities in her and introduced her to his motorway clientele. She knew the night life of Sweetwater better than the other two. She had lived through it. She stared curiously at the back windows, trying to guess what and whom they concealed, perhaps someone she knew? She had no doubts that, just as she had, they had survived the low life in the city when it had been at its height and would hold the best cards when it came to surviving in the present situation of chaos and lawlessness. The law of the jungle governing here, the destruction they had seen on the way, worse than any of them had imagined, indicated that. And the fact that there was no one around. Epidemics had claimed hundreds of thousands of victims (and the numbers were sure to be even higher than those the authorities had issued in broadcasts on disasters they had heard on Doc's radio), no one knew the numbers of refugees who had got away before the authorities put their evacuation and internment plans into action, and it could only be guessed how many were now living temporarily in camps. The present population of Sweetwater was but an insignificant fraction of what it had been. None the less Mary reckoned a city such as Sweetwater could never be totally empty of people. Where were they, those who remained?

It was foggy outside, not heavy with the oppressive, sulphurous smog so common before in autumn and winter, but with a pall of acrid smoke. She could smell it as it seeped in through the broken panes upstairs. She thought about the fire they had seen last night, apparently allowed to burn with no action from the Fire Service. Was the smell from that fire? Or other fires? Or was it from small stoves and provisional fireplaces round about, people warming themselves and perhaps having something to eat? Boiling their drinking water?

Then she saw two men coming out from the back entrance in a yard opposite, beyond the fence. One appeared in the doorway, took a few hurried steps out, then stopped, then the other came, bumped into him and the two hurried along the wall in the direction of the street entrance, glancing quickly around all the time. Their clothes were ragged and they looked clumsy and awkward, presumably because they had on several outdoor garments to keep warm. Mary suddenly remembered the intruders she had come across at the Dump. She found it hard to believe that was only two days ago. The two men had had the same helpless indecisiveness about them in their panicky hunt for *something*.

She saw something else as well. She saw that both were carrying short, sturdy sticks which could only be weapons. She shuddered, imagining the two men setting about each other in a wild fight over something edible one of them had seen first. The law of the jungle. Everyone was the enemy here. The sky darkened in the west and she heard a distant rumble. Was that shooting? More explosions? Or was it thunder, predicting rain?

She decided to wake Allan so that they could rig up something to collect rainwater, and she had to tell him about the two men.

Allan already had a plan for collecting rainwater. The idea had struck him the moment he had seen the house. An old villa of that kind must have old-fashioned gutters and metal roofing, and a rapid investigation when it had grown lighter had proved him right. The gutters under the eaves were metal, some of their fixtures loose, but on the whole the system seemed to be intact. The downpipes ran straight into the drains, so it was a simple matter to break off the pipe at a joint above the ground and put bowls and buckets or whatever they could find under it when it rained.

He worked on this while Mary sat in the window covering him, gun at the ready. What she had told him about the men with sticks had made it quite clear they had better be careful out of doors, at least until the situation became clearer. As far as they could make out, the city was wide open, lawless, free for all to use any means. Occasionally they heard sharp sounds, like shots, far away, indicating fighting round about in the city – perhaps in the central districts? – although who was fighting whom was uncertain and as yet impossible to find out. The radio receiver Allan had taken from the jeep bellowed out music on three wavelengths and, on a fourth, spoke in a language they did not understand, while the fifth wavelength was all brief, incomprehensible messages – presumably in code. None of this gave them any indication of what was going on around them. One certainty was that this stillness, the peacefulness, the lack of people, was deceptive. Allan had seen several columns of smoke from chimneys in houses in nearby streets. He looked up at the gathering clouds promising water, water *en masse*. He also had to collect firewood and see if he could possibly make a fire inside the house. It had chimneys, but no fireplaces or stoves. They would have to get some heating somehow if they were to have any hope of getting through the winter.

The rest of the day went on dragging wood, plank ends and stumps of beams back from the demolition site next door. Bean helped, reluctantly and anxiously, as if expecting an attack any moment as long as he was out in the open air. Mary covered them from upstairs. But they saw no one all day, only smoke, and once they heard a shot not far away, then shortly afterwards the hideous wail of a patrol vehicle. So the authorities were still functioning to some extent. But there were no people to be seen anywhere, although they could feel eyes on them as they struggled with the firewood.

By the evening they had accumulated a considerable quantity and stacked it in a heap in the hall. With some iron piping he had found in the cellar, Allan made a hole in the chimney wall in their bedroom and constructed a kind of fireplace with the loose bricks and a metal plate that had covered the sink unit in the kitchen. At first the smoke trickled into the room as the wood smouldered but would not burn, Rain got smoke in her eyes and cried, but then they got a draught going up the chimney and the fire was soon crackling. In only a few minutes the room was quite cosy, although the draught from the window was fiercer than before. Bean wanted to put more wood on at once, but Allan stopped him, saying they had to ration it. The real cold of winter would soon be on them – and then their small store of firewood would mean the difference between life and death.

They had used up the last drops of water they had brought with them, hoping it would soon rain, but the clouds refused to release their moisture. Mary soaked some bread crusts in spit and fed Rain before wrapping her in a quilt and putting her to bed on the floor close to the fire. The adults roasted some withered old potatoes which hissed in the heap of embers. A thorough search of the cellar had produced poor results. A sack containing some of these withered potatoes, a large proportion of them rotten, a few cans of fruit substitute, another couple of bottles of rancid cooking oil, quantities of newspaper, a few tools, some clothes and shoes, rotten and mildewed and in an even worse state than the clothes they themselves were wearing. But the fittings, door-frames and doors, partitions, shelves and so on could be ripped out and used for firewood. Smoke hovered like a veil in their room, but they were already used to it, as they had got used to the grubby floral wallpaper pattern, the linoleum on the floor with its worn patch by the door, the curtains . . . the colours in their cramped square room were rust, ash grey and yellowing paper.

To be shut up between four walls and knowing they were observed when they went out was more difficult to get used to. They had pulled the mattresses over to the fireplace to make the most of the warmth, and Allan and Mary sat close together, staring into the fire, thinking the same thing but saying nothing. How to get food and water? Where to start looking? Hunting?

Bean was curled up on his own, dozing. His sense of hopelessness had caught up with him again, leaving him even more apathetic than he had been out at the Dump, where his increasingly uncertain image of the city had occasionally manifested itself as a desire to be 'rescued', a hope of getting 'back' . . . now he *was* back and his only consolation was the material of his uniform, although that was not much comfort, for every time he felt it, pinching it to assure himself of its quality – or perhaps just to feel *something* – he inevitably thought of the helmet with the Force's emblem on it as it had rattled away down the road, empty as a death's head, glittering with synthetic brightness in the headlights – then despondency descended on him again as he sank into an abyss.

23

Mary had first watch that night, and she heard the footsteps coming up the gravel path towards the house. The outer door had been smashed and could not be locked, but they had tried to barricade it with a couple of beams. Would that be sufficient to stop someone trying to get in?

A few breathless seconds went by, then she heard them – clearly several of them – on the porch steps outside, then a creaking sound as if someone were trying the doorknob. Then quiet. Just as she was about to go over to where Allan was sleeping, something crashed against the outside door, a body, a heavy object, perhaps a stone? She cried out to wake Allan, grabbed the torch and ran out on to the landing to look. The beams had held, but she could hear shouting and hollering outside now. A moment later a splintering blow made the barricade give way, the door swung open and two or three figures tumbled in. She could see some more pressing behind, and a couple of lanterns, or were they torches flickering outside? Mary raised the gun, aimed and pressed the trigger twice. The explosions, the flame from the muzzle and the acrid cordite stunned her for a moment. She thought she heard a scream and the confused sounds of running feet. Then someone grabbed her by the shoulders. It was Allan. When she opened her eyes again, there was only one person down in the hall, a male figure dragging himself along the floor towards the outer door, a stream of tremulous complaints, curses and groans coming out of his mouth. 'Wait . . . for Christ's sake . . . wait for me! I . . . oh! *Wait!*'

He was leaving a trail of blood as thick as an arm behind him on the dusty floor, then on the heap of planks he had to get over to reach the door, blood coming through one trouser-leg, trickling out of a gash by his knee which had presumably been smashed by the bullet.

'Oh my God,' Mary moaned and made as if to run down the stairs, but Allan held her back and took the torch away from her.

'Let him get out to the others. If he stays, we'll have to feed him, if he survives. And if he doesn't, we'll have a corpse on our hands. What would we do with that?'

Reluctantly, she stayed, her instinct telling her to help the injured man, who had looked like a young boy, perhaps only in his teens. But she saw the situation was such that it might be dangerous for them to help anyone. The law of the jungle was even more merciless here than on the Dump.

Bean had been woken by the noise and came sidling up to them once he saw the danger was over. Allan had turned the torch on to the boy scrabbling his way over the last stretch towards the door.

'You got one of them!' croaked Bean. 'Look at that. Finish him off now, before he gets away. Get him!'

Neither Allan nor Mary deigned to answer, but Allan raised his hand slightly, as if fighting an impulse to hit the man.

Bean noticed and backed away a few steps. 'Bloody rabble,' he snivelled, like a beaten, grovelling dog. 'Breaking in. . . . We should have. . . . Pity you didn't get several of them.'

Head and shoulders already out of the door, the injured youth started shouting again, although his companions had long since disappeared into the darkness.

'Hey, help! . . . Wait for me! I can't . . . for Christ's sake . . . *wait for me*. For God's sake . . . *I can't walk*.'

His screams ceased abruptly as he struggled out on to the steps and a sudden gust of wind blew the door shut behind him. Allan ran down and jammed a beam against the door again. A primitive torch had fallen to the floor in the porch and was smouldering. He stamped on it furiously until he was sure it was out. At the foot of the stairs was a long stick, thicker at one end than the other, with two or three large nails hammered into the thicker end.

'Look at this. . . .' Allan held it up to the others. 'No wonder they ran when you fired – they've only got these to fight with.' He studied the club of heavy dark wood with an elaborately carved 'handle'. 'A banister post,' he mumbled to himself. 'Wood is better than iron. Wood is light. You can hammer nails into wood. . . .'

The wind was howling round the corners now, shaking the windows and making the smashed panes upstairs tinkle and rattle.

Before they had time to think about it, the rain was suddenly on them, a battery of small noises in the night, like running, pattering steps everywhere, then the downpour came, hammering on the roof and walls and spurting in through cracks and holes. Allan was prepared. In the course of the day he had ferreted out what there was to be found in the way of bowls, tubs, vessels and containers and now he had to put them out to collect the rainwater. He shifted the beam from the door (tomorrow he would have to make a bolt) and ran out. No attackers out in this weather, that was for sure. He put containers where the water was spurting out of the broken downpipe, trying to catch streams of water where the pipe was cracked or blocked by leaves and trash from the roof. He had too few containers and they were all too small, so he had to keep rushing back in and tipping water into the bath-tub, then run out again to fetch more, Mary soon joining him and helping to get as much as possible of the precious water into the house. Bean was told to comfort Rain, now whining and miserable from all the rumpus. Allan had also revived the fire and put the largest saucepan he could find full of water on to it, telling Bean firmly it could be really dangerous to drink the water before it had been boiled. Certainly it was rainwater, but no one knew what infections there were in the house, on the kitchen utensils or simply in everything around them.

As the bath-tub gradually filled and they ran out of containers, their chances of collecting any more water seemed to be over. Then Allan had an idea. He ripped off one of the downpipes, shoved it into one of the others sending water gushing down into an overflowing washing-bowl, and pushed the other end through the window of the little cellar where the storeroom had been, the same place where they had ripped out the shelves and cupboards and anything else they could use as fuel. The water was splashing around on the concrete floor when he went down to have a look at the result. The room was only two metres square, so the floor was soon covered with rainwater. He quickly picked up some pieces of wood they had left behind, went out and closed the door firmly behind him just as Mary came feeling her way down the stairs in the darkness to find out what he was up to.

'Making a cistern,' he said. 'Collecting water in the store-room.'

'But it'll run out,' she protested. 'It'll come under the door.'

'Not this door.' He knew what he was talking about. The door had been made in the old days of good wood, with a doorstep down and a sturdy frame. 'Look how it fits. The wood will swell and be as watertight as the wall. Just you wait.'

The water was boiling upstairs. Allan took out a cloth bag, undid the strings and dropped a pinch of dried leaves into three cups, then poured boiling water into them. A sweetish smell spread with the steam, and a few moments later they could start sipping the tea with its strange bitter-sweet flavour, brewed from herbs Run-Run had taught them to distinguish from ordinary weeds.

It was still pouring outside, a dull, persistent roar.

24

They spent the following days gathering firewood and searching for food. Their supplies were low, and they obviously had to find means of getting more if they were to manage.

The nearby houses, streets and apartment blocks lay deserted and abandoned like vast, unexploited hunting grounds, but although they had neither seen nor heard a sign of life round about since the attack on the house, it seemed risky to start systematically searching for food, or anything left behind by those who had moved away, or fled, or died in the epidemics. Allan was also sure some of the nearby buildings must be inhabited, although the inhabitants never showed themselves outside, not in daylight anyway, and this made him hesitate even more when it came to daring to go out on a 'hunt'.

But it was obvious he would have to soon. Necessity forced them into it, and they were tempted by the lifeless, almost unreal stillness of the city around them, only rarely broken by distant rumbles and thuds like shots or explosions, or the far-away sounds of sirens.

It seemed to be most dangerous to go out in the daytime, when they might be observed from a long way away, ambushed and attacked, perhaps killed by gangs like the one that had tried to get into the house. But the nights were so pitch-dark, finding their way would very difficult, like fumbling around blindfold, as a light would easily be spotted by possible attackers. They also had to save their torch batteries.

Allan decided to go out in the evening while it was still light enough to find his way there and back. With every sense alert, one hand on the gun inside his jacket, he ran from entrance to entrance along pavements strewn with rubbish, blocked drains turning whole streets into lakes after the heavy rain, and kerbstones splintered by weeds bursting through the cracks.

The front doors of several houses were smashed open, and most first-floor windows were broken, furniture and household goods having been dragged out on to the street and rooms and their contents wrecked by lawless mobs in their search for something to eat.

Allan knew he had to take it calmly and be methodical if he were to have any hope of finding anything, to concentrate on what raiders might have overlooked in their search, harassed by hunger and members of the Peacekeeping Force, who shot on sight anyone caught looting in evacuated areas. They had heard that on Doc's radio earlier in the autumn, when the Force's surveillance must have been much stricter than it seemed to be now.

He took house by house, apartment block by apartment block, making sure the building had been emptied before slipping inside and searching from cellar to attic. He sniffed out every corner, opened every cupboard and searched right through them all, even going as far as to rootle in bags of refuse, thumping floors and walls to see if there were any hiding-places where the previous inhabitants had stored away black-market goods, fine-combing cellars, rummaging through heaps of remains left in sheds. Occasionally luck was on his side and he found a small store of cans, or some hidden packs of dried foodstuffs. In one place he found a sackful of iron-hard sugar stowed in a corner of a basement room, here and there a pair of wearable shoes, or a garment that had not gone mouldy. So the trips were worth making, though all in all the results were poor. Allan thought about the most severe part of the winter to come. Although he brought home something almost every evening, a good deal was needed to keep three adults and a small girl. He began to understand how much Doc's addition of fresh vegetables had meant to their diet on the Dump, and how valuable had been Run-Run's instinctive knowledge of what was edible and what not.

He never once saw a human being on his trips. Some houses or apartments looked as if they had been empty for years, others as if they had been inhabited quite recently. Some bore traces of having been used as stopovers for the night by people who had departed again and moved on. In all of them, the contents had been completely cleared out and the rooms fouled with excrement and other filth. Many bore traces of the beginnings of a fire. To protect themselves against the night cold, the intruders had made bonfires out of smashed furniture and anything that would burn. Windowpanes were broken to provide draughts for the fires and in some places he could see where the fire had begun to take hold in the floors and synthetic wall panels (which as a student he had been told were fireproof). Wherever they had not been able to extinguish the fire, nothing remained but blackened ruins. Whole quarters were partly burnt down and derelict as if a war had been raging there.

In some buildings, water was flowing over floors and down stairways. After the wet weather, water had suddenly rushed out of dry taps that had been turned on when houses and apartments had been hastily evacuated. That had also happened in the house in which they had taken refuge. The taps in the kitchen had suddenly gushed a scummy stream of filthy stinking, yellow water which had surged into the pipes. They had their store of rainwater, and Allan said they were not to risk drinking this new lot, even if they boiled it – he remembered Dos Manos's stories about the people who had committed suicide by jumping into reservoirs of drinking water.

As it seemed certain the area immediately round their refuge was totally uninhabited, Mary gradually started joining him on his expeditions. Two could carry more than one, and one could keep watch while the other rummaged round in an apartment. It soon turned out that she was just as well equipped for 'hunting' in this way as he was. She knew the 'landscape'. She was practised at searching for what was edible and usable in all kinds of surroundings, wherever she was. She was persevering and physically strong. As things were, they needed their joint contributions. In this situation, she was equal to this dark, male person she had chosen as her escort. Co-operation meant differences from earlier times were wiped out.

Bean was told to keep Rain company and watch over the fire. It had gone colder after the rain and the old brickwork was so damp they had to keep a small fire burning day and night. Bean's job was to ensure the fire did not go out (matches would be impossible to get if they ran out), but at the same time keep the fire as low as possible to save fuel, as well as look after Rain so that she did not run out or injure herself in any way.

The little girl seemed to be enjoying her new surroundings. To her, the house with all its rooms, passages, hall and stairs was a constant inspiration for activity. She seemed to have no difficulty adapting from the much freer life on the Dump to this more enclosed existence. She found a lot of discarded and defective objects to play with, and other things, doors that wouldn't close, rooms inside rooms, corners, niches, dark recesses, made the house into a world of adventure for her. She never mentioned the life or the people they had left behind, scarcely noticing her dejected guardian and spending hours on explorations round the house, intensely concentrated, singing her own strange, lonely songs, the words a kind of conversation with everything around her, and she met Allan and Mary with loud cries of joy on their return. She greedily devoured everything she was given at their main meal after darkness had fallen, and she still liked sleeping while the others spun out their rations with slow mouthfuls of tea, hardly more than boiled water with two or three herb leaves floating in it.

They had wondered whether it was wise to hand over the responsibility of the house and the child to Bean, who had demonstrated that he was prepared to leave them in the lurch the moment an opportunity arose. But their anxiety was unfounded. There were no longer any plans to escape in the mind of the ex-policeman. The very thought of having to go outside without Allan and Mary threw him into a state of anxiety and confusion. The shock he had had at his confrontation with this unrecognizable battlefield devoid of people which his own city had become had eliminated every impulse of his to act. He clung to what he had now begun to regard as the 'rhythm' of their new life, trying to fulfil the demands the others imposed on him, gratefully eating the food he was given and sinking into apathy when everything was calm and nothing needed doing. Every thought of change in this new order struck him with repugnance, even fear. Although he was still wearing the uniform they had taken off the unconscious man, and at night lay feeling the comforting material until he fell asleep, he usually slipped into oblivion with a grinding anxiety about the next day and an unspoken semihope of being able to sink deeper into sleep and never have to wake up again.

None the less Bean had a secret. He had a knife. He had found it half-way under the pile of wood in the hall the day after the attempt to break in. One of the intruders must have dropped it and Bean had seen the glint of the blade, bent down and snatched up the knife almost without thinking. At first he had gone around with it hidden inside his shirt, his body clammy with anxiety at the thought of being found out. Then it had become a habit having it there, thrust into the waistband next to his body. The knife gave him a feeling of security, not because he thought of using it as a weapon against his captors – he would not have managed more than one of them before the other would be there finishing him off. If he somehow got rid of both of them, what would happen to him then?

The knife made him feel secure because it was *his*, not shared with anyone else, a solution to all problems if the situation became impossible.

They never saw any people. Allan wondered why not, but could find no answer. The attempt to break into their house had shaken them but had not been repeated. The yard beyond the garden where Mary had seen the two men (perhaps they had been among them that evening?) was deserted and dark, no sign of life, not even a glint of light after dark, or any smoke. None of the buildings they had hitherto investigated had been inhabited, although there were traces everywhere to show that people had been there, quite recently too. Perhaps flocks of people moved on like nomads to where food was to be found? Perhaps they had come to a part of the city where almost everything had already been exploited, all reserves used up? Perhaps everyone else had fled from there to richer hunting grounds, wrecking as much as they could before leaving?

The city was not entirely dead, for they sometimes suddenly heard sounds like shots. Even a scream carried a long way in the stillness brooding over the lifeless city. At night, they saw the flaring red of far-away fires. But distances were so great and the structure of the city such that what happened more than three or four blocks away did not seem to be their concern, even less so events in other parts of the city.

Now and again they saw a lone bird sailing low above roof-tops, gliding on outspread wings, predatory birds hunting for prey. Very occasionally a dog slipped out of an open door, or a cat sneaked along the walls, but always out of reach of a missile.

Even in earlier times, when Sweetwater's communication system had functioned in a way, it could take most of the day to get from the outer eastern zones into the centre. Now everything happening in other parts of the city seemed to be in a distant foreign country. Distances had to be measured in relation to the human frame, to its efficiency. The centre of Sweetwater was at least a day's walk away.

So they took each day as it came and did not speculate much on what would happen to them or to the city in the future. The struggle for food, to survive, gave them neither time nor reason for speculation. After the years out on the Dump, their expectations of help from outside for a 'solution' of the so-called 'crises' which *they* had regarded as lack of refuse to live off, were nil, wiped out, if such expectations had ever struck root in human beings growing up as they had in a huge city already stagnating and decaying. They had their physical strength and their experience and their courage to go on fighting for life. Their time on the Dump had taught them to adapt, make use of whatever opportunities their surroundings offered them, be satisfied, eat when there was food, starve when there was none, and nevertheless go on toiling yet another day, then another. That had hardened them physically and mentally, blunting their minds and imagination, making them capable of fighting on like rats in the ruins of this vast city, their background from the Dump making them better fitted for a life among ruins than most people. As well as the fact that they had a gun.

*

One day, from an upstairs window, Allan spotted a black dog sneaking about, sniffing along the ground, then raising its head and sniffing the air. It was a big dog, quite powerful, weighing at least twenty kilos, which meant ten kilos of tough, sinewy meat.

Allan clicked off the safety-catch of the gun, judged the distance, aimed from the window-sill, but then hesitated – the distance was too great. If he missed or just wounded the dog slightly, it would escape and he would never get it. But what were the chances of its coming any closer?

The dog had its nose to the ground and was gnawing at something it had found, quite calmly, fifteen to twenty metres away, sideways on to Allan. He had its whole chest and belly to aim at. Perhaps this was his best chance? But then something frightened it, it started and stood stiffly, head up, ears pricked, ready as if at any moment. . . . Allan didn't dare wait any longer and fired through the pane so that glass floated down on to the hard ground. The dog let out a howl, leapt into the air and bit into its side where the bullet had hit it, then began a crazy ring-dance lasting only a few seconds, until it fell and lay still. Allan watched its dance of death with intense concentration, ready to fire again if necessary, although he knew he had to wait as long as possible – so as not to waste a single bullet.

But as the dog lay trembling in its death throes, something astonishing happened. Loud cries of fear came from behind the scrub where the dog had appeared and Allan suddenly saw two people beyond the derelict fence between their garden and the yard beyond – two men in rags, their hair and beards in unkempt manes round their heads. At first they looked utterly confused, yelling at each other and pointing in the direction of the house, then they rushed across the yard and out through the entrance, the slap of bare feet echoing against concrete.

Once he had recovered from his surprise, Allan realized they had been hunters creeping up on the dog, but had fled in panic at the sound of a shot. He thought about the pack of intruders and the way they had retreated as soon as Mary had fired. Perhaps this was why the area around them was devoid of people? Perhaps respect for firearms was *that* great in the ruins of a Sweetwater where life had returned to the Stone Age?

They roasted a whole leg of the dog that evening and slept contentedly, for once not bothering to keep watch. The shot that had killed the dog would have frightened off anyone roaming around for several blocks away, just as Mary's accurate salvo had chased their previous neighbours off to other hunting grounds.

25

One day in January it began to snow, and it went on for several days until it was almost a metre thick, covering everything.

They had never seen so much snow. Snow in winter was more or less unknown in Sweetwater, and in the past when it snowed, it never stayed longer than about an hour or two in that mild coastal climate of warm winds coming off the bay. But the climate in recent years had changed.

So now, to cap everything, they were kept indoors by the severe cold. The snow did not melt, but lay like a quilt, thick, heavy and immobile, re-creating the landscape, making everything different, so it was almost impossible to orientate. At the same time, it was almost impossible to get from place to place because of the snow-drifts filling the streets, in some places right up to the windows.

They stayed indoors for the first few days, this new phenomenon unsettling them, the cold frightening them. Allan thought about tracks – if they took a few steps outside, it would be the equivalent of announcing to everyone that the house was inhabited. Announcing to whom? Nothing, not even a footprint broke the even surfaces as far as they could see in every direction – no life anywhere. Yes, perhaps there was. One morning they saw a small path across the yard from the entrance to a cellar window, a cat, or perhaps a rat? No trace of human beings. But they knew they had to be careful.

The snow seemed to have prevented ordinary noises from reaching them. No more sirens, nor the dull thumps they had occasionally heard, explosions or gunfire from a distant battlefield. Sounds they had got used to became absorbed by the thick layer of snow, sounds in which they had finally found a kind of inverted, illogical security, as if they had been signals confirming that there were other people in the city apart from them, that they were not the only living creatures in the ruins.

They were now living in a sparkling, frozen stillness which told them nothing except that they were utterly alone. Stars sparkled from a clear, frosty sky throughout the long nights, the light of the snow reflected in through the windows, a pale, shadowless winter light that came from everywhere and nowhere, turning night into day and frightening them, for they had never seen a winter sky before, or such stars and light. So they reverted to their old habit of keeping watch. In a darkness which was not dark, they felt unsafe, although the untouched white fields of snow around them showed no impressions of any other life apart from an occasional cat, a roaming dog or rats scurrying from cellar to cellar. The endless darkness and the sparkling expanse of sky above them, above the ruins of Sweetwater, gave the watcher a feeling of cosmic loneliness, of being abandoned, alone on a dead planet surrounded by a universe of hard crystal, a sense of loneliness like nothing else they had ever known before.

They stayed indoors, restless, uneasy, uncertain as to how to cope with this new situation, this new trick the capricious, man-made climatic circumstance had played on them. They stayed indoors, freezing, looking out for tracks, for some indication of what was going on elsewhere where there were people, hoping for a change in the weather, at least an end to this cold, just waiting.

Hunger drove them out after a while.

They trudged along unrecognizable streets, plodding through porchways where snow had drifted through open doors, into passages, far up stairways. They forced open doors frozen into a plinth of ice where water from leaking taps had been flowing freely only a week before.

The work was laborious and they froze, ill-equipped as they were, their feet suffering most, for they had no suitable footwear. They tied rags round their hands, which soon froze stiff from searching through cupboards and drawers in icy apartments, sheds and cellars, frozen heaps of things discarded by previous inhabitants − or by hunters who had been there before them and had left everything scattered behind. Searching took time and they found little. They had been through all the buildings in the streets in their immediate surroundings. Now they had to go further in the hope of finding anything. But walking was difficult in the deep snow. Their feet went numb with cold and even short distances were exhausting. Their fuel supply had also diminished in the cold. Much of their time was spent breaking up and dragging home anything combustible they could find in the apartments they searched, for the next-door demolition site, like everything else, was also covered in a thick layer of snow.

Then, as if that extra worry were not enough, it turned out that Bean was having difficulty tending the fire, the snow and cold apparently sapping the last of his vitality. One afternoon when they came back, they found the fire out and Rain whimpering on a heap of rags on the floor, weak with cold, and Bean lying on his mattress looking like death. Allan vented all his rage on the wretch, reducing him to a bleeding, snivelling bundle in a corner. But even if that might subdue him for a while, they could no longer hand over responsibility for the child to him. The result was they took Rain with them, taking turns to tie her firmly inside their outer clothing, which limited their freedom of movement even more and reduced their field of action, although the child complied with the treatment and never complained. Somehow she seemed to understand the seriousness of the situation and helped by clinging to the body of the parent carrying her, as if trying to be as little trouble as possible. But she was now over four, no infant to be bundled on a back any longer, and when she fell asleep, overcome with exhaustion and falling into the secure rhythm of her parents' movements, in the warmth of physical contact, she soon became an almost impossible burden for whoever was carrying her.

Bean was also made to go out and help them, however much he protested and complained. They tied newspaper and rags round his legs, pieces of cloth round his hands, and made him go and find firewood from nearby. The cold spell had reduced their reserves and they were all now aware they would be finished if their heating failed them. Firewood became as important as food.

This was when they saw their first dead person.

In an apartment with a broken-down door, but nothing touched, an elderly woman was lying in bed in her night clothes. She had clearly been dead quite a long time, for the body was beginning to decompose and the stench was like a blow in the face even in the sterilizing cold of the winter's day. All round her lay a dreadful jumble of empty cans, boxes and food packs, rotting, half-eaten remains of various items that had kept the poor woman alive before death had overtaken her. They found a small store of untouched cans and dried food of various kinds under the bed, and bundled it all up before leaving the apartment. Such riches were rare, and presumably the stench of the corpse and fear of infection had frightened off earlier visitors.

At another place they found three dead men in a basement of an apartment block. They were still wrapped in ragged blankets on layers of newspapers and cardboard which could not have given them much protection on the concrete floor. They were curled up close to an oil drum in which they had made a fire, one of the windows smashed to create a draught. The smell of smoke still hung heavily in the room. The three men must have starved and frozen to death. They looked emaciated and even in death their expressions were of defiance, a wild prayer that conditions would soon improve, a protest that people should be driven so far that they lived and died in this way. In their death throes, their hands had curled like animal claws, grasping at the empty air.

Whatever was left after they had eaten in the evening was carefully collected up and put aside for the next day. Touching anything before they were all gathered for a meal was unthinkable, like breaking an absolute taboo. Even Bean respected this, not because he was idealistic when it came to sharing with others, but because he knew that he in particular was in the spotlight when it came to taking odds and ends from their dwindling food store. With a certainty that sent a shiver of anxiety through his dazed mind, he also knew that they would throw him out if they ever caught him thieving. If he were thrown out now, it would mean succumbing in a few days, and he knew that. So he kept away from their little store on a shelf under the stairs and felt fairly secure.

He knew he was one more mouth to feed, but he tried to make himself useful by dragging in door-frames, banisters and other firewood he ripped out of apartments, particularly from the older houses nearby. His hope was that Allan would not kill him in cold blood, even if conditions became still worse. He knew Allan had had a good excuse once, when they had left the Dump, when his life had hung on a thread. But he obscurely sensed it was a resistance to the kind of barbarity Run-Run represented that had held Allan back from doing what was most 'sensible' at the time, putting a bullet through his head and leaving him on the Dump. Bean was hoping that attitude had not changed and he did the best he could. Beneath the chaos of his fears lay a desperate hope that Allan and Mary would think he was useful. He wanted to live, despite everything. He suffered from the cold and lack of food as much if not more that they did. He suffered from stomach cramps, hallucinated from hunger, wept at the pain in his fingers when out gathering fuel. But he did not dare touch any of the little they had. Instead he went hunting on his own in the buildings from which he fetched fire-wood. The months on the Dump had made him enterprising. He scraped the burnt layers of grease off the stove plates, licked the shelves of cupboards where there had been sugar and flour, perhaps oats or something which had leaked out of a bag. He upturned garbage bins and chewed on semi-dead leaves of pot plants.

One day as he was struggling to get an old door loose with a piece of piping he used as a jemmy, he found the wood had been eaten away by woodworm under the paint. Fascinated, he stopped and stared at the labyrinths of burrows the woodworms had made, then he started digging into the wood and found eggs and grubs, glisten-ing fat larvae he poked out and ate, chewing and swallowing, without disgust, without pleasure, without thought, mechanically, as if mindlessly obeying the imperative of hunger his body imposed on him.

Weeks went by and it became steadily more and more difficult to find food. They rationed what they had, froze and starved. Some days, a small lump of sugar from Allan's sack dissolved in tepid water was all they had. Lack of nourishment weakened them and the cold also severely reduced their strength. Their hunting expedi-tions in the neighbourhood became almost impossibly demanding. They mostly kept to the streets they had already tramped in the snow, but every step was still an effort.

The thought of food which could simply be eaten became an obsession. They were on the go all the time, searching through apartments and empty shops where no one had ever worked or lived, locked up on the day they had been completed as specula-tions. Most had already been gone through several times, either by themselves or others who had been there before them, everything usable removed and everything else smashed, as if rage at the results had found an outlet in destruction. They systematically trawled through building after building. From top to bottom, scrap-ing up a handful of flour, picking up a dried crust out of a garbage bin. Food was the only thought in their heads. Food. *Food*!

They made severe demands on themselves, eating nothing where they found it, taking it home and portioning it out at their main meal in the evening. Without anything being said, they both felt that kind of discipline was their only hope as human beings of getting through this nightmare.

Even so, Allan did occasionally feel his determination wavering, as if his very will to survive were being worn down. His body was starved but still strong, and it made demands he had to struggle against every hour of the day. He was often so hungry he turned dizzy as they set out on their hunts and had to stop and prop himself up, breathing deeply to find sufficient strength to plod on. If they found anything edible, it was only by forcing himself that he could stop himself devouring it there and then to deaden, if only for a moment, the pain in his guts. It was an extreme struggle with his own tortured body, doing violence to himself, knowing all the time, enfeebled as he was, that he would soon be a shadow of his former self if this went on. The knowledge frightened him as much as the thought of what would happen the day when there was no more food to be had, neither that day nor the next, nor the next . . . if that came. Occasionally it seemed frighteningly near.

Then came the only occasion he weakened, all because of a packet of raisins, real raisins, old and as hard as stones and in an old-fashioned packet of the kind he could remember from his boyhood. The packet was squashed between a mattress and bedstead in the only bed in a shabby little basement apartment otherwise stripped of everything. Almost without thinking, he grabbed it and thrust it inside his shirt instead of in his bundle. Mary was just beside him turning over the meagre contents of a cupboard. He pretended to be searching further under the mattress. He could feel the packet, sharp and square against his skin. He thought about the colour of it, the familiar brand name, and he seemed to be able to taste the sweet, slightly sugary taste of the hard dried grapes with pips that got jammed between his teeth. His thoughts sent a glow of sheer pleasure racing through him, and when Mary disappeared into the next room, he thrust his hand quickly inside his shirt, ripped the lid off the packet and stuffed a pinch of raisins into his mouth, almost swallowing them whole, shaking, digging out a few more, so eagerly that some fell to the floor. He had to get down on his hands and knees to pick them up, fatigue and the enjoyment of the sticky mass in his mouth, the slight resistance every time he chewed, making him feel faint, as if his mouth, tongue, gullet, stomach, his whole digestive system were screaming for more.

Then she was suddenly there, just beside him, before he had got back on his feet, while he was still on his hands and knees, trembling, his mouth full of the precious raisins, and a kick sent him flying sideways, a hard boot descending on the hand holding on to the packet of raisins, her strong, dark hand wrenching it away from him, her voice shrieking at him that he must stop, that all hope was gone if they could not trust each other, that all was over if they *stole* from each other, that she would kill him if she caught him at it again.

There was no doubt she meant it. The muzzle of the gun was pointing straight at his temple. If her hand was shaking, it was from emotion not lack of determination. She was starving, too, her face grey under the dark skin, her eyes sunken. She still had her upright posture, her authority, but she was markedly thinner. Rain lay dozing under her jacket, hungry and exhausted. Mary was holding the child closely to her with one hand, the other holding the gun directed at him as he half lay on the floor, his mouth full of raisins and his head empty of thoughts, as if stupor were his only hope, his only defence against the stream of words pouring over him, repeating what he knew only too well. He had betrayed them all, betrayed them all. Treachery of that kind meant the end for them. She would kill him, shoot him like a dog if she caught him again. And she meant it. She was stronger than he was, she knew that now. She was just as hungry as he was, needed just as much to eat, and yet she endured while he broke down. She told him this, her breath coming out of her mouth in a cloud in the cold of the basement, her fingers frozen, her knuckles blue in the cramplike hold on the gun. She was the strongest now, and she would be the strongest from now onwards. He knew that without thinking about it, without taking in what that had to do with him. A sickening rage rose in him at this attack on his authority, a bitterness directed at her, this great dark-skinned woman who endured everything and was now standing over him pointing a gun at him that he had given her himself, showering him with a sudden articulate scorn, full of words and expressions he had never heard her use before. But his rage evaporated as suddenly as it had come, and he remained where he was, trying to ward off his thoughts as they sank into a pit of despondency that finally filled his body like a purely physical indisposition, turning his stomach and forcing him to vomit up the unfamiliar and indigestible mess of raisins.

But she would not even allow him this humiliation in peace. In a flash she was at his side, holding a hand under his chin, as if trying to stop a gulping infant from soiling the floor, and she caught up a good handful of the mess of raisins. Then she left him lying there, throwing up his sour bile, while she carefully tried to get a little of the sweetness mixed with saliva in between Rain's half-open mouth.

The child woke and whimpered as Mary held her tight and went on feeding her from the hollow of her hand. The child soon began to suck up the sweet gruel, the most nourishing food she had had to eat for several weeks.

Outside, the winter evening had begun to lay its bluish darkness in the shadows below the high-rises, in basement passages and narrow alleys, and above the silhouette of the roof of the tower building that had once been the health centre of the East Zone swayed the delicate chalice of the moon. A dog was howling at the bottom of the street where the icy rime-frosted buildings widened into an open space, unbroken and bluish white in the twilight, like a plain in the wilderness.

26

It thawed at the end of February and warm winds and more rain came and melted away most of the snow. Again it became almost impossible to move about, this time because of the melting snow and water flowing in the streets, overflowing where the drains were blocked. The mild weather also brought a stench with it, the stench of death. Dead animals floated along on the flood waters. Dead dogs, corpses of cats, rats and mice, other creatures that had succumbed to the cold, lay washed up everywhere, in gutters, on pavements, in courtyards and on basement stairways. In contrast, the air was full of life, flocks of great black birds floating round high up on wide, ragged wings, the vultures that lived on the tower blocks feasting on the corpses thawing out in the mild weather.

Mary and Allan, Bean and little Rain were now living in extreme need, largely off newspaper dipped in old cooking oil, a clip of hard sugar or a mug of tepid sugar-water when an attack of fainting came, threatening what was left of their strength. They had to move further and further away on their hunts, and there was less and less to find. They had decided to search in a northern and westerly direction, but it was clear they were getting close to areas which had been inhabited not all that long ago and had already been thoroughly searched. They found more dead people, and the stench and fear of infection made them ultra-cautious. There had clearly been a number of fires in the area, whole quarters were partly burnt down, black skeletons grinning out of the grey landscape of melting snow. They found traces of people who had lived in the ruins and slept in the ashes to make use of the warmth long after the fires had been extinguished. In some places they also found traces of the Force's attempts to clear up – apartments, stairways and pavements, even whole office blocks and stretches of street strewn with evil-smelling white powder that stung when in contact with skin. Allan recognized it – quicklime. Rainwater and the melting snow had probably washed most of it away, but what was left made it unpleasant and often quite dangerous to walk through.

Twice, they had come across other people like themselves, once two youths, young boys almost, who hared away the moment they saw Allan and Mary. The other time they were three or four adults led by a bearded giant who at once prepared to attack, picking up stones and starting to throw them. Allan pulled out the gun and aimed at the giant. For one insane second he caught himself weighing up the huge man's body and converting it into tempting fresh meat . . . but then he pulled himself together and swung the barrel up as he pressed the trigger so the shot went high. The little group took flight, the giant bellowing in the lead. Two of them found it difficult to keep up his wild pace and stumbled and fell, their hands pressed to their chests as if fighting for breath. They seemed to be just as weak with hunger as were he and Mary. As they fled, they dropped a sack. Allan at once leapt on it and emptied it. Out fell the still warm corpse of a scrawny dog they must have caught and killed, two cartons of milk substitute, some squashed tubes of indeterminate contents which tasted sweet, a little bottle filled with colourless liquid – could it be liquor? – and two packets of coffee substitute (what a good day they had had!) plus two whole boxes of matches and some clothing.

Treasure trove!

They had not found so much in one swoop for many weeks. It meant they could go on for a while longer.

They collected the things up again, glancing suspiciously at each other. The worsening conditions, the labour of finding food, had reduced all contact between them to purely practical and concrete matters. The thought of the theft of the raisins remained with them both and did not make the situation any easier. She suspected him and he suspected her, because he suspected himself. It had also happened – and did so more and more often – that he would stand with something edible in his hand until he felt faint with the desire to devour it, eat and eat, to have something in his stomach. He had to take a grip of himself and suppress the impulse, which was so strong it wiped out all reason and threatened his actual sanity. Now and again he 'cracked'. At such moments he seemed to be the only person in the world, the distance between him and everything else endless, and any thought of there perhaps being others and that the others were as hungry as he was and needed food just as much simply vanished with the thought that he held rescue in his hand, hunger raging through him, burning, devastating, as if his actual body were very slowly being dissolved by acid. But he knew he must watch out, because of Mary – she would undoubtedly carry out her threat to kill him if he stole again, which was how it had come about that they watched each other, intently, almost with hostility, without a word more than was absolutely necessary. Things are the same for her, he thought. She does it, too – I must keep an eye on her. But he never saw *her* secretly putting her hand to her mouth when they chanced to find something. At the most, she chewed on dead grass collected in the back garden where the snow had melted, or she tore off a strip of wallpaper and chewed on the floury cellulose glue.

Allan also sometimes thought Bean had become an impossible burden on their soon totally depleted reserves of both food and strength. He would calculate just *how* much Bean ate, and how much more there would be for *them* if they didn't have to share with him. Now that it was warmer, it was easy to overlook the fact that Bean made himself useful every day by collecting up firewood and keeping the fire going. If only we could get rid of him, Allan thought. We can't feed him any longer. We must somehow get rid of him.

But even in the position they were in, he could not bring himself to plan cold-blooded murder. His thoughts circled vaguely round throwing Bean out and letting him cope on his own, but the snag was that there was a small chance that he might get to a patrol or somewhere where the Force was stationed (if such places still existed) and report them, then show them the way to the villa. That worried Allan, although he doubted there was any systematic surveillance of the city any longer. They heard the wail of sirens even more rarely nowadays, and even the inexplicable thuds and bangs like shots apparently coming from the northern and north-western zones had gradually ceased.

Nor were the short coded messages they picked up on the radio receiver any use, for they might mean anything. One frequency broadcast continuous music, interrupted by the monotonous announcement: 'During the state of emergency, the population is requested to keep calm. The situation is under control and help will soon be brought to everyone.' The same message day in and day out. They could pick up nothing from transmitters further away.

Their constant fear of being attacked was great, increasing their vigilance, just as hunger sharpened their senses. From indoors they could hear a dog scuttling round the house, a rat scurrying in the cellar, the wingbeats of a bird above the roof. Steps in a deserted street were like a shrill danger signal. Steps in the street after dark could mean the end for them.

They all heard the footsteps and exchanged looks, tensing their muscles without saying anything. No words were necessary. The steps – more than one person's, perhaps three or four – sounded sharp and clear on the wet asphalt and were undoubtedly coming closer, already so near that whoever was approaching must have long since localized their dwelling, not because of the faint light from the fire – they had blankets over the windows, sealed with newspaper to stop the light of the flames attracting attention and revealing them, as well as to keep out the cold. But the smoke in the primitive fireplace with its kettle simmering on it might have guided an intruder, should the wind be favourable.

The steps came closer.

They could hear subdued voices now. Far too close. That could mean only one thing.

Allan and Mary took up positions on the landing, each with a gun ready. The door behind them was closed, so it was only just light enough to see the entrance door. They could hear them outside now, and wondered how the attack would come, as a sudden assault, a break-in through the street door, or a silent entry from behind? Perhaps they would surround the house and try to get in from several directions at the same time? The door was barricaded as usual, but that wouldn't hold long against three or four men. They could hear that there were at least that number outside. Allan waited for the assault, crouched down with his gun resting on his lower arm, waiting for the crash . . . instead they heard a cautious knocking.

They listened, holding their breath.

'Hullo. . . .'

The tension . . .

'Go away. Get away!'

Allan shouted it out at the top of his voice, almost without knowing he was doing so, firing a shot at the same time. The bullet hit the door-frame, sending splinters flying. Through the ringing in his ears he could hear several voices, a scream of fear, loud and shrill as if from a child, then a furious banging on the door and shouts.

'Don't shoot! For God's sake, let us in! Don't shoot. It's us!'

It's us . . .

He recognized the voices, the cries, and his body reacted before his mind could function. Half-way down the stairs, he heard Mary's warning: *'Be careful.'*

But he ignored her, ran across the hall, kicked away the beam, his mind registering that that was dangerous, an insane chance to take, but he was sure, he knew without really knowing what to expect, and he stood still, his arms hanging down, the gun pointing to the floor as he stared as if bewitched at the door slowly opening, the crack widening until he could see them outside quite clearly.

Run-Run in front, a head taller than the others in his long, dark coat, his teeth flickering in his eternal half-threatening, half-accommodating grin. When he saw Allan, he bowed and, with a lightning movement, thrust the long knife back under his coat, Boy's chalk-white, malevolent face glowing just below his elbow, and behind Run-Run was Felix, his arm round Lisa, who was sobbing, then behind them two other figures, indistinct in the darkness, but Smiley's voice was unmistakable.

'Bloody fine reception, old boy. I don't think this neighbourhood has had a very good influence on you. Aren't you going to invite us in? I assure you, we've had quite a trip. . . .'

He tried to take a step forward, but stumbled and had to clutch at the man next to him, whom Allan at last recognized. It was Dos Manos.

As he realized who they were, and in a passive way he was pleased to see them, Allan felt panic inside him at the sight of this crowd outside the door. Too many. They would fill the whole house. How would they keep it warm? How would they find food for all of them? The thought of their food reserve, now almost non-existent, of the fearful daily toil to find something – more or less anything – to eat, the thought of the days when they found nothing, the days they had had to live off newspaper soaked in rancid oil, and again the thought of these people, his *friends* on the doorstep, Lisa and Smiley who were both useless – it all filled him with an unbearable anxiety that made the distance between him and them insurmountable. They didn't exist, *couldn't* exist, not for *him*, as the situation was. They would be too threatening, too impossible to cope with in the present circumstances. He grabbed the door and the door-frame as if to bar their way. He wanted to say something to them, but felt terror overcoming him. Instead something deep down inside him was screaming, and horrified, he heard his own voice shouting: 'You must go! You can't come here. Go away! Just go!'

'Listen, Allan. . . .'

Felix spoke as if quite unmoved by Allan's wild outburst. His face was sunken and he had a week's growth on his slack jaws, and not much left of the immaculate clothing, but he still tried to preserve his tone of voice, courteous and quiet, with a touch of a foreign accent.

'We just thought. . . . We wondered whether we could stay here. Just for a while. We brought Lisa with us to you. . . . We thought, if we could stay overnight. If you want her. . . .'

Gently but firmly he took the weeping Lisa by the arm and led her a few steps forward. Run-Run stepped aside. Apart from Lisa's sobs, it had become deathly quiet on the steps. Allan realized they were offering Lisa to him as payment for a roof over their heads, and the situation sickened him, though he knew full well that only three or four months ago he had offered Doc the same 'payment' for his gun. And Doc? Where was Doc? He could see no one else out there in the dark behind Smiley, who was leaning against Dos Manos, breathing heavily. Although he fought against it, it all now became real again for him. He could not protect himself against it, the moment he understood that they shared his fear.

'You can come in then,' he mumbled, kicking the door wide open. 'Come on in and we can talk about it.'

Their story came out little by little.

It had become impossible to live on the Dump during the winter once the tipping of refuse had ceased, and when the severe cold had set in it was only a matter of time before they also had to leave and set off in search of another place to settle, other hunting grounds. And the only possible 'other hunting grounds' were here, in Sweetwater.

It had been almost chance that they had got hold of Dos Manos. He had taken routes he knew, past patrols and guard posts, out to the Dump to see his old friend Doc. He had had to do the last stretch on foot when his old van had finally given up on the motorway.

'So he walked straight into our arms,' said Smiley.

Not until they came into the passage, into the light, did Allan discover that Dos Manos and Smiley were tied together with a thick rope, long enough for both of them to be able to move freely, but firmly tied round Smiley's right wrist and Dos Manos's left. They had simply captured Dos Manos and threatened him to bring them safely into the city!

'There's no better guide than our friend Dos Manos here,' said Smiley, clearly doing his best to maintain his arrogant, ironic tone of voice. His face was grey, his eyes glowing and he was sweating profusely. As he leant against the wall, his whole figure gave an impression of extreme exhaustion. He clearly found it more difficult to walk than before. A filthy bandage of rags and strips of cloth was wound round his injured ankle and he had pulled a rubber boot with the leg slit open over it. But he kept trying to maintain his derisive grin, his voice grating and jerky, though still mockingly nasal.

'Military iron ring round the city. The Force's terrorist squads inside the city. Nothing to Henry Dos Manos! Did *you* know there are sewers from those building sites in the south-east, right in to the sewage works here by the quays? *He* knew. Sewers so large you can walk in them if you bend your head a little. Never used, because the buildings were never completed. All you have to do is to slip down a culvert and walk underneath the patrols and barricades. By the way, it's not bad in the south-east, not yet, anyhow. It's up in the north they're fighting. Finding you was worse, but he knew some of the gangs operating in the quay area and contacted them. They had heard of an armed group which had moved into the North-East Zone. People who had escaped from there told him. They described a wild man and a huge woman . . . so we took a chance that it was you, and then all we had to do was set off to look – and keep ourselves alive at the same time.'

He laughed, the laugh soon turning into a painful attack of coughing which racked his thin body so violently he almost fell. When he finally got his breath back, he went on: 'If Run-Run hadn't smelt your smoke this afternoon, then I don't know how the hell we'd have got here to hand over the fine presents we have with us.'

Another attack of coughing forced him to his knees, and he

bumped into Lisa, making her stumble towards Allan – he was now behind a wall of stillness, trying to take all this in, this new situation, and what it entailed. The girl fell and stayed moaning on the floor, as if too exhausted even to cry.

'Look at this. . . .'

Felix began opening the leather bag he had had on his back, taking out bags and packs which Allan thought he recognized, somehow connected with Doc. The fire crackled and threw warm light over the white face. All these people filled the room, making it crowded and claustrophobic. The bandage on Smiley's foot smelt foul. As if in panic Allan thought, I must get them out. Although he knew they had come to stay.

'Why did you come? Why did you come here?'

He blurted out the question to stop Felix unpacking, to put an end to this even greater obtrusiveness from the newcomers. But Felix went on undisturbed, putting bags and packs on the floor, and Run-Run's wide grin lost none of its mad glee. Dos Manos replied. He was squatting with his back against the wall beside Smiley, who had fallen over, the rope tying them together too short for the one to stand upright when the other lay down.

'It was the only solution. They would never survive here in the city without a gun . . . and out there. . . .' Dos Manos shrugged his drooping, angular shoulders and looked gloomy. 'Out there they were already at each other's throats.'

A dreadful certainty began to dawn on Allan. 'Doc,' he whispered. 'Where's Doc?'

'Dead,' said Felix curtly, without looking up or ceasing his unpacking.

Run-Run nodded and grinned, running a forefinger in a semicircle under his chin.

'He was old and sick anyhow,' said Smiley from the floor. 'He hadn't long to go. We really only did him a good turn. . . .'

He was interrupted by Lisa's scream. She suddenly seemed to be having a fit, screaming loudly and shrilly, as if the very last of her strength, the ultimate her emaciated body could achieve of vitality was being burnt out in her scream, a terrible wail, as if from an animal at the moment of death. For a moment it paralysed them all, then Allan knelt down at her side, held her shoulders and said something to calm her. But then she drew on yet another reserve of strength and tore herself free, got up and stood there, swaying, staring at him, the whites of her eyes showing as she screamed:

'Don't touch me! Don't bloody well touch me!' She swung her head from side to side as if searching for a way out, a bolt-hole, a dark corner where she could hide, then turned and fled. She staggered the few steps to the door, leant against it to get it open, then she lost her balance as she stumbled into the doorpost, tumbled out on to the landing towards the banisters . . . but the banisters had long since been ripped out and burnt. She could not even manage a scream before the loud, sickening thud told them she had fallen to the stone floor below.

Even from up on the landing, they could see her head was at a fatal angle as she lay there, half on her back, birdlike and brittle, a discarded, useless rag doll on the flagstone floor.

When Allan got up from examining her as best he could and had established what they had all been perfectly aware of before, that Lisa was dead, Boy suddenly tore himself free from Run-Run's protective arm and ran over to Allan, his features twisted with hatred. For a moment he stood still, tense and trembling, as if about to leap at his father's throat, then he started gesturing, twisting his body into a kind of wild pantomime of hatred and desire for revenge, not a sound coming from him as he carried out this mad dance in front of Allan, a dance in which he accused his father of killing his mother, swearing to avenge her. It lay in all his movements, in every nuance of his distorted features, the expressiveness and intensity stunning them all – until he suddenly stopped and ran for the door, out on to the steps, down the gravel path and out on to the street, where his footsteps soon disappeared as if the winter darkness brooding over the desolate city had settled over them and swallowed the fleeing figure. A cold gust whipped in over those standing in the open doorway, frost again in the air.

27

After stowing away what they had saved from Doc's precious store of seeds (they had eaten some on the way to keep alive), they seemed to calm down somewhat, as if the fact that they were again a group belonging together was an indisputable fact. Lisa's death and Boy's flight had affected them all, binding them together. The work of storing away the bags of seeds in a dry place, then finding mattresses or anything the newcomers could sleep on, also emphasized a fellowship that perhaps in this situation was not as welcome or favoured by them all, but, for the moment anyhow, was a reality not one of them could disregard. Although Allan had ensconced himself behind a wall of silence, he led the work of finding quarters for the others. And although Mary kept having to take Rain in her arms to calm her as she was constantly woken by the noise, she made sure there was a kettle on the fire so there would be tea for everyone. And despite his exhaustion and hunger, his anxiety at the sight of his old tormentors – Smiley, with his malicious look and Run-Run's unchanged inhuman grin – Bean stayed obediently tending the fire, making sure it didn't go out and that no firewood was wasted.

Lisa's body had to be left in the hall until the next day, or the day after, before they could bury it. The cold had become steadily more noticeable again and meant that they could leave it indoors for a while without any risk. Outside, it would soon be eaten by rats and dogs.

They each had some tea made with Doc's tea-leaves and the very last of the sugar, and as they sat there, Dos Manos started outlining the situation in the city for them. He was the least changed of them all, the acute circumstances making less impression on him, outwardly anyway. He was still the story-teller, the one to tell the tale of the last few days as it had happened around them.

Civil war was raging in Sweetwater, with open fighting between the two 'forces of occupation'. They all listened to his stories of confrontations between Army units and patrols of the Force as a result of the two commanders' desire to control the city. The fighting had largely gone on in the northern and north-western zones, but it was only a matter of time before it would shift to other parts of the city. It would be slow, for both ammunition and fuel on both sides were as good as used up, and the battle had gradually become increasingly hand-to-hand with casual weapons, ambushing and trapping, a merciless guerrilla warfare in this jungle of concrete and skyscrapers frozen in ice. Disease and starvation had thinned out the ranks of those willing to fight both inside and around the city. The military forces had superior troops and stores, but the administration of the enormous refugee camps had made great demands on them. Epidemics had spread from the camps and played havoc with the troops. The shortage of motor fuel curtailed their freedom of movement and radius of action. So the Army was recruiting people from within the camps to make up for their lack of efficiency and unmanageable forces with superiority in numbers.

The aim was to put the whole city and the districts – in its turn the whole country – under military command to gain control over the situation and set up an effective administration from their own ranks, and on that foundation start the work of bringing about normal circumstances, if the propaganda steadily pumped out over the military short wavelengths was to be believed.

But the Peacekeeping Force had no intention of giving up their mastery over the city. Rivalry between the two branches went back many years, but had now flared up with increasing intensity, for during the crisis the Force had recently expanded and had been given increasing powers to maintain what the administration called 'law and order'. As the situation worsened, both financial and legal resources had also been increased in order that their command over these extended police functions should be administered more efficiently. The result was that the Force had become an independent arm of the State and was able to operate fairly freely with no effective public intervention. Gradually more resources of manpower and arms were put at their disposal. But no one really knew just *how* far this extended police function had really gone, as large parts of the activities of the Force were kept 'secret in the interests of State security'.

Anyhow, the Force had been strong enough to take up the fight against the conventional military forces when co-operation broke down under the pressure of the panic evacuation of Sweetwater and their opposing interests were exposed to the light of day. So they began sabotaging military attempts at aid, which grew from minor confrontations into regular street fighting, then finally outright warfare in the northern zones.

Over recent years, an active progressive movement had grown up inside the military organizations as a result of their widespread discontent with international 'police actions' into which the country had been drawn as a result of an obligatory alliance policy. Perhaps that also had something to do with the recruiting campaign started just as unemployment began to set in. The campaign had gained ground among young people from all social layers, a large number of young men from professional backgrounds as well, who despite everything found the thought of a future in the Army more tempting than long-term unemployment.

In this new wider combination of manpower, thoughts and ideas arose and caught on, ideas which only a few years before would never have been associated with military thinking, so the battle between the two giant powers thus gradually acquired an ideological perspective. Progressive forces within the military were sceptical of traditional power structures, and the disaster situation which had now reduced a stagnant society to collapse called for new organizational and working forms, if what was left of human civilization and dignity were to be saved.

The Peacekeeping Force, on the other hand, considered their interests lay in fighting to protect the present, which was after all their only *raison d'etre*, and even now, after most of what they had fought so hard to preserve had been wiped out, they were still carrying on the fight in the ruins of what had once 'existed'.

It could be thought that this would be an uneven struggle, that the military units with their numbers and superiority in equipment would soon crush resistance and counter-attacks from the Peacekeeping Force. But the crisis in supplies that had lasted a long time had also affected military stores, the flu epidemic had afflicted military personnel as severely as the civilian population, and low morale and desertion had become huge problems. Finally, fighting in city areas put the military leaders in a difficult dilemma. They were neither trained nor equipped for urban guerrilla warfare. To fight effectively, they would have to use heavy equipment, artillery and bombs, reducing large parts, perhaps the majority of Sweetwater, to rubble and thus killing thousands of people still living in the deserted city. Was mass murder of their own countrymen, even if leading to victory over the Force, compatible with the new ideas that had swiftly spread through military ranks, and had also found favour with a large number of officers?

On their side, the Force were neither small nor badly equipped. In contrast to the Army units, the Force were armed, equipped and trained to fight in cities in case of civil disorder. The riot squads were experts at urban guerrilla warfare, the city favoured material and tactical conditions of the Force, and the Force also carried out their recruiting in the form of a drive among the unhappy creatures still in Sweetwater, living their ratlike lives in the skeleton of the city, by crawling round and sniffing quietly in cold, abandoned buildings, by looting, stealing, killing for something to eat . . . when the Force's brutal squads, still called 'cleaning-up squads', tracked down and captured a group of these rat-people, the procedure was simple – a choice between joining them or being shot. During the state of emergency, courts martial had been brought in for anyone caught with arms. As the situation stood, almost anything, bread-knives, clubs and screwdrivers, was considered arms. And also, who was to prevent tyranny arising? Massacres occurring? In a city where all communications had broken down, where liaison between individual sections of the Force was lacking after Army units had blown up the main power stations in the northern and north-western zones?

'They'll come here, too,' Dos Manos predicted. 'In the end, they'll come here as well. It's a slow business without vehicles, but they are not far away. We saw them on the way here. They appeared to have set up some kind of headquarters in the Laguna Hotel near the East Terminal, which was crawling with police. And dogs. And all the usual parasites and hangers-on. We were lucky as we had chosen to avoid the avenues, so we didn't run straight into them. Had they been the Army, at least we wouldn't have been slaughtered. But as far as I know, the military hold the North Zone and Sargossa. They're the most valuable to them. They probably haven't the manpower to start down here.'

Allan remembered the abandoned road-block they had driven through on their way into the city, the ruined guardhouse, the shattered vehicle. It was not hard to imagine what had happened there. Perhaps the military units were operating in the South Zone as well, although Dos Manos thought there was little possibility of that: 'My God, you talk as if you wanted us to leave again, just when we've got here.'

Smiley was on the verge of collapse, but the condescending grin was still there. Nothing seemed to have had any effect on him, nor did he show any feeling of friendship or gratitude towards Dos Manos, who had half carried, half dragged him most of the long way there. On the contrary, his sickness, the fatal symptoms he bore within him, seemed to have provoked a savage hatred in him, as if that meant he had to provoke Fate itself while he still had the power of speech. The others heard him, too exhausted, or too unpleasantly affected to be able to reply.

But Allan looked his old enemy straight in the eye. 'Anyhow,' he said, 'I think *you* ought to get yourself ready for another stroll.'

'What do you mean?' said Smiley. 'You're not going to throw us out, are you? After all those presents we brought? Even if it did end miserably for . . . her.' He waved his hand vaguely to indicate Lisa's fall from the landing.

'We won't throw anyone out who can keep himself alive.'

'What about him there, then?' Smiley pointed at Bean, anxiety in his voice where arrogance usually reigned, the anxiety that always overcame him whenever he saw that his irony, his scorn and mockery were wasted on his opponent. 'You've got that spook to feed!'

'Bean can manage,' said Allan curtly.

'And what about me? Don't you think I could "manage" just as well as. . . .'

Smiley's voice died away as he realized he was begging for his life because he no longer had anything to barter with.

'No, I don't,' Allan snapped back. 'You bloody well can't even cross the floor! You stink like a corpse. Do you think we can feed you? You're as good as dead already.'

'But. . . .' The content of Allan's statements slowly sank into Smiley. 'Do you mean you're going to throw me out?'

'Yes, I do.'

This brutal information rang in all their ears. Smiley opened and closed his mouth, but could get nothing out except a jerky, whimpering laugh. A change came over him as this sentence of death at last sank into his dazed mind, his expression gaping, foolish, almost childish. For once his silly grin had been driven out by *genuine* emotion – the fear of perishing from cold and hunger in this freezing desert of streets and porchways, burnt-out buildings, high-rises and courtyards, where death lay in wait in the form of rats, dogs and vultures, which would follow him watchfully, closing in on any injured creature. By the time he finally regained the control of his voice, it had become a panic-stricken, falsetto whine.

'But . . . but . . . no one can cope *out there*! You can't . . . you can't just let . . . let a person die!'

'You'll probably die pretty soon, anyhow, with that leg of yours.'

'No, no . . . it's getting better. . . . Listen! I'll soon be all right again.' He was weeping now, rubbing his bad foot, the stench rising from the filthy rags round the huge, unpleasant swelling almost up to his knee. 'You couldn't . . .'

'Yes I could.'

'Mary?' Smiley was pleading as he lay on the floor, reaching out as if trying to touch Mary's boot. 'Mary, tell him he can't do it. Tell him I'll be OK again in a few weeks, that I . . .'

'He's right, you know, Smiley.'

Mary's dark eyes gleamed in the light from the fire, her face white and drawn. There was no hatred in her eyes, nor was there any compassion.

'It's every man for himself now, Smiley. No one can be a hanger-on here. We hardly know how to manage from one day to the next ourselves.'

'But . . .'

'Take it easy. No one's going to throw you out tonight.' She exchanged looks with Allan. 'But you can't stay here long. At the most two days. We'll have to think something up.'

'*Think something up*! What do you mean, *think up*? What shall I do . . .?

Smiley's voice had become an hysterical wail, echoing round the room and bouncing back off the closed faces all round him. But his appeals did strike home in one place – Dos Manos suddenly intervened.

'I know something you could do.'

'*You*? What do you know, you bloody preacher?'

'You could try to get to one of the military camps on the outskirts of the north-eastern zone. The Army is in control there. You could get medical help there.' Dos Manos seemed calm and unaffected by the sick man's bitter scorn.

'*The north-eastern zone*!' A series of hoarse sobs supposed to be laughter came out of Smiley's throat. 'And how do you think I'm going to get all the way across the city, eh? In a motorized wheel-chair? I'm not so nippy on my feet as I used to be, you know.'

'I thought we might try together.' Dos Manos was imperturbable, holding a mug of tea and talking as if he had been thinking about getting Smiley to a doctor for a long time. 'I thought of trying to get there myself. We'll never survive here, not with so many of us. Just to try would be madness.'

'Well, now, just listen to the preacher,' croaked Smiley. A little self-confidence had come back into that hoarse voice, which only a moment or so ago had been shrieking, weeping, begging for mercy. 'Follow me, stand up and take thy bed with thee . . . wasn't that said once upon a time?'

'You must get that foot to a doctor,' said Dos Manos, ignoring Smiley's babble. 'If you're lucky, we'll get there in time to save your life. But I'm afraid no one can save your foot.'

'Help yourself,' said Smiley, uncertainly. 'Take an arm, too, by all means. I must say you're very generous with other people's rotting limbs.'

Dos Manos shrugged and sipped at his tea. The others looked at him with increasing interest.

'One poor leg here or there doesn't really matter, does it, here where we've survived the Black Death.' Smiley bleated on, his face deathly white, his eyes glassy, but he was regaining a little of his previous arrogance. 'If His Reverence here can get me to a field surgeon, you'll see, I'll survive you all! But listen. . . .' He grabbed Dos Manos's arm. 'They have anaesthetics there, don't they? The military have anaesthetics, don't they? Amputation out in the open with rusty field tools sounds a bit medieval, don't you think?' He tried to smile again, but with little success. 'Do you know, I think I need a booster. I think I'll reveal my very last reserves of happiness, and toast the pastor here, who is about to commit an old – I almost said incorrigible – sin, showing genuine missionary spirit, yes, real Old Testament high-mindedness. Cheers!'

As he spoke, he extracted a bottle from beneath his layers of clothing, a half-bottle, half full of liquor, the very last from his previously bottomless store.

He took a gulp and passed the bottle on.

'Here you are, help yourselves. Let's finish it off. If things get bad for old Smiley later, there's always something intravenous to be got at the field hospital.'

Felix, Mary and Allan all had a pull. Dos Manos took a great gulp and rubbed his lips. Bean was over by the stove, apparently asleep. Run-Run was sitting cross-legged, his eyes closed, isolated, unaffected. Smiley took back the bottle and put it to his mouth, then was seized with another fit of coughing, his eyes rolling.

'Listen now, just take it easy.' Dos Manos put a hand on Smiley's arm. 'We've a long way to walk tomorrow, don't forget. We'll start early, preferably before it's light, then perhaps we'll get past the Laguna Hotel before they start up for the day. I'm scared of the dogs most of all. They're trained to find people. If they scent us, then. . . . Try to get some rest now. I'll wake you when we've got to leave.'

'Just listen to the preacher,' said Smiley. 'You may certainly join me in Paradise . . . but that's quite a way to go!'

The irony was lost on his listeners, for none except the priest himself knew what 'in Paradise' meant.

28

Bean wakes, stiff from his curled-up position, reaches out automatically to put more wood on the embers, his mind struggling with something he has been dreaming, captivating but frightening images, voices exciting him and filling him with fear, but at the same time tempting him. . . .

The others are all sound asleep. No one is keeping watch — as if exhaustion has suddenly overcome them all. Then he spots the empty bottle close to Smiley's hand and makes the connection.

It must be just past midnight. It is dark, a little grey light trickling in between the blankets over the windows. The voices, the visions will not let go. Bean's mind is spinning wildly, but dangerously near the decision sparked off last night as he had listened to them talking. The voice saying: ' . . . headquarters in the Laguna Hotel, near the East Terminal . . . headquarters in the Laguna Hotel . . . headquarters. . . .' And the visions in his dream, columns of the grey and steel-blue vehicles of the Force, the helmets of the Force, gleaming on the heads of military policemen in line, patrols of the Force, four or five men in a vehicle or on foot, armed, ready to move in on disturbances, the man-high emblem of the Force in stainless steel and gleaming enamel above the entrance to Headquarters . . .

Headquarters in the Laguna Hotel. . . .

He knows it well, the Laguna Hotel. He took Stella there in the old days, before he had his own apartment, when he was living in one of the Force's hostels. The hotel suited them well, in the East Zone, sufficiently far away, just by the Terminal, so easy to get to at weekends when he was off-duty. The small square rooms with their practical furnishings, completely impersonal comfort and dry hygienic smell of disinfecting detergents were the ideal framework for their purposeful love-making. The double bed did not creak, always had cool clean sheets on it, and the monotonous hum of the air-conditioning accompanied their love-making, wrapping its sonorous base note round the words when something had to be said, parcelling them up and thus effectively drowning any attempt at conversation. Both of them liked it like that.

But it is not the images of Stella's trim, hairless body exciting him — it is the images in his dream, the occupation of his weekend hotel by the Force. He sees a busy operation-room in the dining-room, an arsenal of arms in the lobby, the men billeted in the rooms, waiting, sprawling about, their tunics unbuttoned, in those standard beds with their cool, clean sheets.

The others are sleeping like the dead all round him.

He is on his feet without knowing why, slipping silently over to the door and taking an eternity to cover the four or five metres, following up a decision that has been taken for him, somewhere in his dream, in his subconscious. The headquarters of the Force in the Laguna Hotel, an hour's, perhaps two hours' walk in the slush and the cold. But he thinks he can find his way. After months in this house, he has again begun to orientate, the longer and longer trips out for firewood providing him with a new perception of the desolate geography of the city.

He presses down the handle. The others are asleep, prone, lifeless. Even Run-Run is asleep, immobile, face down like an animal. Bean is worried by his weakness, but feels the promise of wild joy as he stands holding the door-handle, looking at the others sleeping, relaxed, helpless. He has his secret knife. He could dispose of them . . . but he comes to his senses. At most, he would manage two before the others woke. He lets them live awhile longer, until he can return in triumph. The dream is still churning through his mind. The thought of the men of the Force lined up in the car-park of the Laguna Hotel, ready to move out, fills him with jubilant delight.

Out on the landing, reaction sets in so that his head spins, his legs refuse to obey him and he has to sit down. Exhaustion overwhelms him. He is sweating in the harsh cold as he makes his way downstairs, soundlessly, soundlessly; nothing must happen now. But he stumbles at the bottom of the stairs and falls over Lisa's body lying on the cold flagstones.

His idea is to get to his feet, get away from the corpse, but his wretched body refuses to obey, exhaustion demanding that he must stay where he is and rest. He stays lying across the dead girl's cold limbs, breathing heavily, wheezing painfully. The long period of starvation and the excitement have for the moment taken control over his body. He can only lie there gasping as his muscles twitch with the effort of trying to control his movements as images flicker past his eyes and voices from his dreams ring in his ears – the songs, the battle songs of the Force, the words, the brief messages from the Commandant.

Bean does something mad as he lies there feeling his body as the useless, tormented container of a pain he has had to live with so long, it has become a habit, a part of his life. He feels it stronger now than during the shower of images sparkling on his retina, the voices calling words he understands, absorbing them without the co-operation of his ear-drums. The pain of defeat, of degradation, the pain of the helpless, the hopeless, not least the pain of the starving, the pain of always noticing the weakness in his own limbs without being able to do anything to still the eternal scream for food, for nourishment, for *something*. (The images: Stella. The hotel room. Hairy arms on the pillows. And the weapons. The beds. The beds.) In this state, he sinks his teeth into the not yet rigid corpse, flicking the skirt away from the thin thighs, where some of the youthful softness still gives way as he presses his face against them. Abandoned to his raging hunger, he bites, tearing with his teeth into this flesh which will give him the strength to get up, go over to the door and make his way out into the street. Yet something in him registers what is happening to him, and something shatters within him as he registers it – that he is lying over a dead body, this dead girl he knows, and with the mindless savagery of an animal he is committing the most terrible, the most inconceivable of all crimes.

Yet he doesn't stop. He bites and chews, he *has* to find strength from somewhere. Meat is strength – the images command him . . . but it is difficult, tough, almost hard, impossible to get anything down. He has to get out the knife and hack away like a madman, trying to chew, trying to get it down, going on like a madman until he notices he must stop in order not to lose everything, until he notices his strength is coming back sufficiently so that he can stand upright, until he can no longer bear the increasing knowledge of what he is doing, and he gets up, leaning against the walls, his hand pressed to his stomach because of the cramps which would soon go . . . must soon go. . . .

The air outside is cold, making him gasp for breath, and his feet hit the frozen asphalt so loudly he thinks it will be audible many blocks away, so he hurries in the direction he thinks must be right, determined, hunched up, limping along oddly, crookedly, his teeth clenched in a wild protest against his weakness, his lack of courage always lying in wait, threatening to overcome him if he relaxes for as much as one single moment. For he knows he has a long way to go.

Hospital Street, Jasmin Street, Transport Road East . . . he tries desperately to orientate, thinking all the time he has kept on a more or less steady north-east course, but he has nothing except the shifting formations of the demolished city to keep to, and the deceptive lack of parallels of the streets. But the names, the names should tell him something. He took that course in locality knowledge as a recruit, studied the plans and projected expansion, he knew the names of all the important main streets and intersecting avenues and a large number of other important streets from where it is practical to orientate. Now he remembers again. . . .

Transport Road East — that rings a bell. Transport Road East goes to the East Terminal. Of course. He remembers now. He *remembers*! It is one of the main streets radiating from a star shape to the East Zone from the centre of the Terminal. Transport Road East . . . just follow Transport Road East, then he will come to the Terminal. And from the Terminal . . . he remembers the location of the Laguna Hotel, even more clearly now after his dream — only two blocks from the Terminal, to the left of the main entrance. A large neon sign on the top of the building . . . and inside the glass doors under a striped awning . . . guards in the uniform of the Force. And in the rooms with numbered doors, men resting, guns leaning up against the walls, pistols on dressing-tables, helmets on the bedside tables, shoulder-straps, cartridge belts, boot heels deep in the hygienic clean white quilts — men resting in bed where he and Stella. . . .

The images urge him on. The cold squeezes the breath out of him. He has not put on his outdoor clothes, just staggered out, got away, escaped . . . but he's made it! He *has* escaped. He has broken the spell the Dump and its people cast on him, the destructive, despairing state of mind that has turned the human being in him more and more into an animal. He has broken out of it and has made it! This thought becomes an obsession, driving him on along the dark, deserted street, block by block, over patches of ice, heaps of frozen garbage, piles of scraps, refuse and splintered fittings flung out on to the pavement, out on to the wide street where there are no vehicles.

He doesn't know how long he has been walking. He doesn't know how far he still has to go, but he feels his legs obeying him. He notices he is going on and he knows he will, and *must* make it as he lurches along the pavement, stumbling and getting up again, trudging on, propping himself up against walls, on and on, steadily onwards, as if fleeing from despair, deathly exhaustion in his limbs, in his whole body, a numb indifference, a creeping sleep which tries to take over if he relaxes for one single moment and lets go of those images and closes his ears to those voices. . . .

But not now, not yet. They still obey him, his frost-bitten feet still bearing him through the cold, clear darkness, now greying in the east – like a sign, he thinks, an encouragement. He can still hear his own voice, croaking from the effort of getting out words, gradually, between curses and groans, merging into stanzas, lines of verse from songs they sang in the days when he was a recruit, cocky, male, pornographic songs. He goes on, his frost-bitten feet still obeying him, the visions of his dream of the Laguna Hotel still beckoning him on.

The East Terminal.

At last he knows where he is. Icy sweat keeps pouring into his eyes, making it impossible for him to see properly. The Terminal building has partly collapsed. It must have been shot at by artillery or been bombed. The destruction is terrible. Bean thinks he can just see something like a tank under the jumble of concrete blocks and twisted girders. Here there has been open warfare!

Bean feels faint, his mind spinning. He must not, *must not* stop. None the less. . . . *No! Go on!* One foot in front of the other. Hand on the wall. *On!* None the less a terrible thought occurs to him – what if the Army . . . what if the new headquarters have been attacked, bombed out? What if . . .

On! Go on without thinking. Reasoning beyond the control of his will helps him. The ruins are cold. There is no smoke here, not even the smell of smoke. The twisted girders are red with rust. The whole place is deserted and empty, not a movement, not a sound except the dragging of his own feet. It is a long time since there was any fighting here.

He looks to the left as he clutches at a wall to keep himself upright. A semi-wrecked building blocking the narrow street. Was that where the hotel sign used to be, gleaming blue and turquoise? Or. . .?

However well he knew this place, he is still disorientated now that the shape of the landscape has changed, smashed as if a gigantic fist had played with whole blocks. Chunks of concrete lie in vast piles, whole façades leaning precariously, a sound alone, a small sneeze bringing down tons of concrete, dust and iron reinforcements with a colossal crash.

Bean staggers across a clear stretch of street, trying to orientate. On the left . . . the buildings on the left have been pulverized. Impossible to know where the streets ran, if there were any streets at all. He goes on, his strength of will gone. The sight of the destruction has swallowed all his initiative. Only an automaton is keeping his body upright, steering him along one more stretch of the wilderness to which the Terminal has been reduced. Where to? Keep to the left? On the left of the main entrance – where the main entrance must once have been, two or three blocks, that's where it should be, under that brilliant sign.

He is gasping with exhaustion. It's all over. He can't think any longer, or hope any longer . . . he falls headlong over some rubble and through the rasping sound of his own breathing he can still hear fragments of those songs from his dream, swaggering, bold, interrupted by stray shots in the air. Yes, they did sometimes go too far . . . the songs, the shots, the intoxicating climax of fellowship. He had never liked exaggerations.

Yelling and shooting. . . .

Yelling and shooting. Suddenly he *hears* it. Really hears it. Shots! Voices! They sound quite near. It is here! Once again he finds the strength to get up, shaking his head, focusing his eyes through the mist of dream and fantasy. There's the hotel, the Laguna Hotel, perfectly visible, even more visible than ever before because the nearest buildings have been shot to pieces. It is not his imagination, even a shred or two of the awning are still there. One side of the building is scorched, some windows broken, but he can see it, the hotel, he can see it so clearly and so close in the grey light, he doesn't understand how he could have missed seeing it a moment ago.

He can also hear the voices quite clearly, and they are singing.

He hurries on before paralysis descends, knowing he won't make it if he doesn't cover this last stretch, the ridiculously small distance separating him from his buddies. He tries to call out, to wave as he staggers on, but he doesn't know if the sound comes from his throat or is only in his head. He stumbles and falls, but manages to get up again and go on, step by step, waving his arms about, his mouth wide open, hoping his screams for help in his dream may make their way out past his chattering teeth. Then he sees a sign of life, a figure over by the hotel entrance, then some more, and he notices the distance has been halved – his cries become hoarse shrieks filling the air as he tries to wave to them, hearing the voices, the shots, even seeing the puffs of smoke much as in the old days, and the ricocheting bullets send dust and mortar into his eyes, a rough game he doesn't like, but he has played it before. He straightens up, waves, holds one hand up in the air as if to catch one of those careless projectiles, and feels a blow through the air, a current of air which seems to pluck at his fingers, and he stops and stares at his hand which they have shot to pieces; he is so absorbed by this, he doesn't realize the firing is at him, into him, paralysing his body and throwing him backwards.

Laughter and shooting. Laughter and shooting as in the old days. Laughter and shouting just as when they had come back from on leave in their time as recruits. They are coming towards him, smiling, shouting, and in one last flickering puff of awareness Bean thinks calmly, pleased they have discovered their mistake and have come to help him, to find him a doctor . . . and he is dead before they reach him and start removing his shoes.

Allan had found an axe and was struggling to make a hole big enough, the steel striking sparks against stones frozen into the ground. Must get it deep enough so the dogs don't. . . . Run-Run was helping, heaving hunks of soil out of the grave as Allan hacked them loose.

It took them nearly all morning.

Then they put Lisa's body down into the oblong hole and covered it over. Mary was watching from the window, trembling as she thought about Lisa's mutilated body, about Bean, who must have gone mad. From hunger? From despair? Where was he now?

Dos Manos and Smiley had set off early that morning, side by side, close together, as if tethered to each other, Smiley shaking, limping badly, one hand on the priest's shoulder, Dos Manos tall, dry and confident. They were heading north-east and had a long, dangerous march ahead of them.

Mary shuddered again and thought about Boy, who had run away. How long would he be able to survive in this dead city? How long would they themselves. . .? Left were Run-Run and Felix, Rain, Allan and herself.

That evening they dipped into one of Doc's bags of seed-corn and baked some hard slabs of bread on the metal plate over the fire-place, washing it all down with hot sweet tea.

'Wonder where Bean has got to,' Allan muttered darkly. Even he had been upset by the sight of Lisa's body.

'Probably trying to make his way to the Force,' said Felix. 'But I hope he takes off that tunic before he gets there. Otherwise there'll be fireworks.'

'*If* he gets there,' said Allan. 'And *if* the Force don't finish him off, then we can expect him back any minute. Didn't you say they were out to get people?'

Felix nodded.

Run-Run signalled, raised an imaginary rifle and fired, pointing north-north-west, then looked up at the sun, then to the east. He had heard the distant rattle of shots early that morning and thought it came from a north-easterly direction.

'Anyhow,' Allan went on. 'We'll probably have them here before long.'

29

The strange sound came nearer.

Allan dropped his load and slipped into a porch entrance. What could it be? He could hear it all the time, a scraping, clattering sound, unlike anything he had ever heard before. It was coming closer, but slowly. What *was* it? Animal, man or machine? He peered down along the long, deserted street, but could see nothing, although the noise was coming steadily closer. He cursed the fact that he had no gun. Mary had it. She felt unsafe alone in the house with Rain and she had no more ammunition for her own gun. They had only a dozen or so bullets left for his, so they had to save them. Two days ago he had wasted two on an emaciated cat. A cat! Not much to fill their stomachs. But they had to take what they could find. Two weeks had gone by since Bean had run away, and they had neither seen nor heard a sign of the Force approaching their zone. Perhaps they had been worrying too soon? They had started foraging again.

He was seven or eight blocks away from the house. He did not usually go that far without a gun, but today it was warmer and good to work out of doors, so he had gone further than he had meant to — he had intended only a quick trip for firewood.

The sound came from the other direction, from the indeterminate place where the street parted and formed a small square. 'It' must be coming from one of the side-streets. . . .

Perhaps he ought to get back to the house where their weapons were? Perhaps Felix and Run-Run were also back? But what if he didn't make it and was attacked as he fled, perhaps even giving his pursuers a pointer that there were several of them? Shouldn't he try to head off whatever was approaching? Take up the fight?

'It' seemed to be coming from several directions at once, the rhythmical, clattering sound echoing between the walls of the empty street. It couldn't be any kind of machine, but what was it? A kind of animal? A gigantic creature? A monster?

Yes, it *was* an animal.

As he put his head out and saw it, he froze at once, thinking he had never seen anything like it before, but then he realized what it was, recognizing the phenomenon from pictures in books and films, although he had certainly never *seen* a living horse before. But horse it was, large, brown and frightening, clip-clopping along, a rider in shining armour on its back, or rather a glinting helmet and a long plastic anti-demonstrators shield reflecting the light. The Force's Riot Squad! So they had come. But on horseback? Did that mean their fuel supplies had run out completely? Or had he bumped into a chance scout out reconnoitring? Or a deserter? It was too late to retreat to the house. He swore again about the gun he had left behind. He hadn't even a knife with him – was he getting careless?

The horse was trotting towards him. He had to get away, but how? Where to? Not up the street towards the house. The courtyard behind him was small and surrounded by high walls, impossible to get over. A hopeless trap if the rider caught sight of him. Only one entrance. The horse was now so close he couldn't possibly leave this damned porchway without being seen. There was a narrow alley diagonally across the street in front of him. He knew it well. It went nowhere, but ended in fencing round the Park and that shouldn't be too difficult to climb. Perhaps the rider would have to abandon any idea of following him in there? Perhaps he could shake him off?

No time to think. He raced across the street and dived into the alley with its high, blind façades and courtyard walls on both sides. He heard the quick clatter of hoofs. Was the alley too narrow for a horse? No, he could hear it coming after him. But there was still the fence . . . he leapt as high as he could, grabbed the wire netting, hauled up his legs, catching a lace and kicking it free, then scrambling on up; he got one hand up and, with a heave over the top, he let himself down on the other side. He had seen the rider drawing his gun and aiming, and he thought the end had come, but he ran on, realizing from the sound it was a gas cylinder. My God, hadn't they even got any firearms left? A gas-gun was just a toy in the open air. As a schoolboy, he had learnt how to protect himself against tear-gas and had practised before planning demonstrations with various cloths over his face. Lots of stuff which could be used as filters. He hardly even recognized the smell now.

The horse was thundering down the alley. He had at least a head start and now he had to find a hiding-place, or somewhere where the horse couldn't follow. He looked around, but what had previously been a recreation ground was wide open and empty, the few bushes and trees leafless, so providing no shelter. He ran along a path searching desperately for some alternative. Far away, he could see the thicket around the allotments which had not been cultivated for years, the high fence around the sports ground towering closer to him.

Then he heard the hoofs again. Horse and rider had gone right round and were after him. He ran faster, though he could feel his exhaustion. Nowhere to go . . . he set off towards the sports ground with no particular plan in mind. He was tired, but knew he had to struggle on through the rough, frozen grass thawing into slippery patches where the winter sun had caught it. He could sense the horse galloping closer and closer behind him, the rider leaning over its neck and driving it on, helmet and shield glinting. It became a race for the fence which Allan only just won. He leapt over two or three rows of rusty fencing and slipped in through the public entrance, tumbled on through the wide passage between the now partly collapsed stands and out on to the stadium.

But the horse was following. Allan swerved to the right and ran along the broad strip of overgrown gravel which had once been a running-track. But they were just behind him now. Too late, he saw pieces of wood in the way, an overturned hurdle, stumbled, but managed to twist his body away as he fell and rolled aside to escape the horse's hoofs. Up on his feet again. Everything was moving crazily fast now, sports equipment from smashed crates lying all round him, wrecked, rotting, half buried in mud and slush, just as it had lain for years since the mob had broken in and destroyed it all. He spotted a bright point shining in the grass in front of him and grabbed it, anything he could use as a weapon . . . it was attached to a shaft and he hauled it out, a javelin, long and intact. He grasped it with both hands – he had a weapon against the rider, a lance!

The man from the Force was trying to turn his steed. He was clearly no rider. Allan saw him digging his heels into the horse's side so that it screamed and reared, terrifyingly. The rider obviously also thought so, for Allan caught a glimpse of a panic-stricken face behind the transparent visor of the helmet, a young man with wide, frightened eyes, a face he suddenly thought he recognized.

But this was no time for speculation – they were coming at him, the rider with his helmet and shield, swinging a club, charging at Allan, standing there with a javelin, the empty derelict stands all around them. There was something oddly anachronistic about the scene. Allan associated shields and helmets of that kind with riot troops in skin-tight uniforms, on powerful motor bikes which could make their way swiftly through city traffic to wherever disturbances were taking place. But here, on a charging horse . . . no time to think. He leapt aside as they came charging down on him, raised the javelin and thrust it in, trying to unhorse the rider . . . but the javelin struck the shield and the shaft snapped, knocking Allan down. As he lay there he saw the point of the javelin had stuck in the shield and was flicking back and forth in time with the horse's movements.

The next time they came at him, he grabbed whatever was nearest and flung it at his opponent, but the swerving discus simply glanced off the man's helmet and Allan had to roll round again to avoid those murderous hoofs. This time he saw the rider's face quite clearly, its scornful, triumphant grin. At once he knew who it was – he was fighting for his life with Roy Indiana, the boy at the PAC station who had been sacked for stealing, but had come back with his friends, looted the station and murdered Janson, the owner. So now he was in the Force. Not surprising, after what Dos Manos had told them.

The next time, Roy Indiana managed to strike Allan a paralysing blow on his left shoulder with the club. As Allan got up again, dazed, he felt around but found nothing, then he heard the horse neighing shrilly and again the thunder of hoofs.

Allan was now without a weapon, exhausted, his legs giving way. It was only a matter of time before he would no longer have the energy to evade the charging horse. A better rider would long ago have ridden him down. Also, his opponent appeared to be taking the outcome for granted, taking his time, pausing by the empty stand, striking the horse and carefully deciding on his course before charging again, his club swinging, as if enjoying slowly weakening his victim. Another fall into the cold mud. Allan was being pressed back to the end of the sports ground and he could feel his strength ebbing. His left arm was as good as useless as he tried to get up, the thunder of hoofs coming up behind him. His fingers grabbed something. A rope? A kind of net? He at once realized what it was and collected his wits. The netting was a piece from a broken football goal, but was it strong enough? Big enough? No time. The horse's hoofs were right behind him. He grabbed the netting with both hands and whirled round, flung out his arms and hurled it as high and wide as he could above the heads of both horse and rider. Nor did he let go, clinging on, jerking and tugging at the coarse netting as the horse dragged him along the ground, dancing and stamping and neighing, tossing its head until it got free and reared up before bolting at such speed that Roy Indiana, who had also been struggling to get free of the netting, lost his balance and fell with a thud to the ground.

His helmet protected his head as he hit the ground, and also protected him from Allan's fists as they rained down on his face. Roy Indiana was lithe and strong and Allan was exhausted, his left arm so feeble he could only just manage to keep the man down. Then Roy Indiana tried to knee him in the groin, so he thumped like a madman at his enemy's shoulders and chest, at the shiny helmet, with little effect. Then he spotted the weight, a rusty iron putting-weight lying on the ground nearby among skipping-ropes, running shoes and other equipment half hidden in the rough grass. He grabbed it, tested its weight, then, with both hands, heaved it high up above his head. Roy Indiana also saw the danger and started kicking and twisting, but too late, far too late, for Allan had swung the weight up and let it fall with shattering force against the gleaming helmet, with crushing force against the screaming face, swiftly bringing this mad gladiatorial fight to an end with a sigh.

The horse was not far away, tugging at withered tufts of grass, the reins dragging behind it, a brown horse with glossy flanks and splashes of mud up its strong legs, the largest animal Allan had ever seen in his life – a veritable mountain of flesh! But how was he to get at it?

He had managed to pull himself together after the wild scuffle, sitting on the ground with his head in his hands, trying to think. Don't frighten it. That was most important. How did one handle a horse? Were they dangerous? Could they bite? Kick? The horse was nibbling at the grass and stretching out its neck to thrust its head under the bottom seats of the stand to get hold of whatever was growing there.

174

Allan gave the horse a wide berth, thrust his hand into the gap between the rotting seats and pulled up a handful of grass flourishing among the empty bottles, cigarette packets, plastic bags and programmes, so high the tips came up and over the seats. Holding out the grass, Allan approached the horse. It raised its head when he was about ten steps away and stood there watchfully, ears pricked, looking at him. Allan made some clucking noises, but they sounded peculiar. He had no idea what people said to horses. As he approached, step by step, the horse clearly became more nervous, blowing through its nose and nodding its great head until it suddenly shied round and moved off, trotting defiantly in a semicircle round Allan, then grazing again at a safe distance.

He tried again, collecting up a large armful of grass and cautiously approaching the horse. It did not move until he was quite close, then it again raised its head and trotted off. They went on like this . . .

He did once manage to get it to nip the nearest bit of grass, but when he tried to get hold of the loose reins with his free hand, the horse snorted loudly and nervously, then set off so fast it almost knocked him over.

Then he remembered the sugar, the two or three lumps of sugar he always had in his pocket for when he felt hunger buckling his legs. He suddenly connected the sugar with this great unapproachable animal – he must have read or seen on television somewhere that horses liked sugar and accepted lumps of sugar from the hands of children . . . he dug out the sugar and tried again, walking slowly, saying a few words when he got near enough, persuading it to stand still, talking soothingly, as if to a person, holding out his hand . . . and the horse did actually seem to take a different interest in him as it smelt the sugar. It stopped with its neck outstretched, nostrils quivering until Allan was quite close. He was unsure how to give sugar to a horse – perhaps it would bite off his fingers? But the horse stood still and stretched out towards his hand, and as the moist muzzle started seeking between his fingers, he grabbed its bridle.

There was no tug of war. The horse submitted as soon as Allan held the reins. It allowed itself to be led across the grounds and out through the wide entrance below the last remaining couple of flagstaffs, the way people heading for the main stand had once streamed in on hot summer afternoons to football matches, athletic meetings and speedway races – once upon a time, long long ago, in another world.

Now they were plodding through the uncut grass as if across a rough meadow, spotlights dangling in the wind, smashed and rusting in their battered, rectangular frames, the stadium clock lying on the ground, its great circular face wreathed in nodding grass.

Allan thought the sound of the horse's hoofs would wake the dead as they clomped down the street towards the house, but he saw no one. He stopped in the gateway and shouted.

'The gun,' said Allan, when Mary came out. There was no time for explanations. Roy Indiana would be missed and others would perhaps come looking for him. He had to get the slaughtering out of the way first.

Mary brought the gun. Allan led the horse over to the open garage door, and although the roof was too low for the horse to keep its head raised, he finally persuaded it inside. In the semi-darkness, he moved up close to the horse's head, put the barrel of the gun into the horse's ear and fired. The horse fell like a stone with a terrible thud and lay still without a twitch. He opened the door again and called to Mary. She brought a knife, and he slit the great horse's throat to let the blood run out as he had seen Run-Run do. Blood spurted out across the cold, oil-spotted concrete floor, and the smell of horse and the warm, sweetish steam from the blood mingled with the acrid stench of petrol. The blood flowed all over the garage floor, so much of it, far too much – it would attract dogs, rats . . . but he would have to think about that later. First they must rescue as much as possible of this meat. There was a colder snap in the air again so perhaps there would be a frost? In which case, for once it would be welcome. The meat would keep for weeks in cold weather. He had also spotted half a sack of coarse salt in a corner of the garage, no doubt used by the owner of the house to thaw out his drive during recent cold winters. Perhaps that would be used? But the animal had to be skinned first . . . he stood over the dead horse with the knife in his hand, hesitant, wishing Felix and Run-Run were back – they were better at this kind of thing.

30

The black Alsatian was sniffing at the gatepost. Allan could see it from the window, large, muscular, glossy and well cared for – undoubtedly a police dog. So they were here.

The dog moved over to the garage door and stopped. The

horsemeat had been hung inside and there was no mistaking the smell. To his horror, Allan saw the dog start scratching at the door. If its owner came and saw that, they were done for. But how to get rid of it? A police dog meant a policeman somewhere near, perhaps several. A shot would be heard miles away. To tackle a well-trained police dog with a knife or bare fists would be madness.

As the dog sat down and howled to warn its owner, Allan heard the outer door bang and suddenly saw Run-Run racing along the gravel path towards the dog, which now had its hackles up, its head low, ready to attack, baring its fangs. Run-Run drew his knife. For a moment they stood measuring each other up, then the dog leapt at the man in black and clamped its jaws on to his right arm, the one with the knife. His overcoat absorbed the bite, so Run-Run was able to shake the dog off and give it a well-directed kick, but that had no effect. It came at him again, a ball of aggression in one lightning bound snarling at Run-Run's throat. But he had collected himself and his long knife made a great gash along the shoulder of the raging animal, clearly trained to avoid attacks from weapons. Impaired but undeterred, the dog attacked again, but Run-Run was quick enough to twist away and wound it again, in the same place, so it fell, rolled around and had difficulty rising again. This time it was Run-Run attacking and the dog retreated, limping, snarling, as if gathering strength for a last fight to the death. But as Run-Run ran up to put an end to it, another raging, snarling Alsatian suddenly entered the fray – large, brownish-yellow, a bundle of well-trained killing instinct appearing from nowhere at incredible speed and flying at his throat, sinking its cruel teeth deep into his shoulder. Run-Run threw himself down, rolled aside to get rid of this new enemy, while the injured dog took the opportunity to grab his foot, hanging on until some fierce slashes from the long knife sliced its head from its body. But by then the other dog was already on him again, knocking him down, and Allan, frozen in the window, saw Run-Run was bleeding from a wound in his neck. Although his thick overcoat absorbed some of the worst bites, clearly he had also sustained injuries from the fierce attacks.

Allan seemed to come to his senses when he saw Run-Run bleeding – the dumb man was not invulnerable, not invincible, he was in danger. Allan moved away from the window, collected his wits and was about to run out when he felt a hand on his arm. Felix had come silently up behind him, watching the fight. He shook his head, retaining his hold on Allan's arm as if emphasizing that he should not interfere. Allan couldn't decide whether he meant Run-Run could manage on his own, or that the outcome of the fight was already clear, but he obeyed and stayed by the window.

They were rolling about on the ground, the wild man's teeth gleaming like the dog's. One arm came free, steel flashed and a long-drawn-out howl told Allan that the knife had struck again. But then a third dog appeared, just as unexpectedly, just as suddenly, just as incredibly quickly and as ready to kill as the other two. With that, the fight was over, for Run-Run had not yet got to his feet and was unprepared for another attack. The dog had him by the throat before he could lift a hand to defend himself. Allan saw him flinging his long arms round the dog's body and squeezing and squeezing until the blood spurted out of the wound in his throat, squeezing as if this last show of wild strength would crush the life out of his last enemy. The dog sensed the man's strength was crushing its spine to breaking-point, crushing its chest and it howled and twisted, struggling to get free, but nothing could save it, for the wild man's arms were locked in a violent embrace deep into unconsciousness as dog and dog-hunter lay intertwined above and below each other, a rigid dead organism on the asphalt.

By then they could hear footsteps thundering along the street, and Allan retreated from the window far enough to be able to look out without being seen. The others needed no command to keep quiet. They had all heard the footsteps and knew what that meant.

There were three of them, all on foot and in the uniform of the Force, or partly so, their helmets and cartridge belts recognizable, although only one of them had a gun in his holster. All three looked dirty and shabby, but they were moving with such energy and speed, they were obviously not suffering from undernourishment. They ran the last stretch up to where Run-Run and the dogs lay, and stood around talking for a moment. One of them bent down and picked up Run-Run's knife and thrust it into his belt. Another started pulling off Run-Run's boots, but was stopped by the other two. Run-Run always wore rubber boots, and a pair of tattered rubber boots was not worth the bother. They stood there irresolutely for a moment, talking excitedly to each other and pointing in various directions, clearly uncertain whether Run-Run had been alone, as he had finished off three dogs.

Allan had drawn his gun. He had eleven bullets left. With a little luck he might get two of the men before they realized where the attack had come from, but hardly all three, and they themselves had a gun. What if there were more of them nearby who would appear the moment they heard shots?

The three men seemed to want to start searching. Two crossed the street towards the buildings opposite, the third approaching the gateway. This was even worse — a desperate situation. Allan would be able to get only one of them in the first round, and that would be an unarmed man — the man's holster was slapping emptily against his thigh as he came up the gravel path. Allan put his finger on the trigger and decided to wait three more steps so that he was as close as possible and there was the least risk of missing and wasting precious ammunition.

But they were saved from another quarter.

What was first a hum soon grew into a growl, a roar, so familiar and yet so unexpected, the sound of an engine in low gear — none of them had heard that for months, so the noise seemed tremendous in their ears. The men had also reacted and were back in the street, looking nervously around. Were they trying to decide where the noise was coming from? Or looking for somewhere to hide? They soon found out, for round the corner came a large, covered Army truck. It set course straight for them, looming and terrifying, roaring down the street. They ran off in panic, the truck's loudspeaker laughing after them, or rather, two of them ran while the third, the one with the gun, knelt, propped the gun on his elbow and started firing wildly at the charging vehicle, aiming at the impenetrable tyres and the reinforced windows, the loudspeaker's repeated exhortations echoing up and down the street.

'Surrender! Drop your guns! No one will be hurt. Surrender! Throw down your guns! No one will be hurt. Surrender. . . .'

The man with the gun went on firing desperately until he had emptied the magazine, then ran — too late. He stumbled to his feet but was hit by the truck and flung into the road. The front wheels and two double rear wheels ran over him as the loudspeaker continued: 'Surrender! Thrown down your guns! No one will be hurt. . . .'

The two fleeing men had given up and were standing with their hands above their heads. The truck stopped. Two men in civilian clothes and with rifles jumped down from the back of the truck, took a man each and helped them in, then climbed back inside themselves. The gears ground and the truck vanished in a cloud of blue-black fumes. For a few moments, they could hear the roar of the engine and the loudspeaker: 'No one will be hurt. . . .'

179

Run-Run's body lay in the street. Run-Run, the man of instinct, the wild man from another era, who could adapt to all physical conditions, the hunter, created to survive any extreme situation, now savaged by wild animals. The shapeless body of the policeman lay, flattened by the truck wheels, his empty gun winking near one clenched fist, his uniform now unrecognizable, earth-coloured, mangled, his flattened helmet a little way away, the emblem of the Force wiped out. Three dead dogs, three bundles of terror trained by the Powers for use against the population, savage animals against people, symbols of the savagery of oppression, the primitiveness of the oppressors, were now three mutilated corpses on the pavement.

After the cloud of blue fumes had drifted away, the dead bodies lay there in a picture of relaxation, the fighting over. They looked small, unreal, harmless, carbonized traces after a fire had burnt out. Flotsam left behind after waves had retreated.

There is nothing frightening or horrible about a corpse. A corpse is an object, a dead form with human features, a human-like object death has left behind as it has raced by – and raced on. An object *life* has left behind so that the cleaning-up can begin.

Felix said a brief goodbye. He had collected his few belongings up into a small bundle and been given a little horsemeat and some maize to take with him. They had lived well on the horsemeat and regained some of their strength. Felix had no doubts he would have no difficulty getting through to the nearest military camp.

'I'll volunteer,' he had told them. 'I'm an economist. They'll need all the qualified people they can get hold of. No worries about identity cards any longer. No current to run the central data bank. Nor any operators. A lot more important things to use people for, those who are left and can do something. Perhaps you didn't know I was trained in economics and business administration? I never completed the course, as I had to escape from my country, but I do know a little and I can learn more. There'll be a lot to learn for everyone now, when this is over.'

And he left, upright and correct in his ragged clothes, no hat and a month's growth of beard, but with measured steps, heading north-east.

Mary glanced at Allan and he shook his head. 'We'll make it here,' he growled. 'They're bloody well not going to put me into any camp.'

He shrugged and looked away. It was mild and the snow had melted. It must be March or perhaps April. Rain had asked to be allowed to play outside, begging and whining until they had let her. Things seemed less dangerous now. In the sunlight they could see how pale she was as she crouched down below the steps picking the first pale-green grass shoots and putting them into her mouth.

It was no use any longer. Whatever they did was hopeless. The very thought of another winter like the last one made him wilt, as if what they had gone through, the brutal events, now caused him physical pain, as if it had destroyed something in him, as if the wound inflicted on him had bled all strength and courage to keep going out of him, a wound that would never heal.

His thoughts ran on like this despite the spring warmth, and though for a while they had enough water and meat. He jammed the spade into the ground as if in rage, then went and squatted down to brood, things all round him sprouting and the garden literally vibrating with wild lushness. Every step he took, every thrust of the spade into the ground produced a warm fragrance of sap and weeds flourishing, entangling themselves into an almost impenetrable thicket. The shoots would no doubt grow well if only he managed to keep the weeds at bay, if anyone could possibly stop this insane growth turning every inch of soil into a steaming hot-house and every chink into a foothold for sprouting seeds and thirsty roots. He could see a whole network of runners winding their way over the ruins of the neighbouring garden, a protective framework of vegetation already covering the worst effects of the fire.

Sounds of vehicles and loudspeakers.

He had got used to them now. They came at irregular intervals, did nothing except drive through the streets repeating their message, the same every time – it was dangerous to stay in the ruins of the city and survivors should report to the nearest Army camp to be accommodated. No one would be mistreated. And so on and so forth.

The loudspeaker was now so near, he hoped Mary and Rain were not out in the street. He had not seen them for a while.

' . . . and survivors must report immediately to the military com-
mander. Everyone will be accommodated and supplied with what is
needed. The sick will be given medical attention. We repeat that it is
dangerous to stay in . . .'

Allan was struggling to turn the soil in the back garden with a spade
with a broken handle. He tried to remember what Doc had said
about sowing, which sorts should be sown when, and he tried to
work out what was left in the bags. What the different kinds were
remained a constant mystery to him. He frowned, trying to remember, but nowadays he was finding it difficult to recall life on the
Dump, and details of Doc's explanations had become a distant fog
of words that had increasingly lost their meaning. Though perhaps
he was increasingly losing his ability to think coherently, to connect
the meanings of words with anything concrete?

The sun was bright and clear in a sky bluer than he had ever seen
it before. Even his weather-beaten skin could feel sunburn after a
day working in the garden. Mary and Rain were searching for edible
grass to make up for the consequences of their one-sided diet of
horsemeat.

But how to bring some order into sowing? Allan's irritation
fought with a growing sense of despair. He had never bothered to
find out about growing things, nor learnt anything about plants and
seeds. That had been Doc's field. To Allan, all nature, and things
that sprouted and grew wild, had always been alien, rather mysterious, almost frightening. Whenever he saw a cat moving lithely
through the grass, slipping along high fences and leaping from
place to place in the ruins of a building, he shivered with both
admiration and loathing, but most of all with alienation.

Now, these bags of seeds. He would have to leave it to chance,
sow them and hope for the best. But was the bed large enough?
How much more would he have to dig over? There was not very
much left in some of the bags, as they had had to eat some when
hunger had been at its worst. Would what they had left be enough
to keep them through another winter, together with what else they
could find? There was so little to find, far too little. What did a few
bunches of carrots, a cabbage or two, some lettuce and maize cobs
mean when they were talking about a whole winter?

Allan tried to think, work it out, but found he couldn't.

Was there anyone apart from them? Allan wondered. Hadn't the

Army better things to do than use up the last drops of petrol? He tugged angrily at a tussock which refused to budge and simply left his fingers green.

Mary and Rain appeared.

She stood in front of him on her sturdy feet while he stayed sitting, not looking up. 'We're leaving,' she said.

'Leaving?'

He found it difficult to find the strength to raise his eyes and look at her.

'To the north-east camp. There's no point in staying any longer.'

'Do you mean we're to *give up*?'

'It's not a matter of giving up.' She was clearly agitated. 'It's a matter of saving our lives. The War's over. People have to start again.'

'Start again!' Allan spat it out. 'When we've got water and horsemeat.'

'The meat's beginning to rot. It stinks.'

'Cut out the bad bits. The bits that didn't get enough salt.'

'It's *all* got too little salt. And there's not much left to cut out. Who wants to die of food poisoning in this plague pit?'

'We'll make it.'

'Maybe so, for a few more months, but there's no *sense* in "making it" any longer. We need help, and we can get it now before it's too late. Look. . . .' She pulled Rain to her and ran her fingers through the child's hair. Hunks came away from the thick mane she had inherited from her mother, from Lisa. 'Malnutrition. She's lost three teeth, too. Amazing it hasn't happened before, for that matter. I know about this from the Palisade. After a year of substitute bread and cheap canned food, the gums rot. We've got to leave.'

He did not reply. The last time they had departed, the decision had been his. Now it was hers.

'There's no way out, Allan. If you don't come with us, I'll go on my own. I'll take the girl with me, and if you try to stop me, you'll have to kill me. I've made that decision.'

It took only an hour to pack the things they would need. They left the door open and did not turn round as they trudged up the street in a north-easterly direction, Mary ahead, Allan a few steps behind, holding Rain's hand. They carried equal burdens and would take turns carrying Rain when she was tired. With a bit of luck they would reach the camp the following evening, if they met a patrol car, perhaps even sooner. . . .

Fish Street, Oak Avenue, Great Eastern Road, she in front, he a few steps behind with Rain on his arm, vegetation and flowers growing through every crack and crevice in the asphalt, climbers winding round the gutters and stems reaching up to the light from cellar entrances and porches, greenery from flower-beds flowing over and under fences out across the pavements. As she walked, Rain gazed at all this green life covering the dead city. She counted flowers. She cried out. She sang. She saw a flower that seemed to free itself and fly on its own until floating down and settling on another. The streets round about were alive with flying flowers.

The asphalt was blossoming all around them.

Rain sang.